Catching Feelings

Scarlett Demonbruen

Protagonist Laboratory

Contents

To Harvey, my very own big charming athlete—sorry I wrote about the offense instead of a certain strapping young defender.

1

Amanté

My career was over. It hadn't even been six years since I was drafted, and my career was over. My coach was shit, my quarterback—good guy—was shit, the entire team was shit, if I was being honest. Every post-game interview was the same: I sat, half listening, muttered something about how everyone just needed to get on the same page, and went home knowing the entire fanbase was talking shit online. I knew I wasn't the problem, but if one more idiot reporter said one more idiotic thing, I was going to become one. Fuck the fines, fuck the fans, all of them. Five years of my physical fucking prime, gone forever, and this year was the worst yet—we hadn't even won one game. Not one. Six games into the season, on our third quarterback, and as much as I try to be an optimistic person, it seemed completely and entirely hopeless.

Two weeks ago, I'd finally caved and asked for a trade. When I went pro, I imagined staying with the same team my entire career, earning whatever city a billion championships, and retiring a beloved hero. It was becoming abundantly clear that this miserable, flat, empty city was not my salvation. The Captains were making it near impossible to get rid of me, which I understood. My leaving would be the sign to the entire city that their franchise was well and truly shit. Absolutely shit. *Fuck them*, I thought, over and over, while I finished my workout. My house here was probably the only part of the city I liked, and it was mainly because I could lift here instead of at the compound. I had big windows, a few pieces of art on the walls, a massive kitchen I never cooked in, and a four-car garage I turned into my gym. Today, my frustration was fueling a squat PR. It wasn't smart, squatting heavy in season, but I couldn't be assed. It had to be a bad sign—that I was willing to neglect my health. I'd never been willing to risk my health, even in my college career. I would go out with the guys, dance and drink and fuck, but I'd always be home chugging a gallon of water with enough time to get at least five hours of sleep before practice. That hadn't been an issue since being drafted to the Captains. The city itself was bigger than my college town had been, but there genuinely wasn't shit to do. There wasn't even a good restaurant with a nice bar. So, I spent my time at practice, shooting endorsements, or at home. Here. In this gym.

My phone rang, interrupting my deafening music, and I dumped the barbell back onto the rack with a grunt. Looking at the name—Amelia Ardent, my agent. My agent was calling after dark on an off day? I picked up.

"Do you have a realtor?" She asked, not waiting for my greeting or any pleasantries of her own.

I tried to sound like I wasn't breathing heavy. "What?"

"Are you decent?"

"Amelia, what the fuck are you talking about?" I asked, and my doorbell rang. I didn't have to glance at the preview to know who was outside, so I threw a shirt on and walked through the house, grabbing a protein shake from the fridge on my way, and opened the door.

Amelia Ardent was still dressed for corporate success even at this odd hour, and she was flanked on either side by men in red t shirts. They entered my house with a single nod from her. I tried to stifle my excitement—this could only mean I'd been traded, right? She allowed a smirk to twist on her otherwise stone-cold facade and handed me a phone. It began to ring the moment I touched it, and I tweaked an eyebrow at Amelia's always-impeccable timing. I answered.

"Amanté Houston?" The man on the other line asked.

"Speaking." I replied, trying to read the look on Amelia's face.

"Amanté, welcome to the Saints." I couldn't stop the shock on my face—and Amelia couldn't stop the smug look that overtook hers. "I'll let you get everything together. See you on Friday morning for a press release. Can't wait to get you on the field, brother." He hung up. It had been unconventional for me to leave all the details of my trade to my agent, but I'd been so bitter and frustrated that I didn't want to get my hopes up. The Saints... I blinked tears out of my eyes. One look at Amelia told me she understood just how much this meant to me. I was going to the Saints. I was free.

2

Calla

I knew I was the hottest bitch in the club, and judging by the amount of free drinks I'd procured for myself and my friends, everybody else knew it too. My friends were bad, too, but they were lacking the absolute undeniable glow of confidence that I was sporting tonight.

"To Calla!" Shay raised a shot—tequila, it smelled like—and the rest of the girls raised their own, shoving a shot into my hand. It was tequila, and even as I scrunched my face I smiled. Even if I didn't get this job, I finally had an interview for something I actually wanted to do. I deserved to be celebrated.

I pushed out of the booth as the DJ transitioned into one of my favorite songs, the bass pounding, and dragged Shay out with me. Shay was our resident high roller; she'd been making crazy money since we'd graduated, and she never made me feel bad about bouncing around shitty customer service jobs trying to figure out how to make my living. She'd seen more of my struggle than anyone—and she'd been the one to invite us all out to celebrate. I hadn't gone out on a Thursday night in years, and it felt good. I felt younger than I had in years, which struck me as a funny thing to think as a 25-year-old woman, but Jesus, retail really aged me.

My hips were fused with the music, taking me to the floor and back, tequila keeping my energy up, and the DJ playing the best set I'd heard in this club in months. It was unseasonably warm, and I was in a tiny skirt, and when I looked across the floor, I found myself catching the eye of a shockingly attractive man. He towered over the rest of the dance floor, standing on the edge with a drink, and when our gaze met, I could have sworn I felt my cheeks flush. If they weren't flushed from the alcohol already. He just watched for a minute, Shay and I dancing, and I gave him a little smile when his eyes dragged themselves back up from my legs.

When he made his way to me, pushing through the sweaty crowd, the music shifted again, pulling into a pounding beat. He fell perfectly into step with me, like we were riding the same wave, and I couldn't help but smile when I looked up and he had a little grin on his own face. I grabbed his hand and pulled him closer, turning around and placing his wide, strong hand on my hip—this was exactly the kind of energy I needed after today. His hand on my waist, just the one, fingertips digging into my hip, guiding me through the beat, I could feel the hardness of his body; I was doing my best not to be vulgar, but the feel of him against me had me biting my lip.

"Can I get you a drink?" His voice was soft in my ear, despite the chaos, deep and masculine.

"Please." I replied, and threw an excited look back at Shay as he took my hand and lead me across the floor. Not to the bar, I realized, but to his table in VIP. Fuck yes. Today was fucking perfect. When he sat down, he pulled me onto his lap, and it took every ounce of my self control not to ask him to meet me in the bathroom expeditiously. Instead, I leaned forward to try to listen to the other guy who was trying to say something over the music.

He leaned across too, finally close enough to hear. "What you drinking?" I took a look at the table—tequila, vodka, and two bottles of champagne.

"Y'all celebrating?" I asked, nodding at the champagne, and he laughed loud enough we got some looks. "I interviewed for my dream job today." I continued, and the man poured me a generous glass of champagne—plus another for his friend.

"I'm Isaiah." He introduced himself, holding out his hand.

"Calla." We shook hands, which felt funny in the club, but was a solid distraction from the man whose lap I was occupying, and his fingers tapping the beat along the crease of my hip, and I drank deeply from my glass of champagne. His hand stretched further across my waist, settling on the band of my skirt.

I turned enough to whisper in his ear, "Stop playing if you're not going to take me home."

He had me up against the door of his hotel room in fifteen minutes, his mouth on mine, my tongue flicking at the roof of his mouth, his hands indecisive, but I knew what I wanted; I pulled on the hem of his shirt, dragging it over his head and tossing it indiscriminately to the floor. He took my breath away, for a moment, his body was perfect, tantalizingly muscular, cut and tattooed and round shoulders with arms that could absolutely, definitely throw me around. I reached for his bulge, relishing the involuntary moan he released, the way he grabbed my ass, and unbuckled his belt, practically tore at his pants until his dick was in my hand, velvet and warm and freshly groomed, I noticed—nothing sexier than a clean man, a man who took care of himself. I knelt and took him into my mouth, and he braced himself against the wall, knotting a hand in my hair, head thrown back. I took as much of him as I could, hand wrapped around the girth of him, imagining the length of him inside me, fuck, I was wet and aching—he could probably just put it in and I would come, I wanted him inside me so bad.

Like he could read my mind, he grabbed my throat and pulled me to my feet, kissing me again, kicking off his pants and picking me up easily in those strong, massive arms, walking us back until he tossed me onto the bed. I was wearing a fairly tiny skirt—would he even take it off? God, he was a big man, and miserably attractive, every ounce of him toned, thick muscle. I just watched, enamored, while he put on a condom. He kept himself in incredible shape. I felt like I'd never seen a real man before this moment. I couldn't quiet the groan when he ran a thumb across my soaked thong—the look he gave me as he felt my desire—and he knelt at the end of the bed, pushing my knees apart, dragging my skirt and thong down my legs with cruel patience, and kissed the inside of my thigh.

"Enough." I breathed, reaching for him, and he only laughed, grabbing my thighs and pulling me to the edge of the bed. I had enough of his maddening patience, so I grabbed his hip and guided him inside me, our moans in unison as he slid inside me, perfectly, filling me, I wanted him deeper, and harder, immediately.

"Fuck." He groaned, my hips matching his as he thrust, in, out, I was delirious, he felt unbelievable, his hands gripping my hips, he was in complete control and I could hardly breathe, my hands gripped the sheets. He slowed, taking my ankles and hooking them over his shoulders, and he was deeper than I could have imagined, so deep I could feel my release building, I could hear myself vaguely but all I could focus on was his incredible dick. He picked me up and moved us back on the bed, until I could brace against the headboard. "Good girl." He muttered, one hand bracing himself against the headboard, the other squeezing my breast, tracing my nipple with his thumb, his thrusts slow, I wanted more, more.

"Please." I begged, pulling his hips even closer to mine. "More, please." I cried out as he acquiesced, pounding into me with fervor, deep and hard and fast enough that my pleasure built, and built, until I was screaming with the incredible feeling, and I was clenching around him, and he was coming, his grip on my waist so tight it almost hurt as he released, and we collapsed together, breathing heavily, and I realized I still didn't know his name.

I woke up to the buzz of my phone. I flung my hand out to feel around the nightstand, finding it and squinting at the bright screen that read: 7:00am. I did not want to be awake yet, but I was pleasantly surprised to find tiredness being my only hangover from last night—that's what drinking top shelf will do, I supposed, and leaving early. I smiled, holding the phone to my chest. This hotel room was nice, nicer than I'd realized when we'd come back last night, which was understandable. I hadn't cared to look at anything but the massive, delicious man who was on me. He was still sound asleep, covers half draped over him. Still attractive. The muscles of his back taunted me, begged me to run my hands over him, find myself under the covers...

My phone vibrated again. I swung my feet out of bed with a sigh and walked into the main room—yeah, this was a nice hotel. He had a whole suite, almost an entire kitchen, with windows that spanned the entire wall and overlooked the city. Home. I'd lived here my entire life, gone to university here, spent every day working towards somehow, someday, working for the Saints. I loved all sports, but something about Saints football brought me so much pride in my hometown that I knew I would end up working for them someday. When I was sure I was far enough from the bedroom, I looked at my phone again. Two missed calls, one text, all unknown numbers—I checked for Shay's location and was relieved to find her at home—and nearly dropped the phone when I finally read the text. *Good morning, Calla! It's Connor, from Saints HQ. Give me a call back when you see this.*

Connor. The guy who'd interviewed me for my dream job covering the Saints yesterday. Connor, who had called me twice before seven in the morning. Fuck. I wasn't sure where my clothes were, but this guy's suitcase was open on the coffee table, and I wasn't above taking home a souvenir, so I dug around until I found a t shirt and sweatpants. They were comically large, but it was better than my tiny skirt and lacy top from the night before, so I rolled up the pants as much as I could, slid on my sneakers, and snuck out the door. To call Connor. Connor, from Saints HQ. My heart was loud enough he'd probably be able to hear it on the phone, and I waited until I emerged on the street, full of morning commuters, to dial. He picked up on the first ring.

"Calla, good morning!" He greeted—how he was already so energized was beyond me.

"Hi, Connor, sorry I missed your call earlier." I wasn't sorry, not really—who called a potential hire before seven in the morning? He laughed, like he was thinking the same thing, and I could hear the humming of an espresso machine in the background.

"Well, let's just get to it." He said, taking a pause. "Calla, we'd love to offer you the position of multimedia associate." I fought the urge to shriek. "I know we discussed this yesterday, but we don't have a senior producer at the moment, so it's more responsibility than the title suggests." I knew that, had been excited about the idea that I would be able to show my growth potential so quickly. Less excited about senior workload for associate money, but—this was my dream job. I'd loved the Saints since I was a kid, and once I realized that I loved documenting sports, I knew I wanted to do it for the Saints. It was worth it.

I realized that I hadn't replied yet, and Connor was sitting in awkward silence on the line. "Incredible!" I breathed, laughing. "Yes, I would love to join the team." Holy shit, this was happening.

"Fantastic! Now, I know it is short notice, but we have a big press release we're doing today and it's going to be complete chaos, and it would make my life significantly easier if you came in to cover it." I pulled the phone away to check the time—still only 7:15am. It was probably a twenty-minute walk to my apartment, another hour to shower and look presentable...

"I could be there by nine?" I suggested.

"Make it nine-thirty. See you soon, Calla, and welcome to the team." Connor hung up before I could. I could barely breathe. What a perfect, flawless, incredible twenty-four hours. I popped into the nearest convenience store and bought an energy drink—two, actually, was probably a good idea—and practically skipped home.

I'd finally moved out of my parents' place six months ago into a tiny old studio right in the heart of downtown. Everyone told me to choose the shittiest apartment on the nicest block, so that's what I did, and living on my own had been wonderful. I walked to the bodega in the mornings for an energy drink or a bacon egg and cheese; I submitted job application after job application in the coffee shop downstairs. Shit. I needed to quit my job. I was working at one of the wildly popular new bars a few blocks away—on the way from the hotel, actually—making shockingly good money doing bottle service. Sure, I was out late, and the outfits were pretty skimpy, but I was hot and the job was painfully easy. My boss was a dick, though, so I didn't feel bad shooting him a quick text telling him that a better opportunity came my way and I wouldn't be coming back in. Whatever.

I could feel the caffeine kicking in by the time I trudged up the four stories to my apartment. God, I needed to decide what to wear—what was the dress code? I should've asked Connor. Like he was reading my mind, my phone lit up: *BTW- Business casual is fine. Professional works. We aren't picky.*

Working as a bottle girl didn't give me too much of a professional wardrobe. I had to have something; I couldn't wear what I wore to the interview literally yesterday... Would a dress be trying too hard? Is there such a thing as trying too hard at the first day of your dream job? I was covering a press conference, but probably would get a tour of the facilities and whatnot—no heels, then. Actually, fuck it. I was wearing a dress, and heels, and if I hopped in the shower now I could do a full blowout.

When I looked in the mirror, my phone flashing 8:30am on the dot, I couldn't hide my smile. I looked like some sexy CEO out of a raunchy high-rise law show. I looked like I knew what I was doing. Maybe I was overdressed, but, dress for the job you want, right? I snapped a selfie in the mirror. Then, I imagined the man from last night—the man from this morning—ut standing behind me, a hand on my hip. He was a delicious man. I should've left my phone number or something, but I'd been so consumed by the text from Connor that I'd lost all sense. Probably for the best. Nobody who fucks that good is anything more than a player.

I sifted through the internet until I found the DJ from last night and put on one of their mixes to drive to the facility. The crack of my second energy drink brought a genuine smile to my face. I was actually doing this—I was actually fucking doing this. I should call my mom.

3

Amanté

I would've thought last night was a dream if it wasn't for the lacy thong by my pillow and my open suitcase on the couch. It wasn't often a girl walked out on me. I would've liked to fuck her again, nothing better than lazy morning sex, especially when all I could think about was how her warm, tight—cold shower. I needed a cold shower, because Amelia would probably show up in the next fifteen minutes and I couldn't be hornier than a teenage boy when that happened.

Amelia knocked on my door at 9:00am with two coffees and a burrito. She stroked my ego for a few minutes, hyping up my fit and my braids, until she finally realized I wasn't listening to a word she said.

"Nervous?" She asked. I took a long drink of coffee. "You wanted this all to be a surprise. Enjoy it."

"Because I was bitter enough I thought it would never happen." Amelia laughed and dug around in her massive bag. When she finally finished, she was holding...

"Fuck."

"I know."

"It's forreal, huh?" I wasn't always sentimental, but I couldn't stop the tears from pooling in my eyes. There it was, my jersey, my real Saints jersey, just like the one I wore when I was a little kid. I blinked once, seeing the number. "You got me number 1?" The energy I was feeling last night crept back in. I grew up here, played high school ball here. Now I was wearing #1. I fucking made it.

"Put it on, Houston, and let's go."

I'd been to the Saints facility before, but never with a warm welcome, and I was surprised by how spacious it seemed. The Captains facility was nice, but cramped, making this feel double the size. I was meeting millions of people, it felt like, but when I finally saw my new quarterback, I grinned and pulled him into a hug.

"Welcome to the Saints, man." Khalil Williams had been in the league at least as long as I had, and while he hadn't won any crazy awards, he was consistently good and consistently hyped. We'd been work friends, I guess you could say, for a few years, but I didn't know him all that well. I'd never heard someone say anything but positive things, though, even if he beat them bad. He also was in need of a receiver like me—someone who could take advantage of his arm and catch those big passes. The Saints had some good receivers, don't get me wrong, but—not to be egotistical—none as good as me.

"Couldn't be happier to be here." I replied, clasping his hand. He looked genuinely pleased to see me, and I was surprised at how good that made me feel. Like I was already part of the family.

"I'll be back later for practice, but really, excited to have you." He shook my hand again and headed past me to the lot. He'd been on what seemed like a time crunch and had still stopped to welcome me to the team? That's the kind of leadership I'd missed for so long—the kind of positive energy you couldn't coach. My twisting nerves softened into pure excitement, and I made my way to the bathroom to make sure I was camera-ready.

4

Calla

Connor was as excited to see me as I was to be there, and he was holding a tote bag stuffed with Saints gear in one hand, a bottle of champagne in the other.

"Calla! Welcome!" He raised the gifts in the air and mirrored the excited little dance I did as I walked towards him. "You look great." I fought away my blush with a coy smile.

He sheepishly handed off the tote bag, then said, "I can't say the champagne is only for you, but I figured it was a nice touch."

"Very." I took a picture of him, and then myself holding the goodies, excited to show off both the manicure and the new job. Connor gave me a quick tour of the first floor, promising a more comprehensive tour later, and then brought me in to set up for the press conference. He wanted me to get b-roll for socials, mainly, because—in his words—the announcement was going to shake the league. I tried to think about what it could be; we had pretty good players all over the roster and a solid coaching staff. We hadn't had a whole lot of success in the postseason, but it was notably better than when I'd been growing up.

"After, if you're okay with it, I think it would be fun if you and Amanté did some kind of 'new in town' bit before we shoot the official stuff tomorrow." He said it so casually I almost didn't notice: Amanté.

I laughed. "Amanté? Houston?" Connor nodded, a mischievous quirk of his eyebrow making me laugh again. "We got Amanté Houston?" Amanté Houston was the greatest wide receiver in the league—possibly the greatest wide receiver ever—and had been under contract with the Captains since he was drafted. Despite being on one of the worst teams ever (worse than our rivals, if I was being honest), he was consistently the best receiver by most metrics. Having Amanté on the team would be... "Holy shit, Connor, we're winning it all this year."

The room was far from quiet, but all my concentration was trained on the little table where Amanté fucking Houston was about to walk out. My first assignment on my dream job was to cover my hometown team acquiring the greatest wide receiver of all time. What if it just never got better than this? I might be happy with that. I got to interview Amanté Houston. I got to make a silly little video with him about the trade. This was the best Friday of my life.

The room hushed, and the door opened, and I didn't even stop my mouth falling open as the man I fucked last night walked onto the stage.

Holy fucking shit. Holy shit. Oh my God. How had I not recognized him last night? I hadn't been that drunk, but I guess I had been decently drunk, and it was dark, but I'd slept with him? I slept with the greatest wide receiver of all time. The greatest wide receiver of all time *had brought me home.* He scanned the crowd before questions started, and we met eyes, the flutter in my stomach eerily similar to the one I'd felt last night. God, he was beautiful. I couldn't read the shift in his gaze, but there was one, and I felt my blood heat as I felt his stare sweep down my body and back. Fuck, fuck, fuck. But it was time to run the socials—so I did that.

The press conference was actually pretty cool, and although I knew the insane engagement was due to Amanté, not me, it still felt very good to see the numbers going up and up. Once everyone trickled out, it was just a few people I hadn't been introduced to yet (plus Amanté and Connor), and Connor called my name.

"Calla, champagne time!" He was cute, I decided, acting like I was remotely the reason we were popping a $200 bottle of champagne.

"Do you have a backdrop somewhere without the table? I have an idea. It might be stupid." I was pointedly avoiding speaking to or looking at Amanté, who was chatting with a lady who must've been on his team. I quickly explained my idea to Connor: stand Amanté in front of a backdrop and spray him with champagne while he caught a football. Or something, I had no idea what I was doing. To his credit, Connor ran with it, dragging all of us to the practice field and changing Amanté into a less sentimental shirt. None of the players were here yet—Friday was a light day, apparently, but they'd be arriving soon—but Connor wanted to throw a pass to Amanté while I sprayed him with champagne. It felt silly, once we were setting up, but I had to commit, so I set up my tripod.

"One problem." I could feel how red my face was. "I've never opened a bottle of champagne before." Amanté looked at me then, for the first time in hours, and I bit firmly on my lip. He was looking at me like—Amanté Houston was looking at me like he was imagining me last night. On his bed. Nails in his thighs. I took a deep breath.

"Why don't I spray you with champagne. Fans like to see the face behind the media." He suggested. I peered up at him, forcing my expression from shy to confident. I could play nonchalant.

"Perfect!" Connor didn't notice (or just didn't care about) the tension building between us, instead corralling us into the center of the frame. Amanté was using the champagne bottle like a microphone, interviewing me like I was the interesting one in this picture. It wasn't a bad idea; it showed us some of his personality, his humility, and I wasn't sure how to feel about that. To my surprise, he knew a lot of Saints trivia—more than me, which I found out by getting sprayed with punishment champagne, which got all over him, and ended the video with the two of us sipping elegantly despite our sopping wet facades. It was easy, laughing and teasing with Amanté. But I knew that already.

5

Amanté

I couldn't take my eyes off her. She was beautiful, and wearing a dress that was sinfully silhouetting her incredible hips, and heels—she hadn't been wearing heels last night, I didn't think—and her hair looked like it smelled good, and when we were standing next to each other for that stupid video I could smell whatever perfume or lotion she put on after she left *my bed* this morning, and there was the faintest hint of my own cologne, and I was daydreaming about bending her over in that dress and fucking her right here. Not that I said any of that, or even alluded to it. No, I was a professional. Usually. And what were the odds that she was here, today, at my new job? Her first day, too, at her dream job. She was cute when I was interviewing her; I felt almost normal. She was cute when I was showering her with champagne, too. Although cute might not have been exactly the word I was looking for.

"Early morning?" I asked, toweling down. Her cheeks flushed. I liked how easily I did that—made her shy or whatever that was when I looked her in the eye.

"I got the call for this job this morning." She said, tying her hair up. She was attractive, really, pulling her hair off her neck like that with her slightly smudged makeup. She was really new, then. "I didn't know you were leaving the Captains." I heard her silent message: *I didn't know who you were last night.* It was understandable. Most people probably look different in real life than on TV. My braids were fresh, too, and she'd probably never seen me without a helmet. The fact that she hadn't recognized me was doing something to my stomach I wasn't sure I liked. I liked it even less when I unwilling identified it as feeling seen—feeling like I'd been chosen for me, not my talent. Not my money. That felt a little bit more intimate, more real, than I was expecting.

"I asked my agent to keep it under wraps. In case it didn't happen." I didn't like how she looked at me—like she heard the depth of that statement, what it meant. Her eyes alone made me feel vulnerable. I cleared my throat. "I guess I should introduce myself. I'm Amanté." I held out a hand. She took it, hands small and soft and freshly manicured.

"Calla Monroe. I'm looking forward to working with you."

6
Calla

"Shay."

"Calla."

"You remember the guy I left with last night?" I was driving home, traffic was terrible, and I needed to vent.

"Tall, dark, and handsome. I do remember because you abandoned us." Her accusatory tone was less scolding, more teasing, but I still apologized.

"I know, and I'm sorry, but I also don't really feel bad, because the sex was unreal, but what's more unreal?" I paused—but couldn't help blurting it out. "He's Amanté Houston. As in, football player Amanté Houston." I could practically see her face in the crackling silence on the other end of the line.

"As in, billionaire Amanté Houston?" Shay asked, giggles bursting through.

"Millionaire." We laughed and caught up, Shay telling me the wild stories of the group of teenagers who came to the shop without fail after school every day, what she was having for dinner, every other silly little detail that didn't matter but felt nice to share. Shay and I had the kind of relationship where we could go weeks—months—without talking, and still pick up without a hitch.

"It's too bad you can't fuck him anymore." Shay said, her voice a definitive bummer.

The laugh that I managed to push out was awkward. "Who says we would have fucked again anyway?" I hadn't thought about it. He'd been a one night stand—a fantastic one night stand, but someone I hadn't anticipated meeting again. I might've left my number, if I thought about it, but I hadn't, and now we worked together? Sort of? And it didn't matter anyway because I wasn't going to like, date Amanté Houston. He was a millionaire. He probably had a standing booty call in every city with a team.

"Hey, Calla, I gotta go. Don't forget wine night. Love you!" Shay hung up quickly enough that I was left pulling into a spot in an uneasy silence. Amanté and I had fucked. That was all. We danced, and we fucked. It's not like we went on a date and I never heard from him. It was sex. I dragged myself up into my apartment, and at the top of the steps there was a half crumpled box. Maybe something I'd ordered online—hadn't I remembered to order a vacuum last week? Or did I still need to order one?

It didn't matter, because I kicked it through the door, pulled the heels off my aching feet, and plopped onto the couch. Those heels were killing me, but I had looked good, hadn't I? Even after toweling off champagne, I managed to maintain my confidence, although I didn't let myself look at comments on the video I was in; not yet, anyway. I didn't want to get hate mail on my first day of work. *Dinner*, my stomach grumbled, and I pushed myself off the couch, stubbing my toe on the box. Right, mystery box. I couldn't find my knife, so I just hacked at it with my keys.

Inside the box was a nearly crushed bouquet of flowers. Roses and calla lilies. I fished out the note: *Text me.* No fucking shot. I typed the phone number, fighting the urge to throw it all away.

Who's this? I sent, feeling stupid, feeling shy and out of my league and ridiculous.

Lots of men sending u flowers? His reply came through almost immediately—and he was typing again. *Amanté.*

I absolutely was not smiling. *How did u get my address? Creepy af.* Sent. Fuck. What if he didn't catch the joke? If I fumbled Amanté Houston on a shitty joke I might actually end it all.

You had dinner yet? No shot.

You asking me out? Holy shit. This was a bad idea. We worked together now, and I couldn't risk my job for good sex. That would be complete insanity. His dick was good, but not destroy-your-career-before-it-starts-good. I typed as much, then deleted it. Maybe I was getting ahead of myself.

There's a car outside. Unbelievable. I went to my window as casually as I could manage, and waved at the driver leaning on his black car—something fancy I didn't recognize—stopped in front of my building. I was going to get kidnapped. Unless. I sighed, shoved my feet back in the heels, slung a purse over my shoulder, and walked out the door.

The driver let me out at the same hotel from before and refused a tip. The front desk attendants saw me walk in and waved me towards the elevators, like I'd know where I was going already. Which I did, but—what did they think of me? Had he given them a description, or did they remember me from last night? From what I remembered, I hoped they didn't recognize me. We had been barely able to keep our clothes on until we reached his room.

I did remember, though. Penthouse, with a view impossible to forget. I was almost surprised he was still in a hotel. Seemed like finding a nice place to live would be the least of Amanté Houston's worries. But really—what did I actually know about the man?

7

Amanté

I was a little surprised when I opened my door and Calla Monroe stood outside. Part of me expected her to be the type who talked and talked and backed down when it was time to play. She looked shy—it was cute, her little blush, the way she was looking up at me like she was fighting the urge to look away.

"You came." I acknowledged, beaconing her in. She went straight to the window, hips swaying with each step she took in the dress that really was far too tight for work, at least for me to focus at work, looking out over the landscape. "You know, I grew up here." I wasn't sure why I said it; maybe I felt awkward, trying to fill the silence, but that wasn't like me.

"What?" She turned around, the now-messy curtain of hair swinging over her shoulder, genuine shock on her face.

I took a few steps towards her. Damn, I really did feel nervous. I wasn't sure what to do with my hands. I took a hopefully casual seat on the arm of the couch. "Yeah, went to school not twenty minutes from here."

"How did I not know that? Why didn't we talk about it for the video?" She sputtered, pulling out her phone. I just watched her thumbs move, the fastest typing I'd ever seen, as she presumably confirmed what I was saying. She scrolled through whatever she was looking at. "Probably didn't want everyone getting their hopes up, huh? Hometown hero coming to save the season." She looked up at me then, playful smirk on her lips. I swallowed. How the fuck did she do that? She wasn't even looking at me and she figured out exactly the little insecurity I'd been hiding from myself. Yeah, I was nervous. Maybe I was past my prime.

"Hungry?" I asked, clearing my throat. "I got chicken and potatoes."

"You got seasoning?" She quipped, walking to my kitchenette, seeing the potatoes on the counter. "Wait, you invited me over to cook for me?"

"What did you think was happening?"

"I don't know, I figured you wanted to fuck." She said it so matter-of-fact, but she couldn't hide the cherry cheeks blooming, or the hands clasped behind her back. I almost laughed, but I didn't want to scare her off, so instead I crossed to the kitchenette with her, pulling a bottle of white wine from the fridge, and reaching over her to grab a glass.

"I won't say that's not true." I fished the corkscrew out of a drawer. "But no, Calla." Twisted. "I haven't been able to stop thinking about you." Punctuating the sentence with a satisfying pop, I poured her a glass. She took it from my hand, gave it a sniff.

"Because of the sex." She met my eyes—something about her eyes just had me leaning in. "Listen, *babe*, I can't fuck up my job. It's been my dream to work for the Saints since I was a kid. So, if this is going to be messy, we can't." Something twisted in my gut. I pushed the feeling aside. I barely knew this girl—no reason to be stressed about something that may or may not have happened.

"Fine. I'm great with casual." I replied, but even the way she smiled at me over her shoulder made my stomach flutter. What the fuck was going on with this girl? What was she doing to me?

"Great. Then get cooking, chef." I could name a few other things I'd rather be doing than cooking, most of them involving her, on the counter.

"How about an appetizer?"

"What did you have in mind?" I smirked at her, and she bit her lip, and fuck, she was hot, and I took her face in my hands, and I kissed her. My body was two steps ahead of me, and I needed to get out of these pants, and she was already pulling them off my hips, bless her. I liked how much she wanted me; she wasn't trying to be coy or cute, she just wanted what she wanted. I took the wine glass from her hand and picked her up, setting her on the counter, and slid my hand up her skirt. I pushed aside whatever sinful piece of barely-there fabric she was wearing and felt how wet she was for me. I wanted to taste her, and feel her, and I wanted her to moan my name.

She pushed me away, mischievous smile twisting her lips, and turned around, pulling her hair over her shoulder. I unzipped the dress, down her bare back, down to where the tiny thong showed, and kissed her neck, her shoulder as I pulled down the dress, feeling her waist, her ass as she grinded against me. Calla stepped out of the dress and turned to face me, her incredible body begging to be taken. I needed to feel her—I needed to be inside her. She closed the distance between us, pulling my shirt over my head and tossing it aside, then kneeling in front of me. She looked fucking good, and she'd tried to do this last night but I was in too much of a hurry to fuck her, and I moaned when she met my eyes and licked up the length of me.

"Calla." I nearly came at the sensation of my dick hitting the back of her throat, especially with the image of her hair in my hand, her sensuous eyes looking up at me like she wanted to see just how good she was. I had no desire to come in her mouth—at least not today, not right now. "Calla, I want to fuck you." I growled, but she was relentless, her tongue doing things that made me shiver, and I tightened my grip on her hair as I came, and Jesus, this girl was fucking good.

She stood, shimmying off her thong, and walked past me into the kitchen, picking up her glass of wine and taking a sip. "Got a speaker in here?"

8

Calla

I would remember the way he looked at me while coming into my mouth probably forever. Casual. Fucking idiot, Calla, but I couldn't let this ruin my career. Even though I wanted to. I badly, badly wanted to. Loads of people had casual sex, though. We would be fine. He was a rich playboy—he would be fine. I put my playlist on his speaker, and soon he was half-cooking as he watched me dance. Naked.

Normally I might be a little nervous, but somehow, I had this man wrapped around my finger. He was naked, too, which I enjoyed, watching him get hard for me, watching him act like he wasn't getting hard for me. His muscles were like a work of art, each striation a detail I wanted to worship. Maybe that was a bit much—but I'd never been with a man like Amanté. In fact, I'd never been with a man at all, if Amanté was a man. He was so masculine, so confident and casual that I *wanted* to get on my knees for him. I'd never wanted that before. In fact, I'd never sucked a man's dick without him begging me to. I told him as much.

"Next time, I'll beg." He replied. I was achingly wet—I wondered if he noticed, if he could smell my arousal the way I could smell his. I'd never been able to smell someone get horny before. It was a fun new dimension of the experience.

"I think I'd like that." I could see him, on his knees before me. It was a pretty picture. "Amanté?" I asked, finishing my glass of wine and walking over to the window. "Do you think anyone can see us up here?" I looked out over the city.

"Probably not. Why, are you into that?" He sounded intrigued. I turned to face him again, and he was putting something in the oven. Amanté Houston was cooking for me—not so casual. I shook my head.

"Probably depends who's watching." I replied, taking a deep breath as his eyes raked over me. I wanted him badly. But I wanted him to want me first. It was a little game—who could be most nonchalant, as though there was anything nonchalant about dancing naked while he cooked for me.

"Come here." He said, his voice low. "We have 45 minutes until dinner's ready." I obeyed, walking towards him. He was pouring me another glass of wine.

"How domestic for a first date." I teased.

"First date?" He replied, and all the blood flowed back into my idiot brain. He was right. I couldn't have it both ways. This was anything but casual—I was dancing naked in his kitchen (well, sort of his kitchen) while he cooked me dinner. After I sucked his dick. He noticed the panic in my eyes. "Calla, I'm sorry, I was joking." I pulled my dress back on, turning my back to him so he could zip it. He didn't zip it immediately, but after a second, did so, and when I turned around, he looked genuinely concerned; my heart jolted. Shay was right. This was a bad idea. I couldn't let anything get in the way of this job—not even Amanté Houston, of all people. The sex wasn't worth it. It wasn't.

"Sorry, Amanté, I just remembered, I'm supposed to be somewhere early tomorrow, I have to go."

"Calla, you don't have to leave like this." He said, pulling his clothes back on. "I mean it, you can stay for dinner, we don't have to do anything. It's not why I invited you." That was even worse, and I swallowed the panic rising. A botched relationship with this billionaire playboy would not be the reason all my dreams fell apart.

"I know, I'm sorry," I couldn't find my underwear, again, but just gave up and slid the heels back on, "thank you for the wine." I opened the door and practically ran into the hallway.

"Wait!" The door slammed behind me and I mashed the elevator button. I needed to get away from this man before I was completely lost to him. "Calla, let me drive you home."

"I'm alright."

"You didn't drive here." Fuck. He was right. I hadn't even thought about it—and he was being such a gentleman—he'd chased me into the hallway to make sure I got home. "I can call you a car, if that makes you more comfortable?" He suggested, and I nearly melted. Fuck Amanté Houston and his twisted flirtation. I didn't reply. "I'll call a car. Don't go anywhere."

9

Amanté

I was unsure how I'd manage to fuck up a perfect evening so completely, but as I ate my dinner, alone, on my couch, alone, I couldn't stop replaying the night in my head. I sent her flowers—a completely insane idea, but I'd asked Amelia if she could get me her address and she pulled through, so I sent her flowers. *Calla* lilies, like a lovesick idiot, with red roses. And I'd felt like a complete idiot, except that she came, and she was fun and sexy and easy to talk to and just as lovely as she'd been the night before, and at work. Not to mention the fact that she'd stripped down to give me the best blowjob I'd ever had as some kind of unbelievably confident foreplay, like she knew she was so good I'd be dying to fuck her afterward. And then she danced around while I cooked for her, and it had been domestic bliss. My mistake was acknowledging that, I guess.

Unfortunately, so far, there was absolutely nothing casual about how I felt around her. I was completely soft—making her dinner? Buying her flowers after one night that would have been entirely anonymous if she hadn't magically been there? I could imagine her face when I walked out—deceptively calm, but I could see it in her eyes. I was sure she could see it in mine. It was like fate put her back in my path. But damn, she'd been terrified when I leaned into the domesticity. Like it was the worst fate in the world. I couldn't be that bad to be attached to, right? I didn't have fifty baby mommas—I didn't have one, I'd never had a girl I was attached to like that. I was focused on football, football, football. Maybe if I'd had time for a social life when I was still a kid, we would've met in high school. I didn't even know how old she was; maybe we would have been at all the same parties and all the same dances. Fuck, I sounded like a lovesick puppy.

I got a text from Ron—my driver—when she walked into her building. A second ping: *never seen u fumble lol*. Fucking Ron.

Smd. I could imagine him laughing at me. He should be laughing—I was days away from my first game as a Saint, and I was on the couch whining about a girl. I needed a good night of sleep. What I really needed was my bed, not this hotel bed, but Amelia hadn't found me a house yet. Living in the hotel made this all seem fake as hell. I texted Amelia.

Can house be priority 1? It was no surprise when she started typing immediately. It's what made Amelia a fantastic agent—she was always accessible.

Not enjoying the $600/night suite I got you? Amanté chuckled under his breath. *Moving it to #1. Enjoy your evening.* That was another thing that made Amelia a fantastic agent—she didn't waste any time. I sighed, looking at the number of unread texts I had. It was one of my worst qualities—I would receive a text, save it for later because I was usually too busy, and then forget about it entirely. Or, I would receive a text, read it, mentally respond, and forget to actually type it. I'd long given up trying to explain to people that I wasn't intentionally ignoring them—I just let them believe I was a 'maybe I'll see you, maybe I won't' kind of guy. As I scrolled through, one caught my eye.

Isaiah, a friend from high school who had somehow ended up my random freshman roommate in college, had sent me a text earlier today. *I know you prolly dont but if you need somewhere to crash I just*

bought a house in Avondale and she gotta empty room callin your name.
I quickly replied.

Offer still stand? In a hotel rn but losing my mind lol. He responded almost immediately with his address. That was the other thing I'd forgotten while I was with the Captains—what it felt like to have real, established friends.

10

Calla

Generally, once I had a taste of someone in bed, any little crush I had on them drifted away like a summer breeze. Of course it was my luck that the same could not be said for Amanté Houston. When I was capturing content, it took every ounce of willpower not to salivate over his powerful body and flirty looks. I would hide in Connor's office to edit, worried that anywhere else in the facility there was a chance I'd catch a glimpse. A glimpse was enough to activate the obsession, the daydreams about his voice and his hands and his perfect little date night. I was going insane. And every time I had to interview him, or shoot some trend, or catch b-roll after games—which was often, considering he was the most talented football player I'd ever seen and all his stats proved it—every single time, he had the audacity to smile at me like I was... well, like I was something special.

"It's because he's rich, Calla." Shay explained, between bites of stuffed crust pizza and gulps of cheap beer. She was typing away on her laptop, too, as we sat, mindlessly watching reality shows and discussing boy troubles. Shay wanted to be an author someday, and probably had fifty different half-written manuscripts stored away on her phone. I wondered how many of our girl chats ended up as dialogue.

"I don't think it's that." I really didn't. There was something about him, this energy, and it terrified me but also felt like, I don't know. "I feel like maybe he's the one." Shay stopped typing and narrowed her eyes at me.

"You had sex once and you try not to flirt at work." She pointed a finger. "You are not in love with this man." I covered my face and fell back on the couch. I wasn't in love with him, she was right, except that I just knew deep down that I could be—or I would be—if I let myself. God, what was I even thinking?

"He probably forgot all about me." I lamented, finishing my now lukewarm beer. "This is disgusting." I knew he hadn't forgotten about me, based on the way he looked at me, the way he oh-so-casually placed his hand on my back or my waist when he needed to get by, the way he just happened to be where I was when he could have been anywhere else. He hadn't made another move, though. Of course he hadn't; he was also having the best season of his already prolific career, carrying our St. Clair Saints to new heights. He was not thinking about me or worrying about me at all.

I wanted him to worry about me, though. God, I wanted to lay claim to him, accept all his generosity and warmth and romance, and never look back.

11

Amanté

Living with Isaiah was fun. I felt more like myself than I had in years, since those first few years of college when I'd achieved my dream of playing football and the pressure of the league wasn't yet standing over me. Isaiah was a good guy: Isaiah Cooper, of the infamous St. Clair Coopers, was a philanthropist and renowned party boy. His family had their name on at least three medical buildings and libraries throughout the city, and his mom once cursed out our high school principal for us. We were good kids, back then, for the most part. We had our moments, like anyone.

Isaiah's house wasn't an ostentatious mansion like I'd expected. He bought a fixer upper in Avondale, an up-and-coming neighborhood that still had a bit of a bad reputation, and was actually renovating it himself. "It feels good to see my hard work, man." He laughed, when I'd asked him about it. It made sense. Isaiah was great at the philanthropy thing—he threw his money all over the city, helping families and communities without judgment or conditions—including the fancy parties and galas and whatever else wealthy people did. In college, though, he'd majored in anthropology, and I'd always expected him to start some kind of foundation that sent every kid in St. Clair to college or something. He was a really good guy. Better than me.

"No girls in your life, Isaiah?" I asked one day after practice, while I propped my feet on the coffee table and iced my shins. He'd had a long-term girlfriend when we were in college, and we'd been out of touch so long I felt awkward asking what happened with her. I didn't even remember her name.

Isaiah plopped on the couch next to me. "Don't rub it in." We chuckled. "I date, a little. Why, you tryna talk girls?" I sighed, dropping my head back to look at the ceiling. Since when did I talk about girls, let alone with Isaiah?

"Maybe." Isaiah clapped his hands and laughed, hopping up from the couch to grab himself a beer and held one out to me. It was Tuesday... a beer wouldn't kill me. I nodded and he tossed it. "It's crazy, man. I've never felt like this." We cracked the cans.

"Tell me more." I wanted to bash my head in. What was there even to talk about? We saw each other at work sometimes, she drove me crazy, and that was it.

"You remember the girl from the club?" I asked, still staring at the ceiling, trying to find everywhere the paint was cracking.

"Yeah, I know Calla." He replied, and I turned to look at him. "She's a bottle girl at one of the clubs I like. Probably seen her out a million times. Haven't been in a while, though." Something about the way he said it irritated me—brought out something almost possessive.

I took a deep breath. Calla was not mine to feel defensive about. "Maybe she used to be, but she's working for the Saints now."

"Oh, shit, good for her." He sounded genuinely happy for her. Again, Isaiah was a good person. I had no doubt that he was actually proud of this near-stranger. "Wait, so you work together?" I nodded. "You're fucked, dude." I smacked his shoulder.

"I don't know why I'm going crazy about it." I admitted. "I want her. I know she wants me. But I don't want to risk her job."

"Very chivalrous." I hit him again and got up to throw the ice packs back in the freezer. "Why don't you just talk to her about it?" I thought back to her naked in my hotel room, dancing like she knew exactly what her hips would do to me. And how quickly she'd gotten out of there as soon as we mentioned the word 'date'. I didn't know how to control myself around her. I could barely do interviews with her without imagining her in white.

"Fuck off, dude." I laughed and sat back on the couch. I should just talk to her about it. I could do that—what's so wrong about a chat? "What would I do, just text her?"

"My guy, there is no way you are this lost." Isaiah laughed and took a swig of his beer. "I'll throw a party. You can invite her." Bad idea. "And I get to show off the new kitchen." He had just done a great job renovating his kitchen. "And," He emphasized, "I get to meet more of your famous football friends." Isaiah leaned back and turned on the TV, apparently tired of this conversation. "Next Saturday—it's your bye week, right?"

Isaiah could throw a damn good party, and he did it fast. He'd made invitations within 48 hours and sent me to practice with them like a kindergartener inviting his classmates to his birthday party. 'Saints & Sinners', a fundraising event for the flag football team the Saints sponsored, which I was now hosting. The theme seemed a little too college frat to me, but Isaiah was confident everyone would think it was funny at the very least, so I passed out the invites at practice and got a whole lot of shit. Everyone who'd be in town RSVP'd, though, so I guess Isaiah knew something about hosting.

By Saturday afternoon, the house was transformed. The island was covered in bottles of champagne, and a caterer had dropped off an astonishing amount of wings. Isaiah had somehow sourced a photobooth, to which he affixed a 'Confess Your Sins' sign. Aside from the champagne, he had a cocktail bar with spicy margaritas, dark and stormy's, any type of mule anyone could ever want, and a scantily clad bartender in a nun costume. Pretty sure that was blasphemous. As I surveyed the scene, I remembered that Isaiah had been the party planner at his frat. This guy went all in. I respected it.

"I bought you a costume and you have to wear it." Isaiah announced, once he noticed that I'd walked in. "This is the first party I've thrown since college and we're going hard." He pointed to a bag on the floor and I brought it up to my room, taking a deep breath as I sat on the bed. I was seeing Calla outside of work for the first time since she'd danced in my kitchen. Since her perfect hair and smooth skin and red lips wrapped around my cock. Fuck. *Cool off, Amanté*. Distracting myself from the feel of her perfect mouth—her perfect pussy—fuck, I wasn't distracting myself at all. I took another deep breath. Distracting myself from Calla, I opened the bag of clothes. Isaiah was not letting me fuck this up, it seemed, because there was no shirt, just a long, somewhat wide white scarf that was soft and so thin it was partially see through. For pants, he'd bought a pair of white workwear pants that were an unexpectedly perfect fit. No wings, thankfully, or I'd have to smack Isaiah after this. At the bottom of the bag there was another drawstring bag made of velvet.

When I opened it, I stifled a laugh. It was an iced-out chain, completely ostentatious, not big enough to be truly gaudy, but pretty close. As I pulled it out of the bag, I laughed aloud, because the pendant was an entirely diamond encrusted goat. Isaiah was ridiculous. I quickly estimated how expensive this must have been Isaiah was doing too much. If it was real diamonds—which it looked like it might be, the idiot, the necklace might've cost twenty thousand dollars. Maybe more. Maybe Isaiah knew a guy. I wasn't sure I could accept a gift like that. My eyes burned a bit as I attempted to blink back growing tears. Isaiah was a great friend, one I didn't deserve, and while this was an insane gift on the surface, it felt deeper than that. He believed in me.

I put everything on with some white shoes, wrapping the shawl loosely around my head and across my shoulders. Did that look stupid? I felt like some kind of desert messiah sci-fi character. Maybe that was the point. Would Calla like it? I flexed in the mirror—I was the happiest I'd been with my physique in a while. Feeling like a little bit of a douchebag for flexing at myself, I closed my door behind me and reentered the kitchen. Isaiah was nowhere to be found; I'd find him later to say thank you.

The party was supposed to start at 8pm, when Isaiah had some kind of fundraising activity planned, and then devolve into debauchery afterwards. My hands were shaking a little. Maybe I'd start drinking now. The slutty nun had a slutty devil friend, now, and he was shaking up a cocktail of some kind. I walked over.

"Hey, I'm Amanté." I introduced myself, shaking each of their hands. "I live with Isaiah."

"You also play football." The man replied, teasing, his red body paint doing little for his modesty. It was probably fun to dress up like a completely different person for a party. "I'm Bishop, this is Natalia." He gestured to the nun.

"You could've had the best costume of the night." I noticed, and he seemed confused for long enough that Natalia and I burst into laughter. When he got it—"Oh, a bishop, ha ha"—he scowled, but poured the drink he'd been shaking into three glasses. Just looking at it, I had no clue what it was, but I took it. We clinked, hit the table, and shot. It was gag-worthy. "What the fuck was that?"

"Nat and I's signature pre-work shot. Shot of espresso, shot of tequila." Nasty. Neither of them looked particularly pleased, either. I didn't get the chance to thank him, because Isaiah burst through the front door, DJ controller in hand, DJ herself coming through after with a stand and a laptop.

"So sorry-" She apologized.

But Isaiah was quicker, yelling, "No! No apologies! Enough! Good vibes! Get a drink! Let loose!" He made his way to the little bar and sighed. "Let me get two fuel and fires." He requested, and to my horror, the nun—Natalia—started measuring coffee for the espresso machine.

"First of all, I cannot believe you also drink this tequila-espresso shit. Second... 'fuel and fire' is hilarious." I scolded. Isaiah clapped me on the back.

"You look angelic, brother." He jokingly complimented. "Nice chain." I elbowed him.

"Thank you. Mean it." I replied, and he smiled. Once he and the DJ (Princess, as introduced) ripped their awful fuel and fires, Isaiah took the espresso machine and hid it under the sink. Then, he disappeared to his room, presumably to change, leaving me with everyone. Watching the clock. Wondering when Calla would arrive. Fortunately for me, everyone was prepping their stations, so I didn't have to make small talk. Once Princess's music started, it was even better. Bishop waved me over and handed me a spicy margarita, which was fantastic. I could do this. I was hot and jacked and confident, and I could talk to Calla Monroe.

12

Calla

It was an hour until Amanté's party, and I was freaking out. I was bringing Shay as my plus one, which I'm pretty sure made her the happiest she's ever been. My hair was already done, makeup too, and I was sitting on the edge of my bed in my outfit, just staring at myself in the mirror. I'd gotten ready too early—stressed about being on time, or whatever—and now I had plenty of time to sit here and think. I checked the clock. Shay would be here in fifteen minutes, and she'd give me a shot of tequila and usher me into her car, and I could pretend there wasn't this pit in my stomach.

It was stupid. I was stupid. The last time we'd seen each other, in Amanté's private residence, I'd been stupid. What had possessed me to suck his dick and dance around naked? We'd barely known each other, but it had been electric, like a buzz in the air every time he looked at me. We met eyes at that ridiculous press conference and instead of feeling dread that I'd encountered a one night stand in real life, I felt... hope. As if that wasn't the stupidest thing ever.

Since that night, I'd gotten to know him in a different way. The way he moved and spoke and looked when he was playing football was unbelievable. He was charming, obviously, and knew how to get down, but the side of him I saw at practice or before games or whenever he was at work was more. He had that aura of someone who was really fucking good at something and who also cared really fucking passionately. He could mess around and have fun, but his true passion was football. And it showed. The Saints hadn't lost a game since he was traded, although he would never take the credit. I thought it was the energy he brought into the locker room. It was like he reminded all the guys that they weren't just playing for money or fame or even to win: they were playing for the little boy who dreamed big. It made me a little emotional, to be honest.

I learned other things, too, like how he refused to wear a jacket even though it was getting consistently colder. I learned that his 'good luck' meal is a bowl of salted and peppered ground bison with blueberries and honey, and I learned that he was great with the team's kids. I learned that he was actually pretty quiet, even a little shy, in a big group. Sometimes, when I found myself interacting with him for content, we fell into this easy banter that twisted my stomach into knots. Sometimes, when I watched him at practice, his powerful body, I could imagine begging him to take me right there on the field with everyone watching. What would I say to him? "Hey, Amanté, I know I said I couldn't do this but I really need your cock." Pass. Hard pass.

A honk outside my building warned me that mope time was over, so I stood and gave myself a once-over. Saints and Sinners was a hilarious party theme for a group of grown ass adults, but I had to admit, I was excited to go to a themed event for the first time in ages. I didn't know how hard people were going to go for costumes, so I decided I'd be a sexy, subtle demon. I wore one of my favorites: a little black dress with the back cut so low it was near-inevitable you'd catch a glimpse of whatever underwear I'd chosen. The pair at large today was barely even a g-string made of soft red lace, and I smirked to myself imagining Amanté seeing it. I contemplated a pair of boots, but assumed I'd be taking them off once we got there and chose a cute little pair of black heels instead. I'd completed my natural makeup look with a sultry red lip. Shay honked again, really laying on the horn. Fuck, I was about to talk to him again.

I grabbed an old Saints puffer as I ran out the door and into Shay's front seat, shivering at the cool air. Shay was blasting music, and once I was buckled, she handed me an energy drink that was—based on a quick sniff—at least a quarter tequila.

"I got you!" She said, and we took off. Shay was a good person to have around. She was honest, even when you needed tough love, and she was the biggest hype man alive. She also cared fiercely—no matter what, if she was by your side, she was making sure you were safe, regardless of the circumstance. And she always made sure I was having fun, like giving me a pregame drink in the car. With anyone else I might be nervous that they'd been drinking, too, but with Shay, I trusted her completely. She'd never be so reckless with my life. It was nice to know she was always looking out for me.

Shay had also decided to go as a demon, but her outfit was far more badass. I had no idea when or why she'd purchased a black leather catsuit, but she was wearing it so effortlessly, like it was an old pair of jeans. Her hair and makeup were understated—letting her body do the talking—and she was bringing all the energy I needed.

"You gonna be able to dance in that thing?" I asked, and she threw me a glare.

"Not all of us can put on red lipstick and become every man's wet dream." She teased, earning a poke in the ribs. Maybe the red lip was too much? "Shut the fuck up, Calla. Turn your brain off. You look sexy as shit and you're going to a party with a bunch of rich athletes. Look alive!" With that, she turned up the music and rolled down the windows. My hair was flying everywhere, and I couldn't even be mad because I felt like I was in some fever-dream sequence in a coming of age movie.

Amanté lived in a far more unassuming house than I expected, although the cars in the driveway proved otherwise, and a glimpse through one of the front windows told me the inside was insane. They had valet—hilarious—and Shay tossed her keys like the villain in a heist movie and strutted her tall ass inside so quickly I had no choice but to follow. The party was technically to fundraise for our girls' high school flag football team, which I thought was cool of him, but I had a feeling the fundraising wouldn't be a huge part of the night. It was already somewhat busy, and a DJ I didn't recognize was warming up her set, and I almost cursed myself when I realized I was just scanning the room for Amanté.

When I saw him, he was already looking at me, and our eyes met, and I swear my heart stopped. His chest was almost completely bare, save a sheer white shawl draped across it—which somehow emphasized his dreamy chest—and I let myself take in every powerful, hard line of his body, his arms, his hands as they brought a drink to his face. I could feel my cheeks flush when I followed that hand right back to his mouth, and then his eyes, and he had the audacity to wink. Tonight could not already be starting like this. I needed a drink.

"Shay-" was gone, apparently, and I swung my head around until I saw her at the bar. She was chatting with the bartenders—one sexy nun, which I thought was hilarious, and one fully body-painted demon. Iconic, honestly. I pushed my way over to her.

"Calla! Here she is." Shay shrieked, and the demon handed us each a drink. I thanked him as politely as I could muster and pulled Shay away.

"Shay, we already made eye contact, and this is so bad and I think I should go home." I blurted out. Shay just clinked our glasses and took a sip—I did the same. Spicy margarita. Couldn't go wrong.

"Explain." She demanded, after another drink, although she was already scanning the room to find someone to flirt with for the night.

"Well, he was already looking at me." She gestured to my drink, so I drank. "And I got distracted because he's not wearing a fucking shirt. And he winked at me across the fucking room." I was gripping my margarita like a lifeline. Shay was nodding along.

She took my hand. "It's poor manners not to greet the host." She said, and we were walking towards him. Fuck, fuck, fuck.

"Hi! Thank you so much for inviting me, I'm Shay, one of Calla's friends." Shay introduced herself, extending a hand to Amanté and then Isaiah—the owner of the house, if I was correct. "Your desert savior thing is really doing it for me." She complimented, and I fought the urge to stare open mouthed as she winked at Amanté, wiggled her fingers at Isaiah, and walked away. Leaving me. Oh my god.

"She seems fun." Amanté remarked, taking a drink. "Thanks for coming." He was looking at me like I was the only person in the room. Was he leaning in, or was I? Isaiah cleared his throat beside us, and to my surprise, Amanté looked embarrassed. "Isaiah, this is Calla, my…" I was definitely the color of a vine-ripened tomato as he trailed off.

"We've met. Night out a few weeks ago, remember?" If I could be any more embarrassed, I would, but I was pretty sure I'd reached a peak. He was the friend Amanté was with that first night—the one whose hand I shook before rushing out of there. This was too much. Amanté was giving his friend a look. "Oh, fuck, something over there." Isaiah was already walking away, leaving Amanté and I in a somewhat private little nook by the staircase where we could oversee everything.

The way Amanté was looking at me was getting me notably hot and bothered. How did he do that—turn me on with a look? It was completely unfair. I finished my margarita, which caused him to raise his eyebrows. God, I was acting like a complete idiot. We got along fine at work, everything was fine, why did everything have to get weird?

"Stop looking at me like that." I said, but it came out breathier than I'd intended, and you could hear the lie clear on my tongue. He opened his mouth again, but I darted away. Sexy. Confident. Sexy. Confident. I forced myself to take a deep breath, settling into the slow, swinging walk that I knew would have him staring. *You can do this, Calla. He's just a guy.* But he wasn't. Fuck, he wasn't.

13

Amanté

I had to go to the bathroom to cool off after Calla walked away from me like that. I mean, Jesus, she walked into the house with her hair looking like she'd just been thoroughly fucked, her dark lips just a little smudged, and it had taken every ounce of my willpower not to grab her right then and there. And when she'd gotten all flustered, it was so fucking cute, and the way she looked up at me did something stupid. And then she'd walked away, that perfect ass swaying side to side, and I could've sworn I saw something red. Fuck, I was like a teenage boy. She could probably look at my dick and I would break. I wanted to fuck her until the only name she knew was mine.

I stepped out of the bathroom. A lot of the guys already had plans for the bye week, understandably, so the room was mainly full of non-players and Isaiah's friends. I scanned the room for Calla. As devastatingly beautiful as she looked tonight, I needed to focus. Needed her to realize that even though it was crazy, I actually wanted to take her out. For real. Like I'd tried to that first time, and had backfired so completely. Maybe this was a bad idea, actually. She'd reacted so poorly the first time I tried to take her out, why would this be any different?

I jumped when a smooth, frigid hand touched my arm. It was Calla, distracting, devastating Calla, and she was actually smiling at me, and she was holding two drinks. I just stared.

"Amanté?" My name on her lips nearly elicited a groan. I nodded, acting like I hadn't just been daydreaming about her. "I noticed you were empty, so I got you another drink." She continued, her voice like beautiful creamy butter. *Get a fucking grip*.

"That's thoughtful." I replied, and it was. Fuck, that was it. The unavoidable hum that filled the air when we spoke, the buzz on my skin when her focus was on me. It was something. "Calla, I'm sorry if this comes off the wrong way, and I know you said you want casual, but these past few weeks have been miserable, and I think..." I gulped, eyes darting between her enamoring ones, "I think this—we—could be something. I want to try. If you do."

She was looking up at me in that infuriating way, biting her lip, and suddenly I felt like I really was a teenager asking my crush out to prom and getting rejected. She handed me the drink—a spicy margarita, same as hers—and held up her glass.

"I'll make a toast." She said, then turned out toward the party and raised her voice, "To Amanté Houston!" She was barely audible over the music, and I started to laugh. "I know it's only week ten but I'm pretty sure he'll be MVP!" She yelled, louder, and I grabbed her by the elbow, spinning her towards me, both of us laughing, and she shocked me by lurching up on her tiptoes and dragging my mouth to hers. I wrapped my arms around her, the delicious dress and all her bare, bare skin.

"Fuck, Calla." I murmured against her lips, loving the way my hand fit around her ribs. She stepped away, the ghost of a smile across her face. "I would never risk your job." I said, trying to read the slight shift in her eyes. Her shoulders softened.

"I really like you, Amanté." She whispered, barely audible. "Dance with me." I let her drag me closer to the center of the party, a shit-eating grin plastered on my cheeks.

14

Calla

I guessed that my anxiety-driven overthinking spiral I'd spent the entirety of the day navigating was entirely unnecessary, because within the first hour of the party Amanté had practically drooled over me, I'd kissed him, and now we were just dancing, his hands on my waist and my hips and the small of my back, which gave me goosebumps, and we'd both stopped drinking after that last margarita, and this DJ was actually really great and I wanted to find out her name, and this was a shockingly, shockingly great party. Shay was having the time of her life, or so it seemed, dancing and flirting and giving me knowing looks across the room throughout the night. We'd rendezvoused once in the bathroom, where I dished what had happened and she told me her top three prospects who she'd ideally be going home with, and then we'd ridden the wave. That was another great thing about Shay—we didn't have to be attached at the hip to have fun together. The whole party was our playground, and we were both the type to see everything.

Selfishly, I wanted everyone to go home so I could have Amanté to myself. It felt like a dam had broken, and now we had a million things to catch up on. Shay had disappeared with one of the prospects, I couldn't remember which, and I was plopped on the couch watching as the DJ closed out her set. Amanté was giving out hugs and farewells. God, he was fucking hot. I wanted to lick his abs. The cushion bounced under me and I looked over to see Isaiah.

"I like your house." I complimented, and he grinned like a kid. "Do you work in interior design?" He laughed at that.

"God, no, but it would be fun. I kinda manage the family business." He replied. I tried to think if I knew the family business, biting the inside of my lip while I thought. Isaiah Cooper. Oh. Isaiah Cooper, like the Coopers. Suddenly, I was a little confused why the house wasn't ten times bigger. He laughed as it dawned on me. "I appreciate that I don't come off like a trust fund brat anymore. My first year at Princeton was embarrassing."

I shoved his shoulder, laughing even as I imagined it. "Princeton, that's impressive."

"Yeah, Amanté and I were roommates that first year, and the rest is history." He placed his fingers behind his head and leaned back as the last few guests trickled out. Amanté walked to the couch and dropped into the space beside me. I looked at him, brows raised.

"How did I not know you went to Princeton?" It was completely unfair. He couldn't be hot, talented, and smart.

"Shit researcher, I guess. Did you even Google me?" He teased, and I punched him in the chest. Fucker. He took my hand. "Well, Isaiah, successful party. See you in the morning." Before I could react, Amanté had me in his arms, sweeping me up the stairs to his room. My giggles echoed off the walls.

He set me down inside a gorgeous bedroom. Avondale was a beautiful old neighborhood, but most of the houses had been restored to be bland and beige. This one looked like we'd pulled it straight out of the Victorian era, with gorgeous crown molding, what appeared to be an original and well-restored fireplace and mantle, and built-in shelves lined with books. There were two large paintings that looked like they probably cost my rent for the year, both of them looking like original Monets if they weren't of St. Clair. The bigger of the two was a view over the river from one of the hills, sun rising over the water. The smaller one was of the fountain downtown, every little detail making it seem more like a fantasy than a real place.

Amanté's room was different than I expected. It was stately and elegant and warm. I spun around to face him, and he was just watching, a soft smile on his face. I pulled his pendant to take a closer look—and laughed. An icy goat.

"I hope this was a gift." I teased, patting it back down against his chest. He laughed.

"You don't like it? Isaiah will be hurt." He framed my face with his hands. "I love that little blush you get." I could feel them becoming redder. "I just want to talk to you, Calla. I really like being around you." The sincerity in his voice made me just a pinch shy. We'd really gone from one night stand to maybe-relationship to work colleagues in just a few weeks. Was this all a little intense? "I can see you overthinking." He smiled.

I forced a deep breath and looked up at him. "This feels like a lot for a couple of one-night-stand-turned-coworkers."

"I think it's because it could be a lot. If we want it to." He replied, and warmth bloomed in my chest. He walked to his bed and sat against the headboard, patting the spot next to him. I sat beside him and dropped a head on his shoulder.

"What did you study at Princeton?" It was rare enough that an actually good player was drafted out of the Ivies, but for someone as talented as Amanté to have gone to Princeton when he probably had offers literally everywhere else, he must have really valued his education. I liked that idea.

He interlaced our fingers together. "Computer Science." He nudged my shoulder with his. "And a minor in Arabic." An Arabic-speaking, computer nerd, professional football player. Amanté was nothing if not completely unique.

"That's so cool. I always wanted to learn another language but I never got past like two semesters before deciding to switch to a new one." I replied, drawing on the back of his hand. "Mine is in Classics." He looked at me with incredulity.

"That's sick." He sounded like he meant it. I swallowed, pushing onto my knees so I could face him, taking a deep breath to push down the nerves.

"Amanté, if we do this, can we wait until the end of the season? We can see if we work as friends first. And I want to prove myself without anyone thinking it's because of you. And, I want to make myself indispensable so if anyone finds out, I'm too important to fire." I was worried about what he'd say. He was Amanté Houston, for God's sake, he could have anyone he wanted without waiting around. The truth was, that feeling that kept streaking down my spine whenever I thought about Amanté was more than fear about my job. It was the fear that I wasn't good enough to be loved. By him, or by anyone. Logically, I knew it was a silly fear. But my heart pounded and my brain created detailed scenarios of him realizing that I actually was nothing special. I cleaned up nice, and that was all. Maybe, if we waited, he would realize he wanted something better before he could break my heart for real. I could live with that.

Amanté took my hands into his. "Friends til the season's over." He looked into my eyes and I could see him wanting to understand. He reached up to brush a stray hair from my face, and dropped it awkwardly. "Tell me something about you."

"I sometimes wonder if I should've left St. Clair when I had the chance." Shit. I was being a sappy sad girl. Why was I sabotaging this?

"You went to college here?" He asked. I nodded. "Where would you go?" I shrugged, but thought about it. I'd never wanted to go to one of the big cities like NYC or LA—too many people for me. I wanted to travel around South America one day, but I probably didn't want to live there. The truth was, I loved St. Clair and my life here. I was independent, I had good friends, my family was nearby, and I just got a job for the team I'd wanted to work for since I was a kid. But it felt like something was missing.

"Maybe I'd go to some romantic little ranch in Wyoming, fall in love with a cowboy, and have lots of babies." I replied. He laughed, a real one that started deep in his chest, and I couldn't help but laugh with him.

"Is that what you want?" He asked. "Couldn't be happy with the professional athlete in a charming mid-size city?" I stayed quiet. He made a show of yawning. "How about I make you breakfast in the morning. Friendly tradition."

"It's a deal."

I woke up to Amanté's strong arms around me. The sun was starting to trickle in through his window, bathing his unexpectedly elegant room in glowy golden light. I snuggled further into his arms, my back—clothed in one of his shirts—nestling into his chest. Last night had been nice. We talked a bit more about stupid stuff, laughing 'til we cried, until I changed into one of his shirts and we climbed under the covers for some of the most pleasant sleep of my life. Amanté let out a low hum, tightening his arms around me, and I could feel him pressing into my ass. I smiled to myself and rolled my hips into his. He pressed a sleepy kiss to the back of my neck, one of his hands sliding down my side to grab my hip. I sucked in a breath.

"Good morning." He mumbled, sliding his hand under my shirt and squeezing my breast. I was aching for him, already, and pushed my ass into him again. He mumbled something I didn't understand, but brought his hand back down to my panties, slipping his hand underneath the band to put teasingly gentle pressure on my clit before he surprised me by ripping them off me with one clean snap. I moaned—unwittingly—and leaned my head back. He placed another kiss on my neck, circling my clit, until I bucked my hips. He growled, sliding a finger inside me.

"Amanté." I breathed.

"Fuck, you're wet." He replied, stroking my clit with his thumb while he pushed inside me. As amazing as his hands were, I wanted him to fill me. I reached back for his boxers, pulling them halfway down until his touch left me and he took them the rest of the way himself. "Impatient." He scolded, then groaned as I took his dick into my hand and pumped.

He grabbed the back of my knee and hitched my leg up, and I let out a whimper when I felt him against my entrance. "Please." I arched my back towards him, and he squeezed my ass, ran his hand over my him and my back and my face. I took one of his fingers into my mouth and sucked.

"Jesus, Calla." He muttered. I grabbed his hip and pushed him into me, drawing a gasp from us both. Fuck, he felt amazing, his dick was fucking perfect. He grabbed my hip and thrust, driving deeper into me; my nails clawed into his hip. "You like that?" He asked, his voice in my ear. "Tell me."

"Yes." He pulled out and I almost whimpered at the lack.

"Tell me what you want." He demanded, his low voice almost enough to make me come, his hands running over my body, gripping and grabbing. His hand made it to my throat, and my eyes rolled back. Fuck, his hand on my neck, I couldn't stand him not being inside me again.

"You." I breathed, and he grabbed my hips, pulling us both to our knees, and pulled his shirt over my head, the sudden rush of cool air bringing goosebumps to my skin. He brought one hand to my neck, the other between my thighs, and my knees nearly buckled at the sheer pleasure of his pressure, the sensation of his hard cock slick with my wetness grinding into my ass as he coaxed an orgasm deep into my core. "Fuck me." I begged, losing patience, losing myself. He didn't relent, just kept his deft fingers in perfect motion at my clit, the other hand lightly squeezing my neck, until my moans turned to screams and I nearly collapsed, the orgasm ripping through me. I was so sensitive, I jerked at his soft touch, tracing over my soaking entrance, squeezing my breasts.

"Tell me what you want." He said, again. I was still panting, and I dropped my head back into his chest. "Be a good girl and tell me what you want." He repeated, and I was throbbing, aching for him.

"Please fuck me, Amanté. I want you to fuck me like an animal." I plead. His satisfied growl made heat radiate through me. He bent me over, my hands on the bed, and squeezed my ass.

"Like this?" He asked, and gently pushed into me. I nearly unraveled, flexing against him, already so sensitive and begging for more, more, more.

"More." I breathed, and he pushed me down to my chest, sweeping my arms behind me and grabbing my wrists in one hand. He thrust again, slow and impossibly deep and I was so, so full of him.

"Like this?" I couldn't think, I could barely breathe, but I needed him to fuck me, not this mean teasing bullshit, I needed to be fucked. "You can tell me, baby. Tell me." Fuck.

"I want you harder." I managed. "And I want you to finish inside me. Please." He tightened his grip on my wrists, gripped my hip in his other hand, and thrust into me, deep, and hard, and again, and again, and I wasn't sure of the sounds coming out of my mouth anymore, I couldn't think, he was pounding into me, he felt so fucking good. He released my arms and reached his hand forward to grip my throat as he loses all control, fucking me so hard and fast and deep I can't even think beyond the rising sensation within me. *It's too much*, I almost say, *but don't stop*, God, God, *God*. He thrusts one last time, rough and wild, squeezing the sides of my neck as he does it, and I flex around him, screaming out an orgasm of my own, arching and quivering around him as he holds tight enough to bruise, filling me, until he pulls me to his chest and we collapse together.

"Jesus fucking Christ, Calla." He muttered. "Fuck." I laughed. "Your body is fucking perfect. I don't think any other could ever compare. You're fucking perfect."

It was our first Sunday off in weeks—a month, maybe—and I wasn't sure what to do with myself. After our lovely morning fuck, we agreed that it was totally platonic (we didn't kiss!). Then, we went down to the kitchen, and Amanté got to work making breakfast. He pointed at one of the hoodies draped on the stool next to me at the island and I handed it out towards him.

He laughed. "For you." I pulled it over my head. It was massive and cozy and smelled like his cologne—vanilla and something smoky, almost? I liked it. A lot. I took out my phone and opened our socials. Even though it was bye week, I still had to post, and I'd had some pretty good engagement. Not as good as after a win, but pretty good. There were a few comments about how much we were paying Amanté, and I realized for the first time that he was getting twenty-eight million dollars a year. Good lord.

I jumped at the clink of the mug on the granite and looked up. Something fluttered in my stomach at the image: smiley, sleepy Amanté making me coffee on a Sunday morning, wearing silly patterned pajama pants and a hoodie that looked two sizes too big even for him. I took the coffee—a latte actually, fancy—and took a sip. He was watching me intently as I tried it and I realized he was waiting for my review.

"It's delicious, thank you." I said.

15

Amanté

I was in domestic bliss and complete denial. Calla was perched on a stool like a little hawk while I made breakfast, and she was wearing one of my sweatshirts with the hood pulled over her hair. She was scrolling through her phone; I guessed that social media people—whatever her job title actually was—weren't allowed to completely take the week off. When she was at work, she always seemed like she knew exactly what to do next and how. Like, she'd come in wearing her heels and her gorgeous hair and she'd beeline straight to whatever it was she wanted to record that day. Mondays were a lot of recovery, so she started an "ice bath interrogations" series that did numbers. Tuesdays, I wasn't at the facility, but Wednesday she'd make sick edits of our full on practice, Thursday was usually interviews about the upcoming game, and Fridays she'd hype us up. She got Saturdays off, I was pretty sure, or at least she stayed inside wherever her office was all day.

I liked seeing her like this, hands wrapped around a mug except when she scrolled through her feed, chin tucked to her knees, sunlight streaming in to turn the back of her head golden brown. I didn't want to be just friends, but it wasn't the end of the world. I was an all-or-nothing kinda guy, but I could give it all in... friendship. It wasn't too long until the end of the season—January, hopefully February. A pit of anxiety formed in my stomach.

It was week 10. I'd been with the Saints for four weeks now and our record was a very respectable 6-3. I hadn't lost with the Saints, which was a great thing, but the longer it went on the more pressure I put on myself not to let it happen.

"Pancakes? French toast? Omelette?" I offered. She plopped her hand into her chin and thought. Calla was a loud thinker; I couldn't always tell what she was thinking, but I knew it was happening, could see the pieces coming together in her eyes.

"French toast, please." She requested, and I saluted. She laughed, and I could chase that laugh forever. Fuck. I sometimes had the fabled 'post nut clarity' but this was nothing, nothing at all like that. We absolutely should not have had sex this morning. I was ruined. "Amanté, did you know you're fucking loaded?" Her voice was nonchalant. I smirked at her and started on the custard.

I did know I was fucking loaded, but I don't think I really understood it. I had a guy who handled my finances—Benjamin, a fellow Princeton alum and someone Amelia recommended—and I told him from the beginning that I didn't need the majority of my salary liquid. Only about $200,000 hit my checking account a year, which was still a fuckload compared to what I thought I'd be making when I was growing up, but was somehow a drop in the water compared to what was going on behind the scenes.

"I did, actually." Was the answer I settled on, but I wasn't sure how to take the question in the first place. She held up her phone and I dropped my head back and guffawed. She was on one of our local fan accounts—@StClair.memes—and it was a picture of me getting into my car after practice with the caption "this guy makes 28mil". The car in question was a red 1999 Ford Ranger, and I loved that thing. I drove much fancier cars when I was on my rookie contract, and I still had the first car I bought (a McLaren Senna that I would keep forever), but when I dropped everything to move to St. Clair I told Amelia to sell my other cars when she sold the house. My first stop when I landed was a used car lot near where I grew up, and I found the truck.

"What do you even do with twenty-eight million dollars?" She mused. I shrugged, dipping the bread into my bowl.

"Save it so I can retire before my brain is destroyed." It was a joke, but not really. I went to Princeton because I was smart and I knew it, and I wanted to be healthy enough to actually use it. She made an appreciative "hm" and turned back to her phone. I finished breakfast, handing her a stack of French toast and sliding into the stool next to her. She loaded it up with maple syrup—the real stuff, thanks to Isaiah's expensive taste, and I did the same once she was done—and took a bite.

"This is the best French toast I've ever had." She said around a mouth of food, and her eyes were so genuinely full of joy that I had to laugh. "I'm not kidding. How did you do this?" I took a bite of my own.

"It's my mom's recipe. The secret is lots and lots of butter." A wave of sadness washed over me. My mom had been dead for a long time, now, and even though it didn't hurt less, it hurt less often. Every once in a while, though, something would make my image of her so clear in my mind that it hurt to breathe.

"I like this woman." Calla smiled, and I hesitated on whether to say anything. She paused, the smile falling, and put a hand on my arm. "You okay?" There it was—that too deep stare I'd noticed in her from the beginning. She saw everything.

"She died when I was seventeen. Multiple myeloma—blood cancer." She squeezed my arm.

"I'm really sorry, Amanté." She leaned over to squeeze my bicep and went back to eating. I went back to my breakfast, too. Calla might be the best thing that's ever happened to me. I just hoped she could believe it.

16

Calla

So, he was a millionaire, he was smart enough with his money to stay a millionaire, and he could cook. Maybe I'd been too hasty to tell him we should just be friends. It wasn't that I wasn't attracted to him—obviously, after this morning, we were clearly attracted to each other—but I thought he was right. He said that he thought we could be something. If that was true, I didn't want it to be foiled by workplace drama or moving too fast. Just friends was a good idea. Although we'd have to reconsider whether 'just friends' spent the night together and had the best sex of my life in the morning. No kissing, though. I giggled under my breath.

Amanté had offered to call me a car again, but I decided I'd walk home. It wasn't particularly close—in fact, we were pretty far from my place—but Shay's job wasn't too far from here and I wanted to stop in. I didn't know how she did it, but Shay could be out until four in the morning and still make it to her Sunday opening shift. She liked opening on Sundays because she got all the church-goers, and according to her, they were all on their best (and well-tipping) behavior when they came through. And, she didn't like making anyone else working what she called the least popular shift on the schedule, so she made it part of her Sunday morning ritual. I hadn't done it since starting with the Saints, but one of our traditions was a debrief at the cafe after the rush. I'd come in, get my coffee, watch the mesmerizing barista routine—measuring the beans, grinding them, that wonderful aroma, pulling a perfect shot, making slightly wonky latte art—and wait for Shay to get off at 11am.

"Double shot over ice with a little caramel and a splash of cream, please." I ordered, and Shay's head shot up at the end of the bar.

"Calla!" She shrieked, "Don't ring that up." She told the cashier, calling out the name of whoever's order she'd just finished and quickly starting on mine. She looked great, somehow, her dark hair in a long braid down her back, no hint of exhaustion under her eyes. When she handed me my drink, I brought it to my usual spot and watched her finish up her shift. She wiped down the counter, made herself a drink, and said farewell to her fellow coworkers before sliding into the chair across from me.

"You look like you had a great night of sleep." I complimented. She raised an eyebrow.

"That's what happens when you drink lots of espresso before your shift at a coffee shop." She laughed, but put on a straight face and leaned across the table. "Dish."

"We agreed to be friends until the end of the season." I stated, taking a sip, watching her closely to see the reaction. She impressively had none. "And his room is surprisingly fancy. It's like some rich Victorian merchant's bedroom."

"Mhmm." She narrowed her eyes. I pursed my lips.

"We also had some of the best sex of my entire life this morning before he made me breakfast." I admitted. Shay was grinning, still silent, and I sighed. "As friends."

"Right." She rolled her eyes. I smacked her hand.

"Serious, Shay. We didn't even kiss." *After the party*, I added to myself. Shay looked like she wanted to burst into laughter but managed to keep it together for my sake. I knew it sounded stupid, especially given the circumstances, but I felt like we owed it to each other to make a real foundation before relying on sex. We were both mature enough to handle that. If it worked, we might have something real. If it didn't, we were both saved a headache. It was a good plan, and I told Shay as much.

"Whatever you say, babe." She teased, but it wasn't mean-spirited. "Want a ride home?"

As nice as it was to have a week working from home, I was excited to get back to the facility. I'd set out a full week of my best outfits, because this week was rival week. The St. Clair Saints and the Ridgeway Eagles were, in my opinion, the greatest rivalry in the league. We always traveled well, with Ridgeway being only a couple hour drive away, so the energy was buzzing all week. Historically, the Eagles got under our skin. I couldn't remember the last time we'd won against the Eagles at home, actually. Having Amanté had the city talking, though. We were a solid team without him, but with him? We were unstoppable. This game would also put us on top of our division, which could be huge for the postseason.

"Hey, Calla." Connor poked his head into my office. I looked up. "My office?" He ducked away, and my heart began to race. It could be anything, right? He'd been in Mexico for the whole bye week, so he hadn't seen anything at the party. We weren't even being super touchy at the party, just flirty. Would someone have said something? I wiped my hands on the sides of my pants and walked down the hall to Connor's office.

Amanté was sitting in one of the chairs opposite the desk, and my stomach dropped. I sucked a breath in through my nose and stepped inside. Connor looked between the two of us.

"Sit, sit." Connor gestured, and I sat on the edge of the chair. "How was your week at home, Calla? Amanté and I were just discussing his party I was so disappointed to miss." Connor leaned back, and I took a beat before exhaling. He didn't know—this wasn't an ambush.

"It was good. Amanté throws a fun party. Well, his roommate does, anyway." I answered, settling further into the chair. If this wasn't an ambush, what the fuck was it? Connor and Amanté both laughed, and Connor leaned forward on the desk.

"Calla, I know you're busy." He began; understatement of the year. I was doing the work of an entire marketing team all on my lonesome. "As I'm sure you know, Mr. Houston is approaching the league record for fastest time to 100 touchdowns. If everything goes well," he paused to knock on his desk, "he'll take the record this weekend." I nodded, feeling an unexpected well of pride blooming in my chest. I risked a glance at Amanté, and found him smugly smirking at me, ankles and arms crossed, the picture of chill.

"That's exciting." I replied, unsure where Connor was going.

"You're going to do an interview for the pregame show." Amanté blurted out, and I snapped my head to him. "They're giving me a ten-minute spotlight before the game and I told Connor I wanted you to do it." I snapped my head back to Connor. He was smiling.

"We have to shoot by Wednesday to get the network's approval." Connor handed me a folder, presumably full of guidelines. "It'll be a long week." He said, looking at me intently.

"I've got it. You can trust me." I said, barely hearing myself. Connor clapped his hands.

"Great! Now let me do some work." Connor dismissed us, and Amanté laughed before hopping to his feet and gesturing at the door. I walked out first, Amanté behind me, and spun on him as soon as Connor's door closed.

"Did you do this?" I asked, my heart pounding so loud I thought he might be able to see it. Amanté shrugged. This was a night game, na-

tionally televised, the biggest game of our season so far, and Amanté…
"I'm interviewing the best player in the league on national television?"
My voice was breathy and I placed a hand on my chest.

"Yes, ma'am." Amanté replied, that smug smirk still on his beautiful
face. "What are friends for?" He winked. I allowed the smile on my face
to stretch into a completely ridiculous grin. I was going to be reporting
on sports on TV. This was unbelievable; this was my biggest goal. I
thought it would take me years to have this opportunity, and Amanté
had handed it to me now. I looked at the folder in my hands and cursed
under my breath.

"Text me your schedule." I started walking down the hall, calcu-
lating just how much unpaid overtime I would be doing this week.
Amanté followed behind as I ducked into my office, and I felt my
cheeks flush at the mess. It wasn't messy per se, but it wasn't visibly
organized either. He stood in the doorway, filling it all even as he
leaned against the frame.

"I'm off tomorrow," he said, "but I know that's a lot of work for
you." I rifled through the folder. "Why don't you come to Isaiah's
once you're off work and I'll order food to repay you for tripling
your workload." My eyes met his. He looked so casual—but his eyes
betrayed the truth. He was testing this. I looked further, wishing I
could read his mind. There was a flicker of—fear? I cocked my head
to the side. This was what I wanted: an opportunity to figure out if
there was more to this than sexual tension. And I was interviewing
him, after all. I sighed.

"That would be nice." I replied. He pushed off the doorframe and
smiled—God, his smile was distracting.

"Text me when you leave." And he was gone. I looked at my very
full desk, and a small smile crept onto my face.

17

Amanté

C alla and I were not very good at being just friends. It only took something like five hours for us to succumb to lust after agreeing to keep it platonic, and I couldn't say I was upset about it. I did want her to know I could be serious, though. Maybe it was stupid to invite her over for this—maybe it muddied the water too much when we were already in weird territory—but I wanted to be around her, and she needed to prepare to interview me, and mostly I just really wanted to be around her. We could be professional.

Aside from the ever-present sexual tension, I also knew Calla was good at her job, and I knew all she needed to get the opportunities she really wanted was a chance to prove herself. When Amelia told me the league wanted to do a spotlight on me before my hopefully record-breaking game, I knew it would benefit us both. So, I went to Connor, proposed that Calla interview me, and that was that. I could hardly believe I was even in this situation to begin with.

When I was with the Captains, our team was beyond mediocre—but we could score, and that was mainly my doing. I was catching insane passes my entire career, and somehow, I was coming up on the fastest player to reach 100 touchdowns. The record was 89 games—if I scored on Sunday, I'd be setting the record at 88 games. One game wasn't much, but it was a record that had stood for years and years. Breaking it, claiming it myself even after having such awful luck in my first contract, would be huge. It would be proof that I was more than my record, that my play was elite regardless of where I played. I knew I could do it; if I was being honest, I was pretty confident it was going to happen—maybe even in the first quarter. There was an exciting energy amongst the team. These guys were excited for me, they wanted me to succeed, they cared about hitting stats and breaking records. It's a whole different game when your whole team has your back and the locker room gets lit. I was hyping them up, too—one of our rookie wide receivers was leading the league in yards after pass, and our quarterback was on track for a MVP season. Everything I did on the field and in practice was for the team. It felt good—really good—to not be so alone anymore.

I thought I might be able to be real friends with most of these guys, too. It was hard with the Captains, because even though they were good dudes, I was so frustrated all the time. It was hard to separate work from my personal life. It was easier with the Saints. Everyone seemed to be well-adjusted: dads, husbands, brothers who managed to get to college volleyball games and sons who weren't embarrassed to shoutout their mom when they scored. It helped me keep things separate, and my game was at its best. Even though I was going crazy, catching feelings for Calla, I was still going crazy on the field, too.

Isaiah was playing video games on the couch when I got home. I dropped my bag at the door and dropped heavily onto the couch next to him. My whole fucking body ached. The good kind—the kind that made me feel like I was doing something worthwhile with my time—but man. My stomach grumbled.

"Long day?" Isaiah asked, not looking away from the screen.

"About to be longer." I replied, and hauled myself up to make a protein shake. My phone buzzed in my pocket—Amelia. I answered.

"Why did you give this interview to a random reporter with no experience?" She asked, cutting immediately to the chase. I rolled my eyes and tucked the phone under my ear, rustling in the freezer for some fruit.

"The random reporter has done really great stuff with the Saints socials this season." I replied. This was a stupid conversation. "If you wanted to choose who interviewed me you should've just done it."

Her sigh was so audible I could imagine the face she was making while doing it. "Amanté, we're talking legacy right now. You could've had anyone." Amelia sounded exasperated, but how many times had I spoken with great quarterbacks? How many post-game interviews and podcast episodes with people who were already famous?

"And I decided on her. Best case scenario, I'm known as the guy who helped a young woman break into the industry. Worst case, everyone's only paying attention to me anyway." I hadn't done it to look good, but even Amelia had to see the potential. She was quiet for a minute. I dumped my fruit, protein powder, and milk into the blender.

"When are you shooting? I need to book a flight." She sounded stressed—unusual for her. Even when there were a million things going on, she was calm and collected.

"Tomorrow afternoon, and I'll be fine. Don't worry about me." I reassured. "If there's any questions she should be sure to ask, send them over. I'm not going to ruin my career, Amelia." I chuckled. She sighed again; something was definitely wrong.

"Promise?" She finally asked.

"Promise." I replied. "I'll send you the script and everything."

"Good night, Amanté." She hung up. That was very, very weird. I turned on the blender.

"By the way, Ben and his sister are coming over to watch the game." Isaiah said around a mouth of popcorn. I pursed my eyebrows.

"Sister?" I asked, propping my feet up on the coffee table. Benjamin—my finance guy, who happened to be one of Isaiah and I's mutual friends from college—was a fairly private person, but I assumed I'd know if he had a sister.

"Yeah, she just moved to St. Clair so he's trying to get her to meet new people." Isaiah explained. "That's fine, though?" He liked to make sure I didn't have some kind of crazy recovery plan before inviting people over; Isaiah was thoughtful like that.

"That's fine. Calla is coming over after work to prep my interview, so we'll have a full house." I very pointedly avoided Isaiah's look. I knew he would be able to tell instantly that there was a lot more to it.

"Calla, huh?" He teased. I just stared at his game, acting like I didn't hear. "Calla the fuckbuddy, or Calla the coworker?" At that I punched him in the arm, and he whined like a kid, but we both laughed.

"Calla the coworker, and we're working on an important project. We also have agreed to be friends." I said, giving him a look. He laughed.

"Oh, is that what I heard yesterday morning?" Isaiah deadpanned, and I briefly considered punching him for real. The doorbell rang, so I took the opportunity to get up.

"Dick." I called over my shoulder, and went to open the door, expecting Calla—but it was Benjamin and his sister. "Hey, man!" I greeted and pulled him into a hug. He hugged back, and I stepped aside to let them in.

"Ben!" Isaiah said, switching off his game and hopping off the couch. They hugged, too, before Ben gestured to his sister.

"Isaiah, Amanté, this is Lucy, my little sister." She waved. Isaiah was looking at her like she was an alien. She seemed somewhat familiar, but it was still so weird that Ben had a sister nobody ever knew about.

"Hi. Thanks for having me." She said, and held up her tote bag. "I brought chips."

"Hell yeah." I replied, and before this awkward situation could continue, the doorbell rang again. Calla. I felt my chest tighten and took a deep breath before going to let her in. When the door swung open, I heaved out a deep breath. How could she look so beautiful even after such a long day at work? Her hair was down—she taken it out of the clip she'd been wearing earlier—and she'd thrown an old St. Clair University hoodie on over her blouse. She was barefoot, her heels in one hand and a box of pizza in the other.

"Hi." She said, and I noted her blush. Fuck, we were bad at the friends thing. I stepped inside, gesturing for her to enter.

"I was supposed to buy you food." I admonished, and she pushed the box into my hand. "I am a millionaire, remember?" She smacked my arm, the physical contact doing stupid things to my brain, and then froze in her place as she took in the fairly full room.

"Sorry, I would have brought more." She said, positively embarrassed. I set the pizza on the counter.

"Everyone, this is Calla. Calla, this is Benjamin, one of my friends from college, and his sister." I couldn't remember the sister's name—oops. Calla shook hands with Benjamin and the sister and waved at Isaiah, who winked at her. I glared at him over her head.

"Sorry to interrupt, work has been chaos and Amanté offered." She explained, and everyone told her not to worry about it, no big deal, happy to have her, and she smiled sheepishly up at me. "Can I borrow some comfier pants?"

18

Calla

I t was surprisingly easy to be productive surrounded by people, football, and food. It was fun, too, sitting on Isaiah's floor writing out potential questions, gasping or cheering when something happened in the Monday night game, and occasionally stuffing my face with pizza. After I changed into sweats, Amanté had ordered more pizza for all of us, and we quickly settled into a solid rhythm. He'd asked me to rephrase a few questions that put the Captains in a slightly negative light, but otherwise approved of all my questions, and sent along the list to his agent for approval. Isaiah, Lucy, and Benjamin were surprisingly helpful, too, pointing out when I sounded awkward or when a question seemed too numbers-oriented for a primetime audience.

Amanté was different among his friends. Not in a bad way, but different—sillier, more guy-like. Every time we'd all laugh, we met eyes, for just a second, and then his would dart away. It felt a little bad, if I was being honest. I liked when Amanté looked at me like I was the only person alive. Of course, friends didn't usually do that. And we were still having fun and getting along, and that was what I'd asked for.

I left shortly before the game ended, before Amanté could offer for me to stay. I was exhausted after spending the entire day coordinating a last-minute video shoot on top of all my other responsibilities—including figuring out who to pawn off my Tuesday responsibilities to—and tomorrow was going to be just as miserably long. I had no idea how the Saints office came to the decision to only hire one person to handle all of this genre of work, but I was starting to realize why the entire social media team before me left for other teams. This was a lot, I was exhausted, and I was making $28/hour to Amanté's $28 mil.

As much as I wanted to pass out on my bed as soon as I could, I forced myself to wash my face, do a half-assed gua sha routine, and pluck my eyebrows. Leaning forward, I inspected my skin, my lips, the circles under my eyes that would never go away and the unevenness of my bottom teeth. The longer I looked, the more I noticed, so I flicked off the bathroom light and found my way to my pillow in the dark.

I was already awake when my alarm sounded at five in the morning. This time of year, the sun wouldn't rise for another two hours, but I'd had enough early morning jobs that I knew how to set myself up for success. I had all my lights connected to a timer that simulated a sunrise, and my little studio was already beginning to be bathed in warm light from my fun lamps distributed about the space. I dropped a capsule into my espresso machine and brewed a double shot, bringing it over to my window. Fuck, it was early.

I took a scalding sip of the espresso and rolled out my yoga mat. Could I call it sun salutations if the sun wasn't yet up? It didn't matter—I was going to do every tiny thing that had ever made me feel good this morning, so I did my sun salutations. It only took about fifteen minutes, and afterwards I finished my espresso and wrote in my journal: *I am confident. I am capable. I deserve this opportunity. I am going to absolutely fucking kill this interview, and I am going to have everything I have ever wanted.* I bit the end of the pen, considering. *I am beautiful and wise. I know what I want and how to get it. I am brilliant and bring joy everywhere I go.* My pen hovered over the paper as I considered writing something about Amanté. The espresso was gone, though, so I closed the journal and turned on my tiny shower.

The shower was barely big enough for me to stand in, but the water was scalding and the pressure was perfect, so I didn't mind it. My lavender vibrator sat on a shelf by my head and I bit the inside of my lip. A glance at my phone told me I had plenty of time, so I took it and leaned my back against the tile, watching the steam rise around me, and turned it on. I loved my vibrator—I got it after a particularly awful relationship made me question whether I enjoyed sex at all, and it had given me ownership of my own pleasure. I closed my eyes, imagining Amanté's hands, his tattooed body filling the shower, touching me, tasting me.

No one was even here to see me, but I was blushing. My vibrator was lovely, but I never came as hard with it alone as I did when I was getting fucked. I imagined Amanté, the way his dick was made to fill me, working in tandem with my vibrator, and slid a finger inside myself, finding another small orgasm as I envisioned him claiming me. Fuck. I did feel more relaxed, though, and I giggled when I imagined thanking Amanté when I saw him later—at the confusion on his face.

Choosing between my natural texture and a blowout was always difficult, but I decided the blowout was the way to go today. I didn't want to be thinking about my hair all day, and a blowout was pre-dictable. I scrolled through my phone until I found a DJ set that looked promising and got started on getting ready. The goal was pro-fessional but undeniably alluring—not necessarily sexy or whatever, but just, elevated. Amanté was the focus, and he should be, but I wanted to be at least a little memorable. Simple makeup: a brush of blush across my cheeks and nose, natural lashes that emphasized my eyes without looking too fake, a natural lip that emphasized my cupid's bow, and brown shimmer on my lids to bring out the blue in my eyes.

Buttoning up the little boy blue blouse, I couldn't help but smile as I swayed to the music. I tucked it into a navy pencil skirt that was secretly stretchy and slipped on my classiest pumps. The DJ was killing the transitions and I let myself dance to the beat. Today was going to eat.

Production arrived right when I did, and I watched them transform the conference room into a studio while I reviewed my questions. I'd had the foresight to hire an external producer so I could mostly enjoy the day as talent rather than the leader of this whole mess. Breakfast was set up shortly after, and we all went to grab bagels and bacon and scrambled eggs and a scoop of fresh fruit, too. Planning a shoot on the Saints' dime was fun.

"You're Calla Monroe, right?" Someone asked, and I turned around with a full mouth. It was a man I didn't recognize, but he held out his hand and I shook it.

"Hi, yes, sorry. You are?" I asked, dabbing my mouth.

"Raul, I'm your sound guy today." He had an excited smile on his face and was decked out in Saints gear.

"Welcome to the facility, Raul. Grab some breakfast!" I replied. Looking at the time, Amanté was due to arrive in the next half hour. I directed hair and makeup to an empty office where they could set up—Amanté's agent had hired them, and I was grateful for the help. She wasn't coming to set today, as far as I knew, and I couldn't help but be relieved. Amelia Argent was an intimidating woman. She seemed so put together—I wanted to embody some of that energy today.

"Good morning, Ms. Monroe." Amanté murmured in my ear, and I clenched my thighs as the vision from my shower returned. Damn. I spun around.

"Good morning, Mr. Houston." I popped a blueberry into my mouth. "You're early." I made a show of checking my watch. He smirked down at me.

"You look beautiful." He was wearing a crisp pair of light wash jeans with a simple indigo shirt that made his chest and arms look... frustrating. His braids looked freshly redone, he had a fully iced out watch on his wrist, a fat chain, and, of course, his ridiculous goat pendant. Somehow, he managed to make all the diamonds look correct— not completely ostentatious. Like, of course he had a diamond encrusted goat around his neck. Of course.

"Thanks, buddy." I replied, remembering what was going on. "You've got like an hour and a half before we start," I pointed down the hall, "hair and makeup are that way," he leaned towards where I was pointing, giving me a whiff of cologne, "and you can help yourself to some breakfast." He raised an eyebrow but walked towards the office, waving at anyone who saw him.

19

Amanté

B uddy. She, for real, called me buddy. I bit down my laughter. Looking at her across from me on this set, it felt like another life. Another world. For a second, I felt all the lights, the production assistants, the weight of the chains around my neck; I felt every hair on my body, every breath inside my lungs. This wasn't just an interview—this was an acknowledgement of everything I'd worked for. Tears pricked at my eyes. When I was getting my shit rocked in middle school ball, I never would have imagined this outcome. When I started ditching my boys for extra training, and I felt so alone, I prayed it would all be worth it.

"You okay?" Calla's voice brought me back to my body. I swallowed and nodded, smile spreading across my face once again. She smiled back, and I thought I would remember this moment for the rest of my life.

"Sound?"

"Speeding."

"Action."

Calla smiled and looked into the camera, and I could see her settle into herself, could practically feel the confidence radiating out of her. She'd worked so hard for this—she'd been killing it all season, and now she looked like an actual angel, and she deserved to be seen for all the effort she was always putting in.

"I'm Calla Monroe, and today we're getting an inside look at the mind of the unparalleled, exceptional Amanté Houston. The league has never seen a talent like Mr. Houston, who has been elevating teams and amassing fans for the five years and change he's been playing professionally, and has shown no sign of slowing down." She took a deep breath and turned to me. "Amanté, you are about to break the record for fastest player to 100 touchdowns. How does it feel to get to this point in your career?"

I took a deep breath, mirroring hers, and adjusted my seat. "It feels amazing, Calla. Feels amazing."

"Looking back, was there a specific moment that you realized you could achieve something like this?" She asked, and her smooth voice set me even more at ease.

"Honestly? At the combine, looking around at all the other guys, I realized how close I was to everything I'd ever wanted." I could still feel the buzzing in my hands from that day; I could still picture the moment it all fell into place. I could practically feel the air entering my nose.

"Coming into a new team, a new culture, can be difficult to navigate. What's been the key to your success in consistently performing at such a high level throughout your career?" She leaned back in the chair, smiling at me with this glint in her eye.

"Every time I walk onto the field, I give it everything. I do my job, I do it well. There's not much else I can do." I replied. We continued like that for a while, answering silly questions and serious ones, making sure there was plenty of content to cut down. It quickly became natural, like Calla and I were just sitting on the floor in the living room, throwing popcorn into each other's mouth, laughing and teasing and learning about each other. It was easy, talking to her, but I wasn't sure this was because of how I felt about her. I thought she might just make it easy for people to talk to her—she brought an infectious confidence that permeated through the whole room.

"I have a feeling that this milestone is just the beginning of what's sure to be a continuously record-breaking career. What's next for you, in terms of personal and team goals?" She asked, and I straightened up a bit.

"Well, I'm planning on getting a ring or two." I answered, and pointed into the camera, drawing a few laughs. "Personally, I feel like I'm feeling as good as I've felt in my career. It might make me a corny motherfucker, but I'm hoping to find someone to share this feeling with." Calla's laugh burst from her mouth, despite her attempting to stifle it, and she covered her mouth with her dainty, manicured hands while she laughed.

"We might have to edit that out." She said, still laughing, but the look we shared was heavy. She looked to the producer, who gave her a thumbs up. "Last question for you, Amanté. Here in St. Clair, we say you aren't truly a Saint until you beat the Eagles at home. What can we expect out of you when you face them, at home, for the first time?" She asked.

I smirked. "You can expect a good fucking show, baby."

I didn't care much for St. Clair sports when I was growing up—far too focused on myself, funnily enough—but they weren't lying when they said the rivalry game was the best game of the year. The energy in the whole city was electric. I stopped for gas and got serenaded; there were parties every night, and from what I could see the Sunday tailgate events started at seven in the morning. One touchdown and I was untouchable. I smiled while I dialed up Amelia, looking through my closet for the outfit I'd show up wearing.

"Good morning!" She replied, surprisingly chipper. "I just got off the plane, heading to my hotel, then I'll see you at the facility, yeah?" Amelia loved airports—no wonder she was in a good mood.

"Sounds solid. How's the interview look?" I hadn't seen anything from the interview on Tuesday—not even a snippet, and Calla had been so busy all week I'd only seen her once, across the parking lot, and she'd given me a huge wave before getting in her car and driving off.

"I have to admit, Ms. Monroe was a good choice. It's a fantastic spotlight." She replied.

"What do you mean?" I asked, pulling out a few tops.

"She edited the whole thing. I thought you knew—she took full creative control. Saved everybody lots of money." Amelia laughed, but the statement rubbed me the wrong way. "Anyway, you'll love the video. Listen, I have to go, this idiot is screaming at me—I'll see you soon." She hung up before I could say anything else.

Calla had edited the entire video? No wonder she'd been so busy; she was essentially producing a commercial for national television. She definitely wasn't getting enough money for that. I made a mental note to send her flowers. Like that was enough of a thank you.

Isaiah wasn't home, but he would be in my box at the game with a bunch of the friends and family of the team. My eyes spotted an old jersey hanging in the back, and I pulled it out. My old St. Clair high school jersey had somehow made it in my wardrobe. I made a mental note to thank Amelia for making sure it was taken care of during the move.

It was a perfect fit: camo cargos, some sick sneakers, and the old ass jersey. I had always been that fucking guy. Rolling up in my 1999 pickup, the first thing I noticed was that there were about twenty times as many reporters and photographers as usual. I quickly scanned the crowd, searching for Calla, but didn't spot her. Weird—she normally took the pregame walk photos—and I kept looking until I saw her. There she was, sitting on her knees halfway down the hall, nearly blending into the mass of people standing in front of her, hair pulled up into a bouncing ponytail. I pointed and winked as I walked towards her, and held out my pendant as I moved past.

20

Calla

This. This was why I wanted to work in sports—this incredible atmosphere. I felt like I'd just snorted a line of cocaine, that was the only way to describe the complete and utter rush of energy and euphoria I felt standing on the field as the crowd went wild and the Saints ran out. These boys—they were my friends, now, and it only made it more special. I wasn't rooting for kids on a screen, I was rooting for actual guys with goals and inside jokes and weaknesses and strengths. It was a perfect day for football: sunny, not a cloud in the sky, and 57 degrees. Amanté was on one, yelling and hyping up the crowd, and they were loving it. Everyone was. This was his game, which meant it was the Saints' game, which meant we were going to fucking beat the fucking Eagles at home for the first time in five fucking years.

They started with the ball and a couple quick completions that put them almost immediately in range to score. *Come on, defense.* I was snapping photos and videos and uploading them, silently praying that the Eagles wouldn't score on their opening drive, when they called a crazy play that we were completely unprepared for. Their quarterback had years to decide where to throw the ball, and when he did, it was to an entirely uncovered tight end-

I started screaming, because Javon—one of our rookie corner-backs—was sprinting at me with the ball tucked in his hand. I hadn't even seen the interception, but the whole sideline was alive, screaming and jumping and racing him down the sideline. He was going to fucking do it. When he reached me at the corner of the endzone, he snatched the phone out of my hand and did a dance for the socials.

"Let's fucking go!" I yelled, catching the phone as he tossed it back at me to get a celebration with the whole defense. Quickly scrubbing through the video, I threw a song over it and uploaded it. Today was fucking good.

I snuck upstairs at the end of the first quarter to get official graphics and higher quality photos uploaded. It was much more electric down on the field, but even in the box the energy was high. The Eagles answered our pick six with a touchdown of their own, and when they stopped us on a fourth-and-one, they hit a kick, too. The crowd was, understandably, subdued as our boys ran into the locker room for the half. Half time was my bathroom break, so I took care of that, grabbed a hot dog, and monitored the socials.

Unsurprisingly, people were coaching from their couches all up in the comments, and I fought the urge to reply like some of those brands that went viral for being sassy. The video of Javon's pick six was doing numbers, which made me smile. I made sure the halftime posts were all going up without an issue before opening my personal phone. I had twelve—thirteen, now—messages, from my parents and Shay and a few people I hadn't spoken to since college. I smiled to myself, pulling up the video. It was part interview, part fan edit, and Amanté looked like a big fucking dog. He deserved it—he was. I had no doubt that in that locker room right now, they were getting hyped and planning on how to get Amanté the ball. He was being double-teamed, sometimes triple-teamed, but if anyone could break some ankles, it was Amanté. I had complete and utter faith in him. Besides, we were only down by three. We could have three touchdowns in the third quarter alone.

With everything in order, I headed back down to the field. The cheerleaders were doing a dance, and part of me filled with envy looking at their cute little outfits and glamor and flexibility. Next year, I was going to try out. I could use a second job, anyway. I imagined working all day at the facility, changing into some workout clothes, and staying another four hours for rehearsal; it sounded awful. They looked good, though. Maybe in another life.

When the boys ran out, the stadium erupted. I liked the energy they were bringing; Khalil had a great talent for keeping everyone level when games weren't going flawlessly, and it looked like he'd done just that. I pulled out my phone to monitor everything—most of my job was scheduling posts and monitoring them, especially on Sundays. Amanté was due for his touchdown, and that seemed to be the consensus from everyone online. Looking at Amanté, the look on his face and the tension behind his eyes, he was about to go off. Fuck, he was hot. The fire in his eyes, the sweat glistening on his arms, those tight pants, everything made me want him. It was unfair. He couldn't do this to me. He wasn't allowed to be fucking talented and fucking sexy. Athletes shouldn't have nice faces, I decided. But damn, I was ready for him to unleash. Tonight was his night—it was time for him to take it.

21

Amanté

C oming into the third quarter, I was locked in. I was no stranger to good defense, and today was no different. I was getting that 100th fucking touchdown, whatever the Eagles thought they were going to do. The guy who was riding my ass the entire first half had been pissing me off, anyway. It would be fun—therapeutic, even—to shut his bitch ass up. Khalil, our quarterback, gave an incredible halftime speech, and we came out onto the field fired up.

"Just get me the ball. I got you, just get me the ball." I told him, patting him on the back and going to get some water. They kicked off, and we got decent field positioning. Play call was bold—coach wanted us starting out with a big pass down the field. Fuck it. I lined up, eyeing my designated defender, and on the snap, I took off. One quick juke and he was behind me, and I had the whole field. Ball spiraled beautifully in the air, and I jumped to bring the ball down easy, turning in to run it home.

My defender, to his credit, caught up to me, tripping me up by the ankle and stopping me at the fifteen-yard line. The crowd was going wild, and after I tossed the ball to the ref, the defender got in my face.

"I'm gonna get your ass, unc."

"I don't know who the fuck you are." I grinned at him, skipping backwards before running to the huddle.

At this point, the game was muscle memory. I could hardly remember anything I was doing; I was just letting my body take over, sprinting and snatching and pushing. I had to admit, the Eagles defense had come to play, but nothing was going to stop me from getting my touchdown, least of all this no name bitch. I told Khalil as much, and as the ball snapped, I cut in on my guy—and ran into the end zone for the easiest touchdown toss I'd ever received. Lil bro was on his hands and knees in the turf.

"One hundred touchdowns for wide receiver Amanté Houston!" The announcers voice echoed through the stadium, and one of the offensive linemen picked me up on his shoulder, and I waved up the crowd, everyone was chanting my name. I scanned the sideline, and Khalil was running up to celebrate with me, and the lineman dropped me to the floor so I could do a little dance, and we sprinted to the sideline. The sideline was going crazy, and holy fucking shit, this was my life.

Tyler ran up to me, my massive goat pendant in hand, and put it around my neck. I crossed my arms and nodded, smiling, searching for a camera to stunt at, and instead locked eyes with Calla. Fuck, she was smiling, and her ponytail was flying all over the place, and she was jumping up and down, screaming something, and something fluttered in my stomach at the pride in her face.

"Greatest of all fucking time!" Tyler was yelling, and it all felt like some crazy dream.

It was still too close a game, and one of our best defensive guys went out with a concussion, and we found ourselves halfway through the fourth all tied up. They were taking lots of time off the clock. I glanced at the clock; if we were smart, we could score a walk-off touchdown and call it a day. If we weren't smart, we could probably end up with a kick. We just needed to make sure they didn't have time to take it back down. Play calling was pretty conservative—I was mostly a distraction, which I enjoyed, pissing off the defenders more and more each time I got open on them for no reason. I got to block a big boy one play, which was always fun because I got to flex my time in the weight room.

We inched closer and closer to their territory as the clock ticked down and down—and Khalil threw an interception. I cursed and started my sprint towards him, taking as best an angle as I could, running him down before he could take it for a touchdown, and launched myself into the guy, throwing us both into his own sideline. He jumped up, standing over me, yelling shit I couldn't hear because the entire Eagles team was screaming. I stood up, throwing him off of me, and bit my tongue when the referee threw a flag. There was no fucking way I got called on that, and one of my guys pulled me away before I could say so.

"Taunting, defense." I didn't listen to the rest, just ignored the idiot who lost his team fifteen yards for acting like he was that guy. When I got to the sideline, I went straight to Khalil, smacking his helmet.

"You're good, man. You're good." He was looking over plays; I could tell he was beating himself up. We had three minutes—more than enough time, even if they scored on the turnover. "Look at me." He did. "Nobody cares about one turnover. You're a good fucking quarterback. Get your head right." They did, in fact, score on the turnover, putting them up one and leaving us forty-five seconds on the clock.

I patted Khalil on the back as he put his helmet on. "Easy money, baby."

We ran out onto the field. Khalil gestured for the crowd to quiet, and to my awe, they listened, and he rattled out the plan in our huddle. The first play was a run—successful, getting us the first down. Next play, slot pass to a receiver—incompletion. I looked at Khalil and nodded. I ran across the field, and when they snapped the ball, I tore across the middle, then cut back down to meet Khalil's bullet, catching both defenders at my back and tearing back up the field, hopping past whiffed tackles and sidestepping defenders, sprinting as fast as I fucking could until I hit the end zone, dropped the ball, and stood there, arms crossed, staring into the first camera I saw, until my boys caught up to me.

We set up for the extra point. The Eagles called a time out. I jogged right to coach. When he looked at me, I knew he was already thinking what I was.

"We're going for two." He said, and launched into the plan.

22

Calla

Watching Amanté was like church. Everything he did was impressive, and he looked faster than humanly possible when he ran the forty-five-yard run after the catch for the touchdown to tie us up. When they iced our kicker, a small part of me wanted us to go for two points to win it outright, and as the time ran out, a shiver ran up my spine as Amanté and the rest of the offense ran back out onto the field. Holy fucking shit—this was it. We didn't have enough time to get the ball back after this; it was all or nothing.

Please, please, please. I inched my way closer to the end zone. Snap—throw—fuck, incompletion. But there was a flag—I held my breath in anticipation. It was defensive pass interference, and the stadium erupted as we lined up on the one-yard line to try for two again. I could see Amanté saying something to the guy defending him; it amused me that he was a frequent trash talker. He'd earned the right to talk shit, at least.

We snapped the ball, and it was like everything was in slow motion. This could've been the final game of the postseason, that's how high the tension was. Our offensive line was protecting Khalil, but only for so long, as it started to collapse, and Khalil scrambled back, side to side, the clock expired, he was searching, searching. Amanté tore through the middle, and Khalil let it rip, a too-high pass that sealed our fate.

Except, Amanté was in the air, one arm outstretched, and the football was in his hand. I gasped as he got slammed to the ground—but he maintained control. We'd converted—we'd won. We beat the Eagles. I ran onto the field with the rest of them. Everyone was running to Khalil, and I searched for Amanté.

He was still on the ground. I picked up my pace, running towards him. As I got closer, I could see him gasping. My heart began to race; I felt myself begin to sweat.

"He can't breathe!" I yelled, running faster, faster. "He can't breathe!" I reached him, sliding to my knees, screaming for someone. The look in his eyes nearly made my heart stop. "Oxygen! Get a fucking doctor! He can't breathe!"

23

Calla

It was silent and I fucking hated it. How had a cacophony of cheering fans become so, so quiet? I could see every detail of the field and the fabric on his knees and the footfalls of the medical staff running out. When I reached him, I didn't know what to do, just grabbed his hand and said shit, I had no idea what I was saying, just talking to him, saying anything.

When the medical staff reached us, they pushed me out of the way, and I stood back up, hovering over them, trying to see what was going on. A breath pushed through my lips when they strapped the oxygen mask over his face, but no one looked happy, and he still had this awful look behind his eyes, and my ears were ringing. The team was kneeling, not too far away, and I jumped when someone touched my back.

Khalil—our quarterback, who I interacted with nearly every day but hadn't gotten very personal with—was standing behind me. He squeezed my shoulder. An ambulance drove onto the field. We watched as he was strapped to a stretcher and loaded on. Then, he was gone.

"Let's go." Khalil said, rubbing my back. "I just have to change."

My car was too quiet. When I pulled out of the garage, my heart lurched, seeing Amanté's little red pickup. I couldn't quiet the slimy voice in the back of my head telling me that something truly, irreversibly awful had happened to him. I blinked, focusing on the road.

The last thing I needed was to get into a wreck. The hospital wasn't far—just ten or fifteen minutes, if I could find parking. I just needed to follow Khalil's car. Breathe, breathe, breathe.

A nurse stopped us in the waiting room. We couldn't see him for at least an hour, maybe longer. My heart dropped. Fans were starting to arrive outside the hospital, waiting to hear what had happened, and if he was okay. The door opened and I breathed a sigh of relief as Isaiah walked in, his eyes quickly finding mine and coming over to give me a big hug.

"What happened? Is he okay?" He asked.

"We don't know." Khalil replied, and a weight settled upon my shoulders. A nurse walked over to us—a man my dad's age wearing immaculately clean scrubs and bright, decorated nurse clogs that said "World's Best Papaw."

"Here for Amanté Houston?" He asked, looking between us all.

"Yes." I said, stepping forward.

"He's suffered a punctured lung. He's going to be okay. Someone will come get you when he's ready for visitors. It probably won't be for a few hours." The man left as quickly as he came, and my vision fogged. Someone's arm around my shoulders pulled me into their chest, and I returned the embrace.

"Fuck this." I breathed.

Isaiah laughed. "Who wants some victory food? On me."

The diner was not equipped to seat the fifteen or so of us crowded into pushed together tables, but they were thrilled to. The walls were lined with Saints jerseys and photos of players, and the sweet lady at the host stand looked about ready to freak out. Most of the guys had decided to go home once we had the news that Amanté was okay, but the ones who stayed were laughing and joking around like we were at a high school awards ceremony. It made me smile—the normalcy of it all. My skin felt like it was still buzzing with electricity. I scanned the table. I didn't know all of their names; there was Isaiah and Khalil, of course, and a few others I knew: Javon, one of our most talked about rookies, and Mikey, who I'd made a video on due to his secret singing talent.

I recognized everyone from the field, of course, and I knew all their names if I thought about it long enough. But I hadn't really forged real relationships with most of them. It was better that way, and it was how I'd always operated: keeping work and work people completely separate from my personal life. Until Amanté, of course. We hadn't had the chance to keep it professional, and when we tried, I just felt this warmth. A knowing. Like I'd been meant to meet Amanté the way I did, so I couldn't keep him at arm's length, no matter how much I tried.

The second night, when he sent flowers and a car and I'd gone over without hardly thinking about it, I'd wanted to lean into it. I wanted him—obviously—and my nude dancing was the least of the ways I wanted to show him that. But he'd been so good and romantic and idealistic that my fear had taken over immediately. Sure, it would be good to date Amanté fucking Houston—but was it worth sacrificing my career if he was only interested on a whim? Sitting here now, my answer was obvious. Yes. Obviously, yes, Amanté was worth it. We were friends, and he had used his own incredible achievement to give me the chance to succeed. He was dedicated and ambitious and caring and I'd told him I wanted to just be friends. What a fucking idiot.

"How are you holding up, Calla?" Isaiah asked between sips of a vanilla milkshake. He scooted a chocolate one across the table towards me and I took a long drink.

"Overwhelmed, I think." I replied honestly. He nodded.

"He's lucky to have you." Khalil said, and I narrowed my eyes. He cleared his throat. "I mean, nobody was paying any attention to him. You got him help." He took a big bite of his burger.

"Come on Calla, everybody knows he has a crush on you." Javon said, halfway down the table, and my cheeks warmed. "Ain't nobody else wandering through that ugly ass building to see you." He continued, and I pushed a laugh out. There was absolutely no way in the world that the team—The St. Clair Saints, professional football franchise—thought Amanté had an embarrassing crush on me. But, as I thought about it, it was true. I didn't know the other guys that well because I didn't see them all that often, but I always seemed to cross paths with Amanté, even if it was just with a quick wave or smile across the room.

Fuck. Amanté Houston was like a sweet lovesick teenager, and I'd been completely oblivious. I'd been worried about him losing interest, but he'd been crushing so hard even his 22-year-old teammates were making fun of him. I laughed again, drinking my milkshake. Someone started teasing Javon, and then everyone was chowing down on smashburgers and chili, and the clamp of fear around my heart released.

Isaiah and I went back to the hospital, promising Khalil we'd update him if anything changed, and sat together in the waiting room for another hour until a nurse—the same man from before—came out. When he saw us, he waved, and I held my breath, preparing for what I was about to see. I didn't know much about punctured lungs, but it couldn't be that good, and when I replayed the tackle in my head, I could see everything, from where the defender made contact to how he smashed to the field. He wasn't in the ICU, which was great news, but they had admitted him. It was now 10:00pm, and the nurse very politely informed us that he was bending the rules to allow us to see him so late, so we needed to be respectful and quick about it.

He looked smaller than he should. How did a 6'2", 220-pound man look so, so small? Tears pricked my eyes. He looked sort of out of it, and a physician was speaking to him as well as the team physician, and he was mostly covered in a blanket. His feet poked out from under the blanket, covered with too-small socks. He was fiddling with the tube that was administering his oxygen, and I swallowed loudly when I noticed the tube sticking out of his chest. When the physician saw us, he turned towards us a bit, and continued speaking.

"The procedure went well—just needed a small repair. No fractures, just pretty good bruising on the ribs. We're administering oxygen to be safe, and we'll keep him a few days to make sure the lung stays inflated and clear. The tube will be removed in a few days, too, as long as everything goes well." He explained, and shook all of our hands, and left. The team physician shook our hands, too.

"If you want to sleep on the couch, they said that was fine. I'm going to head out while he's stable. Thanks for coming." She smiled at me—and then it was just Amanté, Isaiah, and me.

"This straw," Amanté spoke, pointing to the plastic tube that was keeping his lung from collapsing, "is inside my lungs." I wasn't sure that was exactly how it worked, but I laughed anyway. "It's in me, Calla. What the fuck." Isaiah laughed then, and Amanté coughed.

"That is crazy." I replied, walking closer and sitting on the nurse's stool. He tried to shift in the bed and winced.

"My fucking ribs hurt. Fuck that guy." He complained again, and I couldn't help but smile. "But I got his ass. I caught that shit." Amanté paused, looking up at me with genuine fear in his eyes. "I caught it, right?"

"Yes, dude, we won." Isaiah replied. He pulled up a video of the catch on his phone and we all leaned around Amanté's head to watch. We each sucked the breath through our teeth at the hit.

"That's fucking right." Amanté muttered, leaning his head back. I wanted to hold his hand, touch him, something, but I wasn't sure what to do. He sighed. "There goes my MVP season, huh?" I placed a hand on his arm, and he adjusted his head to look at me. It was like looking at him for the first time. He looked so exhausted, and I realized that staying here all night was not what he needed.

"You should sleep. I'll come back first thing in the morning, okay?" I said, and hurt flashed across his face—but not before his eyes closed and he had to fight them back open.

"Thank you." He squeezed my hand as I pulled it away, and against my better judgment, I pressed a kiss to his forehead before walking out.

24

Amanté

My body hurt. I badly wanted to curl onto my side, but even thinking about moving hurt. Looking around, I was alone in a fairly nice hospital room. One wall had a massive window overlooking the river. I didn't know you could get the penthouse suite in a hospital. My phone was sitting on the table beside me, to my surprise. Someone must have brought it for me. I didn't remember much between grabbing that pass and now, which was—about four in the morning. Awesome.

I remembered taking a big hit, not unexpected in the life of a professional wide receiver, making sure to hold onto the ball, and being confused once I hit the ground. After that was mostly a blur. I could see Calla running towards me in slow motion like the climax of a cheesy movie. I spoke with a doctor, I was pretty sure, and Isaiah was here. With Calla, I thought. I turned to look out the window. It almost reminded me of the view from the hotel.

When I looked down at my body, I started to shake. My hands trembled in front of me as I examined them, my fingers, the little device that was tracking my oxygen and the IV stuck uncomfortably at the top of my wrist. I had a straw—a tube, a piece of plastic—inside my ribs, making sure my lung didn't collapse. I remembered that much, that the doctor said they'd had to do an emergency operation to repair the hole in my lung. My ribs ached, too. I couldn't remember if I'd broken any. It felt like it. I tasted salt on my lips, and sniffed. I was crying.

God, it hurt to cry. Even stifling the sobs that were beginning to shake me was painful. I wanted my mom, and then I couldn't stifle anything. Everything hit me all at once, and everything hurt, and my season was over, and I wanted my mom to come and tell me it would all be okay, and she couldn't. Something was beeping and a nurse stuck their head in my door.

"Sorry." I said, not really sure what I was apologizing for.

"No need." It was a man, probably around my mom's age, and he came in to check all the little machines. I took a few deep breaths, trying to get it together. "Lots of pain?" He asked. I nodded. I could hardly think through it all. He messed around with the pump and then stood with me, watching.

"You like football?" I asked. I don't know why I asked.

"I do. I'm supposed to act like I don't know who you are." He smiled at me, and I felt tears prick my eyes again. "I taped the game to watch after my shift, but why don't you tell me how it ended?"

I smiled, breathing easier. "We won." I fell asleep.

Morphine had me groggy as shit in the morning, and as nice as the lack of pain was, I was ready to feel like I had my brain back. When what felt like the entire hospital flooded my room at the crack of fucking dawn, I told them that I didn't want morphine anymore. The nurse wrote it in my chart but told me that was what I'd get if I asked for anything else between now and when the doctor came in. I could handle that. I was still feeling pretty good from my 4:00am dose.

Someone knocked on the door and pushed it open, and I was shocked to see Calla. She looked beautiful—like always—but less put together than she generally was for work. Her hair was in a mess of a bun on top of her head, her eyes were dark, and she was wearing her comfy slacks with a big sweater. I wondered—how late had she gone home?

"Morning, playa." She said, and I burst into slightly pained laughter. "Sorry. I don't know why I said that. Hi, Amanté." She crossed the room to my side. "I brought hot chocolate. The internet said no caffeine, but I thought you'd appreciate a fun drink." I did. I appreciated her. I took the hot chocolate from her hand.

"Are you okay?" I asked, setting the hot chocolate aside to cool. She smiled, but her eyes were watery.

"I should be asking you." She said, and watched the ice rattle around in her coffee. "I'm okay. I didn't sleep very well."

"Worried about me?" I teased, but she didn't smile. "I'm okay. I have enough morphine to knock out a horse." She smiled then. I thought back to last night, how I remembered her being there. "You were here last night?"

"Yes."

"What's wrong with me? I know the lung thing," I gestured to the tubes, "but are my ribs broken? It feels like I shattered every one of them." Right now, it wasn't too bad, but the ache was already beginning to build just from being awake.

"No broken ribs. The doctor said the procedure went well, though, and it wasn't too much damage." I hated seeing her like this, like she was trying not to cry, like she was fighting the frown from her sweet cheeks.

"I am okay, Calla. Thank you. For everything." I said, reaching for her hand. She squeezed it once. She looked at me differently, somehow. It wasn't quite pity, or I'd be mad. She just was looking, really looking.

"I have to head into work. I'll visit after, if you want?" She nodded at the hot chocolate. "Don't forget that." I slowly reached to grab it, and once I went to take a sip, she was gone. It was delicious.

25

Calla

Seeing Amanté awake and mostly well considerably raised my spirits. I had slept horribly last night, waking up in a panic every hour or so, dreaming that I'd received an awful call. Not that I would receive a call at all. Amanté was my friend, and newly so, and even though watching him had triggered some kind of horribly embarrassing come to Jesus moment, it didn't mean that we were suddenly more than friends. As intense as yesterday had been, I was glad for our agreement. If I wasn't careful, I was going to let my ability to always have a good time blend with his endless charisma and find myself moving faster than was smart. He was a good friend, anyway, and some friends were true friends while being attracted to one another. I shook my head—who was I even trying to convince?

Connor was waiting for me when I walked in. "Good morning." He greeted. I smiled.

"Amanté is going to be okay, thank God. Did you see the numbers on our socials last night?" I'd briefly scanned the page every time I woke up—it was blowing up, filling with prayers and questions and tons of views. People were reposting edits of my interview—and I'd even seen a few posts praising me for how I'd handled Amanté's injury. I fought the smile off my face.

"Can we chat?" He asked, and my stomach turned. I followed him to his office, and froze in the doorway when I saw Amanté's agent sitting in the other chair. She stood when she saw us.

I reached out a hand. "Calla Monroe—I'm not sure we've been properly introduced." She shook my outstretched hand, throwing a look towards Connor. He cleared his throat.

"Calla, you're fired." He blurted out. Time slowed. All I could hear was the slight ringing of my ears I got when it was very quiet or I hadn't drank enough. His agent's face was painfully pitying and Connor looked firmly at his hands. The video I'd planned, shot, and edited had received praise from every outlet that wrote about it. The social media had the most engagement it'd ever had, and I'd literally saved our star player's life last night.

My throat made a garbled noise. "Why?" I asked, trying to figure out where to put my free hand.

"Unfortunately, we have a strict no relationships policy." Connor said, busying himself with papers I knew were useless. The color drained from my face.

"I am not in a relationship." I replied, forcing my voice to remain steady. "I'm confused." The woman sighed, and before she could speak, Connor cleared his throat.

"We'd heard rumors from some of the players, and Amelia—Ms. Ardent—informed us that you stayed the night with him last night. Unfortunately, we cannot bend the rules." He sounded genuinely pained, but panic was beginning to rise in my throat.

"This is a misunderstanding. Amanté and I are friends, that's all." This was my worst fucking nightmare come to life. "I watched him asphyxiate on the field, I checked on him at the hospital and went home." My words sputtered out of me. "I brought him hot chocolate this morning. I would do the same if you were in the hospital, Connor."

"Calla, please." He said, eyes flitting to Amelia.

She smiled, and I wanted to smack it off her face. "Mr. Houston cannot be sidetracked by scandal when he is attempting to have a record breaking season." I clenched my jaw.

"Mr. Houston," I spat, "is a human being who nearly lost his life. You're punishing me for caring." I took a deep breath and lowered my volume, realizing I was beginning to yell. "We are just friends. This is a misapplication of the rules."

Her lips pissed me off. "We appreciate the incredible work you did on the interview." Her compliment sent my blood simmering. Connor coughed once.

"Calla, I am sorry, but rules are rules." He still wouldn't look me in the eye.

"So that's it." I said, turning my ire on him. "You invent a relationship in order to kick me out and, what, claim that you did everything I've done for the Saints?" I should not have said that. "This is unbelievable." I was on the brink of saying something else I'd regret, so I threw my head back, silencing myself and blinking away threatening tears.

Someone knocked on the doorframe behind me and I spun around to see Khalil, in office on his off day, a little girl propped on his hip. "Calla, just the girl I was hoping to find!" He said, and his face dropped as soon as he saw mine. I didn't bother trying to smile. "Sorry..." He started, then stepped away. Fuck, this was embarrassing.

"It's out of my hands." Connor said, his voice softer. "We appreciate the work you have done, but the decision has been made." I swallowed. I was going to pass out—I could barely breathe. Everything around me was fuzzy. I turned on my heel and walked out, past Khalil.

"Hey, Calla!" He said, falling into stride beside me. "Are you okay?"
I tried not to feel frustration with the kind man I barely knew who'd
come in on his day off specifically to check on me. The sleepy toddler
in his arms helped.

"She's adorable." I said, wishing it didn't sound like I had a lump
in my throat. The girl gave me a thumbs up. "They fired me." I said,
wanting it out there. Khalil stopped.

"What?" He asked. I relayed the gist of it. I wanted to kick Amelia in
her fucking face and smash Connor's head into his stupid desk. "Calla,
that's insane. They can't do that."

The truth was, I hadn't looked to see if my employment had some
clause about relationships. I'd been worried about it because I didn't
want it to look bad—not because I thought it was literally against the
rules. I felt tears prick my eyes again.

"We're friends, Khalil. I didn't do anything wrong." I plead, and I
believed it. We'd slept together, sure, but we were mature adults who'd
agreed to keep it platonic while we worked together. We made the
right choice and I was being punished anyway. Khalil's arm squeezed
around my shoulder.

"Here," he handed me his phone, "give me your number. I can't
stay today—lil miss has a half day—but I'm going to call you and
make sure you are okay." Something about Khalil was so soothing. It
must've been the fatherly energy coming out. His daughter was now
slumped on his shoulder. I typed my number and handed it back.
"Head up, Calla."

I sat in my car for what felt like an eternity. My guilt and fear and
sadness was beginning to morph into anger. Who the fuck did Amelia
Ardent think she was to snitch on Amanté's personal life to get me
fired? How did Connor just go along with it, even with no concrete
proof? How had I lost my dream job in less than a season? I knew the

answer to that one—by being an idiot. I turned up my music. Then turned it off. I dialed Shay.

"Hi!" She drawled, coffee shop ambiance in the background. She usually did her business stuff at the shop—kept her grounded, she said.

"Hi." I replied, not even trying to hide my mood. I started up the car, letting the engine warm a bit.

"What's wrong?" She asked.

"I got fired. For being with Amanté." I waited. She was silent on the other end.

"I'll meet you at yours." She said, and hung up. I huffed out a sigh and cranked my music up. When I looked back up, back towards the facility, Amelia was walking out—and towards me.

"No." I said to myself, buckling my seatbelt to further protect my peace. My peace that she was unwilling to respect, apparently, because she walked right up to my window and knocked on it. I took a deep breath. She pointed down and smiled. I shook my head.

She knocked on the window again and all the fear, frustration, and rage filled my brain all at once. I unbuckled and threw the door open, nearly hitting her as she scrambled back, and slammed the door shut. I sealed my mouth shut, waiting to hear what she had to say before I let myself scream any of the millions of awful things I wanted to scream at her.

"I'm sorry about all this." She finally said. I just stared. And stared. And then I laughed, throwing my head back.

"I know you did not follow me to my car to apologize when your bitch-ass is the one who got me fired." I finally said, steadying my gaze on hers.

She shifted uncomfortably. "I didn't know it was going to go down like that." She was full of shit. "I didn't show up today to get you fired."

"No, you showed up to make sure Mr. Houston," I spat his name, "was focused, when what you should be worried about is if he's going to fucking recover." I took a step closer to her. She was taller than me, lanky but in a begrudgingly elegant way, but I definitely had some pounds on her and I hadn't yet decided if I was going to break her nose. I probably didn't want assault charges, but it was still on the table.

"I don't know why I said that." She said, then sucked in a breath, stepping away. I narrowed my eyes, but to my irritation, I couldn't detect anything to indicate she wasn't telling the truth. "Look, I was here on other business, but Amanté texted me this morning asking me to tell Connor how much of a godsend you are. I didn't know it would be a problem. He said other people had been saying things about Amanté and you and..." She trailed off, covering her face.

I just crossed my arms and waited. She turned back to me with a sigh. "I can be jealous, alright? There was a little part of me that was pleased you couldn't have it all. So, I said what I said. I am sorry." She chewed on her bottom lip as she looked at me, waiting for my reaction. Almost as quickly as it came, the anger slipped away, leaving only sad, lonely defeat.

"Amanté and I are just friends." I affirmed.

"I know that's not true." She replied, a laugh waiting to bubble out.

"See, that's what's pissing me off, because you are lying on my fucking name and you are ruining my life. How about I go to your agency and tell them you're meddling with my career because you're fucking jealous?" All the good will she'd created was immediately expended.

"No, I mean—I believe you—I just know him, and I know you aren't just friends." She sputtered. I stared her down. "I am sorry. For the record, I never said anything about your relationship. Connor put the pieces together on his own." She watched me carefully and I felt tears prick my eyes. It wasn't fair. We were just friends—that was the truth, the fucking honest truth, even if we both had feelings—we were just friends. Intentionally, so that our careers weren't impacted. Yet here I was. I could feel something awful on the tip of my tongue, so I just got back into my car and drove away.

When I got home, I had the notice in my email, and I read through the whole thing three times before tossing my phone in my freezer to keep from doing anything stupid. I had no idea how Shay got in the building, but she was banging on my door shortly after wearing a hoodie I'd bought her as a joke last Christmas that was decorated with sexy photos of me, holding not one, not two, but three bottles of wine, and a takeout bag from our favorite Chinese place.

She walked in on her own, clearing the various papers off my coffee table and arranging everything. "Fuck them." She said once, then continued, even tidying my kitchen a bit before she took two wine glasses, the TV remote, and a pair of forks. She plopped onto the couch beside me.

"Thanks, Shay." My voice was small; my throat tight.

"Do you want to start with the Albariño, Barbaresco, or Rioja?" Shay presented each bottle. She had a genuinely impressive collection but was a bit of a closet wino. She'd been fascinated with wine since I'd known her, and always prided herself on knowing all about it. I wouldn't be shocked if the next direction for the coffee shop would be tacking on a wine bar and staying open late.

"Does the sommelier have a recommendation?" I asked, smiling her way. I could always count on Shay. She was a really, really good friend. She pushed forward the white wine—it had a nice minimal label, very sophisticated.

"Albariño to cool you off, because if I know you, and I do know you, you're fucking pissed." She opened the bottle and poured. I gave it a sniff—nice bouquet—and a sip—delicious, refreshing. Shay offered a spring roll, and I took a bite. It was a shockingly perfect pairing.

"I love you." I said around the mouthful, and she grinned. "Amanté's agent was sitting in Connor's office when I got there. He said there was a strict no-fraternization policy and that I was being let go." I took a bigger sip of the wine. "I tried to tell them we were just friends but apparently other people in the facility had been talking about his crush on me and then Amelia told him that I'd stayed the night at the hospital last night when I absolutely did not." I took a large bit of the spring roll and closed my eyes, trying to focus on the flavors.

"That's some bullshit. Do we know any lawyers?" Shay asked, and I shrugged. We enjoyed the food and wine for a minute.

"You know what's fucking crazier?" I asked. "Amelia followed me to my car to apologize. After she literally orchestrated this whole thing."

"No."

"And told me it was because she gets jealous sometimes. Can you imagine? She's lucky she was talking to me and not you." I exhaled. Shay burst into laughter.

"I'm proud of you, because I know it took every ounce of your willpower not to say something awful." She paused. "You didn't say something awful, did you?" I laughed, then, and we both laughed until tears were streaming down Shay's face.

When we calmed down, Shay put a rom com on the TV and we finished our food. Before I knew it, the bottle was empty, and she was cozied up under the blanket, looking half asleep.

"What did Amanté say?" She asked, as credits rolled. I didn't look at her. "Please don't tell me you haven't talked to him."

"My phone is in the freezer to prevent poor behavior." I should take that out. Hopefully I hadn't ruined it.

"Calla." She scolded, and I glared at her.

"I know it isn't his fault, but..." I trailed off, tears pricking my eyes again. "I lost my job. My dream job that I've been trying to get for years. What if I said something I didn't mean?" I knew it wasn't fair, but it twisted my stomach anyway.

"You need to talk to him." Shay said, sitting up straighter.

"And say what? Your bitch agent ruined my life because I was distracting you?"

"She said that?" Shay asked. I nodded. She stared at me, a slow blink that meant she was preparing for something devious. "She isn't important right now. What's important is that you and Amanté are friends, right?" I nodded again. "If I got fired because of a misunderstanding surrounding our friendship, how would you feel if I ghosted you?"

"You can't get fired." I replied; she smacked my arm, and we both cracked smiles. "I would feel bad."

"Right. We're going to the hospital tomorrow." She decided, snuggling back up into the couch. I covered my face with my hands and fell back into the pillows.

26

Amanté

It was nearly midnight before I gave up on Calla returning. She was probably exhausted from the day, understandably, but I couldn't stop the disappointment. Not only was I bored, but I was also regaining little spotlights of memory, and the clearest one was the moment on the field when our eyes locked and she ran to me. I could see every hair as it bounced around her face, could see the rapid evaluation she was conducting in her head just by looking at the movement of her eyes, and it filled the memory with her, instead of the pain. The fear. I remembered that, too. I'd been hit in the diaphragm before, but having the breath knocked out of me was a relatively quick discomfort. The panic I felt when I realized it wasn't going away was tempered by the warmth of her hand on mine, the sound of her voice—even though she was screaming. It was soothed by her presence, I guess, and the memory was not so bad.

She may have saved my life. It wasn't a particularly severe injury, according to the team doctor who filled me in on everything later that day, but it could have been. I would still be in the hospital until they were confident my lung wouldn't collapse again, and I likely wouldn't be back to practice or play for at least four weeks—more likely six. As awful as it sounded to sit in bed and do boring physical therapy for a month and a half, it sounded like I'd be able to be back for the postseason. As long as we made it to the postseason—I was hoping the offense could function without me. It seemed like they could. They were talented guys; it was just a young team. They'd needed someone like me to bring a little experience to the room.

The thought willed a smile to my face. When I was playing for the Captains, everyone was miserable. I didn't like to talk bad about anybody, but here was an aura of resentment that filled the locker room. I was still achieving success even though the team was suffering. Getting traded to St. Clair had been a dream, not only because I was playing for my childhood team, but because I was entering a room where my greatness in spite of mismanagement was something people were excited about. St. Clair had talent—some new blood that was exciting the fan base—but they were missing the mentality of a closer. When I walked in the room, when I put on the uniform for the first time, that was when I realized that all of my less-than-great time with the Captains was worth something. I'd learned how to give my everything even when it seemed hopeless.

We'd won more than a few games that way. Shit, we won last night because we would not quit. I had faith that the boys would keep the momentum enough to get us to the postseason. Then I could show up, my triumphant return, and bring a championship to St. Clair. Fuck—I wanted to laugh, but laughing hurt for the exact reason I wanted to laugh. Fantasizing about bringing a championship to St. Clair while strapped to a hospital bed with a tub coming out of my chest and an oxygen line was fucking hilarious. I could, though. This injury wasn't the end—it was time for the boys to level up so I could come back to a team so badass they don't even need me anymore. And then we'd stomp the competition.

I woke up to the sunrise out my big window and couldn't help but smile at the image. I was feeling less hopeless—a good prognosis and less pain was probably the culprit. A nurse came in to do whatever it is they check on every morning, and I dozed off and on for a few more hours, until a knock on the door woke me.

Calla stood in the doorway. She was wearing grey yoga pants and a tight black shirt that made her look simultaneously decadent and chill. She was shrugging off a massive puffer, and hung it on one of the chairs. We locked eyes, and I could see the wall up in hers—something was wrong. Her eyes were pink, and the little smile she gave me didn't quite reach her eyes. And, she wasn't in one of her usual work fits.

"What-" My question was thwarted by Shay, Calla's friend I met at the party, bursting into the room with two trays of beverages and a bag of presumably pastries. I could hear a few nurses yelling thank you from behind her, and she threw them a wave.

"Amanté!" She exclaimed, setting everything down and coming over to give me a very odd hug. "You look a lot better than you did on the TV." She teased, and I made a face. Before I could say anything more, she turned to the ridiculous amount of coffee and held them out to me. "Choose—I told the nurses at the station that they could have whatever you don't want." I looked up to Calla, and she had an iced something already, so I surveyed the options.

"Let me pay you for these." I said, considering each. Knowing how much coffee costs these days, it was probably $80 worth of coffee. She waved me off.

"That one's my favorite, it's our Saints signature drink. Honey infused cold brew with some cream." I took it, and she immediately swept back out of the room with the rest, earning a literal whoop from the nurse stand.

Calla was still hovering by the door, so I took a sip of the coffee—it was pretty solid. "She really should let me pay for all that. It wasn't necessary at all."

"Shay owns the coffee shop." Calla smiled, walking towards me. That was almost surprising, except that every interaction I'd ever had with Shay was direct and purposeful: good qualities for a business owner.

"Are you okay?" I asked, patting the spot next to me on the bed. She shrugged. "What happened?"

"You haven't talked to Amelia?" She asked, a bit of venom in her tone, and I was shocked. What would I have needed to talk to Amelia about? Did the Saints drop me after the injury? She placed a hand on my arm, pulling my attention back. "It's hard to say."

"Take your time." I replied. We each drank some more coffee. Finally, she sighed, twisting to face me.

"I got fired. Because of this." She was expressionless, eyes flitting between mine. I blinked.

"Because I got hurt?" I asked, but that didn't make sense. Air pushed from her lips and she turned to face the window.

"You know that's not what I meant." I could hear the tightness in her throat.

"That can't be true." I said, shaking my head. "They can't police our friendship like that." She laughed, and I swallowed. I was being naive if I thought we were just friends, but no one on the team would've snitched—at least not intentionally.

"Ask fucking Amelia." Calla said, still facing the window, and I reached out a hand to brush her wrist. Her shoulders lowered as I did. Ask Amelia? A slow disbelief began to build. She wouldn't—she had never inserted herself into my personal life like that. I hadn't told her about Calla at all... had I? I couldn't remember now, and I felt so stupid. Calla had specifically asked to keep things platonic so this wouldn't happen, and here we were, a singular week later.

"Calla." I said, taking her hand. She turned to face me, and I fought the urge to wipe the lone tear streaking down her cheek. "I cannot express how sorry I am." I squeezed her hand. She nodded. Her phone buzzed in her hand, and when she read it, she stood up.

"I really like you, Amanté, but I need a little time to figure out what to do." She said, and I felt my heart drop into my stomach, and she walked out, just as quickly as she'd came.

I understood that she needed space, but fuck, I hated it. I wanted to talk this out—I wanted to tell her I'd pay the rest of her salary, or buy her apartment, or refuse to play until they hired her back. I knew that wouldn't fix it. Well, paying her salary would probably help quite a bit, but I wasn't sure I had the power to influence non-football hiring practices.

I wanted to be able to get out of this stupid bed and run after her and tell her I would take care of it all. I'd tell her she's incredible at her job, the Saints are stupid, and that at least with them out of the way I could take her on a real date. That would be phenomenally selfish of me, though—to turn her genuine personal tragedy into an opportunity to romance her. I wanted to.

After a few days, I'd check in on her. Until then, I was going to text Amelia and get Calla's salary transferred. It was the least I could do, being the reason she lost her job. The door opened, again, pulling me from my focus, and there was Amelia—and everything Calla said came back to me.

"You look better than I expected." She said, walking in and setting a briefcase on the side table. "I saw Calla on her way out." She cleared her throat. "I behaved unprofessionally, wildly unprofessionally, and it revealed something that has been growing in me for a long time. I'd been ignoring it for so long, but I've allowed the discontent and jealousy inside me to fester, and it has destroyed the life of an innocent woman who I believe could have been my friend." Amelia sighed, gesturing to the briefcase. When I opened it, I was shocked.

Inside was every headline, every magazine, every article I'd been featured in since Amelia became my agent during my sophomore year at Princeton. There were a few small flash drives, too, and the polaroid we'd taken together at the office the day I'd signed.

"I'm leaving the agency. I asked for a sabbatical," she smiled, "and they've granted it." Her tone shifted back to that professional trill she always used. "Your new agent should be calling in about five minutes, if I timed this right. Thank you for being a wonderful client." She held out a hand, and I shook it, and she walked out of my life.

27

Calla

I only let myself wallow for two days before I asked Shay if I could have a job at the shop. I knew myself, and if I sat at home doing nothing for too long, it would have devastating effects on my psyche, so there I was, pulling on jeans and a flannel that I would let fall casually off one shoulder—classic barista stuff—and braiding back my hair. I couldn't say I wasn't looking forward to being a barista; I loved making myself fun drinks, and I had comfortable enough shoes that my feet shouldn't suffer being on them all day. Not any more than they had when I was wearing heels every day.

Being a barista was nice, honestly. Shay didn't even have me taking orders, yet—just stationed me at the bar and helped me make anything I was unsure about. She had to teach me to steam the milk properly, which wasn't difficult, and the rest was the same as my machine at home. I fell into the routine, lattes and cappuccinos and cold brews, until the rush slowed and Shay told me to make something for myself.

"You're a natural." She complimented, and I rolled my eyes. She didn't usually work on Fridays, but had started to come in to keep me company and make sure I was situated. The shop was small enough that there wasn't usually more than two people on a shift, which was nice. I didn't want to have to socialize while I was at work—that had burnt me so badly that I doubted I would ever seek out a 'work friend' again.

"It's nice, honestly. It's fun." I swirled a bit of cream into my cold brew and chugged it. "Thank you, Shay."

"No problem." But she smiled, and I liked seeing her like this, in charge and happy and happy to help. "Have you texted Amanté?" She knew I hadn't. She asked me every single day without fail and the answer was always the same. What did I have to say to him? He had far more important things to worry about than me, and I needed to sort out the mess of feelings surrounding him and my dream job.

I knew it wasn't his fault. I did. And deep down, I knew that. But technically... I was just having some trouble separating the two. I knew it wouldn't last. He hadn't reached out, either. The bell rang and a tall, glowing pregnant woman with a familiar toddler walked in. Khalil's wife, if his daughter was any indication.

It was confirmed when, a few minutes later, Khalil walked in and kissed the top of her head. My cheeks burned when he saw me.

"Calla!" He waved, and the sweet family walked up to order. "Calla, this is my wife, Amina." He turned back to his wife. "Calla is a friend from work." I wanted to sink into the floor at the way he said it, and the way she seemed to completely understand what he was talking about. He must've told her all about my drama—and of course he did.

"You're the one who saved Amanté's life." She smiled, shooting me a look that told me that she did, in fact, know all my drama.

"The very one!" Shay chirped, stepping back up to the register. "What can we get for you today?" The little girl stepped up and raised her chin.

"One chocolate milk, please!" She requested, and Shay diligently wrote the order on a cup.

"Would you like ice with that, ma'am?" Shay asked, and the girl looked up to her mom, who shook her head.

"No, thank you!" She grinned.

"Name for the order?" Shay asked, and the girl proudly placed her hands on her hips.

"My name is Safiya!" I started on her chocolate milk, drizzling chocolate along the side of the cup while Shay took the rest of their orders, shaking the milk with syrup like it was a fancy drink and calling out her name.

She skipped towards me, sang 'thank you', and skipped to the back corner to take a seat. The other two were a mocha and a 'Saints' drink, which I made and handed over. Khalil smiled at me across the bar.

"Think you could take five and chat?" He asked, and I looked over my shoulder to see Shay already giving me a thumbs up.

I never expected to be enjoying coffee with the quarterback of the Saints and his family, but it was surprisingly awkward. Or maybe, I was surprisingly awkward, because Khalil was very casual and his wife was as casual as a very pregnant woman can be.

"I see you've found a job." Khalil started, and I nodded, sipping on a glass of water.

"You were mad when we saw you at daddy's work." Safiya announced, and I didn't think my cheeks could be any warmer.

"I was, you're right." I replied, not sure what else to say.

"Amanté joined us at practice yesterday." I shot my head up. "They discharged him end of last week, so he got to pop in before going home." Amina reached a hand across the table.

"If it isn't overstepping, I have some friends working in sports media, and I'd love to send them your portfolio if you have one. I can't promise anything, but what happened was deeply unfair, and from what I've seen you're wonderful at what you do." Amina was... offering me a job? Or, trying to?

"That would be amazing." I replied. I hadn't considered that my career in sports didn't have to be over. Just because I didn't work for the Saints didn't mean I couldn't work in sports at all. I felt a little silly, a little pathetic. One setback, over a man, and I gave up entirely? I wrote my email in her phone and we sat and made some small talk while Safiya enjoyed her milk.

"You know, Amanté also mentioned you haven't spoken to him since, how long was it, a week ago? Almost two?" Khalil said, oh so casual, and I found myself smirking.

"And what about it?" I asked, feigning nonchalance while something warm and fuzzy bloomed in my stomach.

"Well, Safiya is turning four next Friday. Maybe you should come." His conspiratorial smile caused us both to burst in to laughter.

"I feel like you knew I was going to be here." I accused, and he shook his head.

"I was going to text you to check in, but," He smiled, taking Amina's hand across the table, "must've been fate."

I wasn't going to watch the game on Sunday as a form of protest, but I there I was, sat on the couch, frozen pizza in the oven, fresh pack of beer in the fridge, taking in the pregame show. I hadn't watched since I'd started, and I realized with a sad twinge that, based on the shots they were showing, I'd probably been on TV—would have been right now. Connor was there, doing what I usually did. I noticed the quality of the social media had gone down notably. Part of me wanted to post something shady about it, but I knew better. Once I got going, I didn't stop. It wasn't who I was.

My timer beeped and I pulled a hoodie over my head before snuggling under my blanket with the whole pizza and a bottle of ranch on the coffee table. While they counted down to the kick, I held my beer, cracking it as the Saints kicked it away. It was weird watching without Amanté, but also familiar. I'd never watched him on TV. It almost felt like the last few weeks hadn't happened, and that was comforting. My life had been completely flipped over since that interview. I went from working a shitty bottle girl job to working at a professional football franchise and pulling the most famous athlete in America, to putting said athlete in the friendzone, to working as a barista at my friend's cafe. I counted on my fingers—how long had it been?

Seven weeks—or was it eight? And I couldn't recognize my life, except that I liked watching football by myself with a cold beer and pepperoni pizza dipped in ranch. I thought about calling my mom, but decided against it. I still wasn't ready to talk about everything. My dad, too, he'd be unbelievably disappointed in me, and I couldn't handle that right now.

Our defense looked pretty good, so I assumed morale was still high in the locker room. Amanté dropping into practice this week was probably good, ensuring that everyone knew he was okay and on track to come back for the postseason. We were leading our division, so I was sure we'd make it, and if the way this game was going we were going to be just fine. Khalil took over after the punt, and I swallowed hard as the announcers began talking about Amanté.

"Word on the street is that Houston dropped into a practice this week."

"Speaking from experience, a scary injury like that can really shake a team."

"You ever puncture a lung in the game, Sean?"

"Never! At least, not one of mine." The two laughed. I should've texted Amanté, but part of me wanted him to text me—even though I knew he was respecting my request for time to think. I had my time to think, and the more I thought, the more confident I was: when I saw him again, I was going to ask him out.

Everything that was in our way was gone. We no longer worked together, and if he decided in a few weeks that he was bored or uninterested, I could much more easily never see his face again. We were obviously attracted to each other, and talking to him was the easiest thing in the world, and the feeling I'd had when I thought he was dying was something I couldn't even describe—like the meteor was coming down to earth and I only had enough time to watch my incoming demise, knowing I hadn't achieved the most important thing in the world.

Needless to say, I wanted to achieve this. I didn't want to be on my deathbed, darkness closing in, realizing that Amanté was the one person I was meant to have by my side yet didn't. Not that I would phrase it like that when I spoke with him at Khalil's, but it would be some less intense version of that. I'd never asked someone out, to be honest. It usually went down something like that night at the club—although that was the first time I'd gone home with a stranger. But I'd catch somebody's eye, we'd flirt, they'd ask for my number, we'd go on a few dates, and... that was about it. It was weird to admit, but I'd never had the—I was sitting alone, but I blushed thinking about it—the raw, animal attraction we seemed to have. I knew I was hot and I loved to flirt, but the sexual draw was somewhat new. Men usually wanted to fuck me, and my response to that was an enjoyment in their desire—not a mutual desire.

Maybe, I'd ask him out by telling him that. *Hey, Amanté, you awakened a succubus within me and I need your body.* Khalil scored a 1-yard rushing touchdown and I took a welcome gulp of my beer. The boys were wearing my favorite uniform combo—sky blue jersey, blood red pants, sky blue socks—and I willed myself to just enjoy the game. No thoughts of real men; just the faceless athletes on the screen.

28

Amanté

I tried not to look too smug at the praise my physical therapist was laying on me, but it was almost impossible with how proud he was. This wasn't exactly difficult physical therapy—I'd had a hip arthroscopy done to fix a labral tear when I was in high school—but it was effortful nonetheless and I was proud of how quickly I was improving. They'd told me I needed to be smart about returning to my usual level of exercise, and I was, even though I wanted to ignore their advice and push myself to get on the field as soon as possible. As a result, though, my bruised ribs hardly bothered me anymore, and my respiratory fitness was at an all-time high. I was proud of myself.

"And I am so, so proud of you." Joe reiterated, as though he was reading my mind. I liked Joe. He reminded me of Isaiah, a little, who was also there. He'd taken to joining me at my physical therapy appointments, insisting that he drive me there and back, and I had to admit it was nice to have him there. He was a relentlessly curious person, and with all his questions, I felt like I was learning ten times more about pneumothorax injuries and how to rehabilitate them than I would have.

"Our shining little athlete." Isaiah teased, clapping his hands together. "I'll grab the car." He stood and left. Joe shook my hand.

"Thanks, man." I said, and he shrugged, walking me up to the front. "Same time tomorrow?"

"I think you can return to some limited practice if that's alright with your team doc. At the very least, you can do your PT at the facility with your team instead of with me. I'm sure they've missed you." The twinkle in Joe's eye told me everything I needed to know—that he knew exactly how exciting that was to hear.

"Fuck yeah. Thank you, Joe." We shook hands again, and I nearly hopped into Isaiah's waiting car. "I'm going back to practice!" I yelled, and we both thrashed around in the car until we realized everyone in the clinic could still see us and Isaiah drove away.

Ben was coming over tonight to play some games and hang out, although it was dual purpose for me—he was helping me get some money transferred to Calla, which was surprisingly difficult without her being privy to it. I didn't care what anyone thought: I was going to pay Calla for the rest of her salary for the season. After I did a little digging, I understood her shocked reaction to my $28 million. She wasn't even making $60k, and to do everything she was doing, plus the extra work she did on my interview, was almost criminal. She deserved more, and she definitely didn't deserve to get fired, so I was working with Ben to fix it.

I'd had plenty of promotional spots since the injury, anyway, and even Ben was starting to ask if there was anything specific I wanted to do with all the unexpected extra. I never thought I'd be in this situation. I'd never been, like, dirt poor, but we were a modest family growing up and I'd only been able to afford the extracurriculars I did because I was an only child and my mom worked her ass off to make sure my talent didn't go to waste. My hardworking nature came from her, and I wished she'd been around long enough for me to force her to retire. Instead, she'd wanted to keep working until she couldn't, and then it was just me and football.

I had fond memories of watching shitty rom coms, eating shit on a shingle—buttered toast with chipped beef and gravy—laughing at all the stupid miscommunication and pretending to be grossed out when they eventually kissed. It had made me a big softie, or so my friends said. I wasn't really into casual stuff. I bought flowers and wrote love notes and planned elaborate dates and wore my heart on my sleeve. When Calla had walked out without leaving her number or even saying goodbye, a little part of me had been offended—a bigger part had been hurt. I'd never been drawn to someone the way I was drawn to her, and I hated to think that the connection we had was for only one night.

The rest was history. She'd saved my life. I laughed to myself, thinking about what I was planning. It was insane—truly insane, easily the most insane thing I'd ever done—but they say that when you know, you know. I knew. I was going to marry Calla. I knew it, even if she didn't yet. I hadn't said it out loud to anyone yet. I knew everyone would tell me I was being an idiot. That I was seduced or traumatized. The truth was, I'd had the feeling from that first night, from the moment I caught her eye across the room and felt a fist around my heart. She'd looked beautiful that night, and everyone was watching her, and she'd only looked at me. It had to be fate.

"Come on in!" Isaiah's voice sounded from the front door, and I stood to dap Ben up, who walked in with a massive backpack and a bag of what smelled like Thai food.

"Been forever, man." He greeted, and I responded likewise. We all got situated on the couch, handing out meals: green curry for me and Isaiah and something I didn't recognize, that smelled amazing, for Ben. "So, Calla Monroe will be receiving some money in the next few business days." He said, taking out utensils.

Isaiah raised an eyebrow at me and I shrugged. "Great, thank you." I fought the urge to tell him I was about to drop a handful of stacks on a diamond, and instead chowed down on curry while Isaiah and Ben caught up. It didn't take long for us to finish and get out the cards, and the night went faster because we were all having fun, and I fell asleep dreaming of Calla.

The jeweler was trying very hard to be nonchalant, but I could tell he knew who I was, and whether he was excited because I was famous or excited because he knew how much money I made, I didn't care. I'd snuck out of the house—even took Isaiah's car to try to avoid being recognized—to visit the only jeweler within ten minutes that came up when I searched. They had great reviews, and when I walked in, I recognized some features I appreciated in a jeweler. First, it wasn't massive and flashy like the box stores, and I liked that. Second, I had to call to get in, and the man who answered the phone had a strong Italian-American accent. That was enough for me, but when I walked in, they gave me a hot towel that smelled like witch hazel and lemon, and that did it for me.

I was looking at diamonds, and I had no fucking idea there were so many diamond shapes until this moment. Round, square, rectangle, teardrop—some were completely clear, some were what they called 'fancy yellow', which I could've named myself. I tried to imagine Calla's hands, her jewelry. She wore silver, I was almost positive, but I pulled up her social media to double check, and she had lovely, soft hands, with long fingers? I thought they were long, anyway, but definitely dainty hands. I wanted to get a ring she would like, and I had no idea what that would entail. She was a cool girl, for sure, but would she want a super unusual ring, or would she want something simple she could wear with anything?

I knew it was risky to buy a ring when I had no reason to believe she would say yes, but something in me knew I had to. Even if she said no, I had to do this. It was like some predestined path I couldn't help but walk upon. The jeweler showed me a fat teardrop—he said it was the most quality diamond he had, but the pear was a less popular shape, so it hadn't sold. I held it in my hand, imagining hers.

"Could you do a custom band? Something a little fun?" I asked, imagining it—an almost woven strand, tying the diamond onto her finger; like a knot or a loop instead of a traditional band. He nodded while I described it, grabbing a little pencil and sketching something out that was shockingly like what I'd been imagining.

"It'll be a bitch to resize, but it will look beautiful." The man reassured me, and we shook on it. Fuck—that seemed too easy. I glanced at the clock and only twenty minutes had passed. Was twenty minutes long enough to choose an engagement ring?

If I could choose a wife in two months, I supposed twenty minutes to find a ring wasn't bad.

I tried not to cringe when he charged my card for the diamond, a lab-grown diamond, almost $10k, and reminded myself that it was a drop in the water compared to the rest of my salary. The ring—finalizing the design, sourcing the right materials, and ensuring the quality—wouldn't be ready for seven weeks, maybe eight. I laughed to myself, tucking the receipt into my pocket. It was seven weeks until I was back on the field, too. Fucking fate.

29

Calla

What does one wear to a four-year-old millionaire's birthday party? I had no idea, but I was pretty sure the answer wasn't in my closet. I'd received a digital invite, but it said nothing about dress code, and I couldn't even tell if it was an adult party celebrating the birthday girl, or if it was a 'kids' situation and I'd be surrounded by munchkins.

If I did have to hang out with a bunch of kids between socializing with fellow adults, I figured heels were a no-go, so I chose a classic pair of black and white sneakers and built my outfit around that, tugging on a pair of wide-legged jeans and a well-fitting sweater I'd bought at the thrift. With the outfit as simple as it was, I decided to curl my hair and paint my nails, all of which left me in much more of a rush than I'd wanted to be.

Big silver hoops, one of my mom's handbags, and a swipe of lip gloss later, I was ready to go. Instead, I stood in front of the mirror, hands on my hips, chewing on my bottom lip. What if it was actually a nice dinner party, and I was wildly underdressed? I looked cute, but...

I pulled the sweater over my head with a huff and tossed it back towards the closet. Jeans tugged off, too, and I stood in front of the mirror in nothing but a pair of underwear and my ruffled white socks. It didn't help that I knew I'd be seeing Amanté—that it was basically the only reason I was invited. I wanted to look effortlessly beautiful and nonchalant. I wanted to look like I hadn't spent every second of every day hoping he walked into the shop while I was working. Like I hadn't missed him.

I had a boat neck dress—tea length, which might be too fancy on its own, but paired with the fun socks and the sneakers seemed fine. With a worn-out, slouchy leather jacket on top, it was kind of a vibe. I checked my phone to see how late I was, and pouted at a notification from my bank. I never got notifications from my bank, so this couldn't be a good sign.

"Motherfucker." I mumbled under my breath, sitting on the arm of the couch to open my account and see what was draining my account today.

I swallowed. I swallowed again. I closed out the app and reopened it. I exhaled, trying to calm my shaking hands.

My balance was $50,326. Which was $50,000 more than had been in my account yesterday, and was about $50,000 more than I'd ever had in my checking account at one time. My heart dropped to my stomach. Who got my bank account information to be able to scam me? What kind of scam deposited $50k?

A giggle pushed through my lips. *WIRE TRANSFER CRED-IT AMANTÉ...* I didn't know whether to laugh or cry. Investigating further, I tapped the transaction. *WIRE TRANSFER CREDIT AMANTÉ HOUSTON.* He'd sent me almost my entire yearly salary with the Saints. The man was—God, he was infuriating—but he was...

I began pacing. Clearly, he was feeling guilty. He didn't need to be, but I appreciated that he was taking some responsibility. Fifty thousand dollars was absurd, though. Not to mention that if he did this and I immediately asked him out, that would look awful. I stopped in front of the mirror and took a deep breath, smoothing down where the tight waist met the wider hips. There was no way I could ask him out. That was okay—as long as I could talk to him, and make sure he knew we were still friends. I could handle being friends a few more weeks, until he knew it wasn't just about the money. And, I could scold him for sending me that much. Not that it was much for him.

I was officially going to be late, so I willed my brain to shut up and left the apartment, locking my door and practically running down the stairs. My foot missed a step, and I went tumbling down the rest of the stairs, probably half a flight, banging my head on the way and nailing my shin. Tears pricked my eyes and I forced myself back to my feet in case anyone heard and tried to check on me.

I examined my legs quickly and noted with some frustration that not only did it hurt to walk on my right leg, but a bruise was already blooming under the skin. No blood, though, so I took that as a sign to keep moving. At least a throbbing head and an aching shin was a good way to stop panicking about Amanté. Until I thought of him again. Fuck.

Khalil owned a gorgeous penthouse suite in one of the nicest buildings in St. Clair, and I felt a little out of my depth as soon as I pulled up and my car was valeted away. For a child's birthday. My ears popped while I was standing in the elevator, bouquet in one hand and a gift in the other, and the now-familiar ruffle of nerves jittered through me. I'd never been someone who was self-conscious—but I was also never surrounded by successful, ambitious millionaires. It was inspiring to get to know people who had it all, and had gotten here on their own, but it also made me feel a little... behind. I was twenty-four, had only recently moved out of my parents' house, and was working at my friend's coffee shop. Khalil was freshly thirty and obviously successful. Amanté was only one year older than me—maybe two—and could retire today if that's what he wanted.

It was intimidating, and I wasn't quite used to it. Not that it was bad; just new. The elevator opened and I stepped out to a stunning, modern apartment. Everything was sleek and clean, and the entire apartment was decorated with baby blue and red garlands. Tears pricked my eyes as I took in the theme and realized it was themed after her dad—the cake had two dolls, Safiya and her dad, both decked out in uniform. And as soon as I stepped out, the birthday girl herself skipped up to me. She was her dad's mini-me, complete with tiny little football pads and a custom jersey.

Amina saw me first and pulled me into a hug. "She's daddy's little girl." She said, and we both giggled at how precious. I squatted down to Safiya and handed her the flowers.

"Happy birthday." I smiled, and she hopped three times, sticking her entire face in the bouquet.

"Thank you!" And then she was off, running to wherever was more interesting. When I stood back up, I was pleased to note that the dress was the better outfit choice. It seemed to be more of a friends and family party than one with lots of kids, and I recognized a handful of people from the team. As I walked further in, I spotted a formal dining room with a massive table, and an elegant lounge space where it looked like most people were hanging out.

I spotted Amanté speaking with a couple people I didn't recognize, martini in hand, and took a deep breath. Amina followed my gaze and elbowed me with a good-natured smirk. I leveled a look back at her.

"How does it feel to have a four-year-old?" I asked, not wanting to talk about him just yet. Amina looked just as beautiful and just as pregnant as she had the last time I saw her, though this time she was wearing a tight dress that showed off just how big her bump was. Her feet were adorned in Saints slippers, though, fortunately, and she just shrugged.

"Some days I can't believe I have a child at all. Some days, I look at her, and I just cry, because—how did she get so big? When?" She sniffed, tearing up as she talked about it, and then laughed. "That might be the hormones talking, though."

I noticed a pile of shoes by the door and toed mine off.

"Calla! You made it!" Khalil spotted me, walking over to wrap his arms around his wife, kissing the top of her head. "Grab yourself some slippers and join us in the lounge. Naji will make you whatever you want." I had no idea who Naji was, but I looked where he pointed, and found that they had a veritable trove of Saints themed slippers for me to choose from. I found a pair I liked and made my way towards Naji—towards Amanté.

Safiya was performing a dance number for the group. One of the guests was tapping out the beat for her on the bar, and when she finished, we all applauded. To my surprise, she ran right to me and grabbed my hand.

"Uncle Naji! Uncle Naji!" She dragged me over to Naji, my would-be bartender, who was the man who'd been making her music. "This is..." Safiya trailed off and looked up at me, embarrassed. I fought the urge to laugh, knowing she wouldn't understand that she was just too adorable.

"Hi, I'm Calla. I met Khalil when I was working with the Saints." I held out a hand, and we shook.

"What's your poison, Calla?" He asked, gesturing behind him to the bar. I found myself blushing at the way he was looking at me.

"Let me guess—spicy margarita?" A deep voice replied, behind me, and Amanté swung Safiya into his arms, close enough I had to crane my neck to look up at him. Now I was quite warm. "It's good to see you." He murmured, and the sight of him with Safiya in his arms, decked out in Saints gear, was enough to tickle my ovaries.

"I doubt they have-" I started, turning back to Naji, but he was already on it, dropping jalapeños into a shaker. "Wow. Thank you." He smiled.

"I think Khalil has mentioned you—you're the one who made that great video of him trying local foods, right?" He asked, straining the drink over ice.

"Yes, that was me." I replied, taking the drink, feeling my cheeks flush yet again as he waited, intently watching to see how I liked it. I took a sip—it was a spicy margarita, but it had a hint of... "Pomegranate?" I asked, and he grinned.

"Hibiscus. Is it good?" I nodded, taking another drink, and turned to Amanté only to realize he and Safiya were on the other side of the room, chatting with Khalil. Naji followed my gaze.

Feeling fiercely embarrassed, I took another long drink and looked back at him. He chuckled, observing my nerves. Fuck, I was embarrassing myself.

"You're Khalil's brother?" I asked, and he shook his head.

"Amina's. I'm just in town for a few weeks." He inclined his head to the couch, and we went to sit down.

"Where's home?" I asked, and his eyes softened. "Tough question?"

"Yes." He sipped his drink. "I live in Beirut, but home is a small town in central Chad." I wasn't sure I'd ever met someone from

Chad—except for Amina, I supposed—or anyone who'd even visited Beirut. "I went to Beirut for university, then made a life there."

"I've never been that far from home. I grew up here, went to school here. Live here now." I laughed, drinking. "It must be exciting."

"It can be. It can be lonely, too." He smiled as he said it, placing a hand on my knee. No fucking way, I thought, feeling my face turn red. This guy was flirting *heavy* at his niece's birthday party. Not that he wasn't nice or good looking—but, Amanté was the entire reason I was here. Except to celebrate Safiya, of course. Before I could say anything, or he could comment on my burning cheeks, Amina tapped a spoon on her glass. Thank God—it was time to transition to dinner.

30

Amanté

I wasn't listening to a thing Khalil was saying as he yapped away in my ear about some stock he'd purchased for his daughter. Instead, I was watching Calla and Naji as he walked her to her seat—assigned, thankfully, next to mine—and pulled out the chair. I hadn't wanted to be rude and interrupt their conversation earlier, but now I was being stupid, because Naji was a very successful flirt and based on the tomato shade of her cheeks, Calla knew what he was trying to do.

Khalil and I had met a few years ago at a post-season gala, and as a result I'd known Safiya since she was born. She had become like a niece to me, and I loved her, and she was beyond excited to have her Uncle Amanté around more. As a result, she was attached to me, and as much as I loved being the little girl's favorite, I really, really wanted to interrupt that conversation now. Instead, I was watching from across the room as I held Safiya and Khalil talked away into my unhearing ear. Safiya wriggled out of my arms so she could run to her seat at the head of the table, and Khalil's hand clapped my shoulder.

"You know how he is." Khalil said, following my gaze, and I sighed. I'd only met Naji once before this, but he'd romanced a girl or two last time I'd seen him, too. Freed from my responsibility to entertain the birthday girl, I walked to my seat beside Calla, who was sitting quietly, staring at her lap.

"Calla." I greeted, sliding into my spot. "Seems like you and Naji are getting on well." I tried to keep the jealousy out of my tone—Calla's a beautiful woman, of course people were going to flirt with her. I didn't get to monopolize her beauty.

"Stop." She squeaked, looking up at me with wide eyes and a little smile. I smiled back, unable to help myself. "You're teasing me! Unbelievable, Amanté, unbelievable." The way she said my name made my heart sink below the belt.

"I have no idea what you're talking about." I replied. She smacked me in the stomach, drawing a true laugh from me. People were still settling in, and I spied Naji chatting with another guest at the other end of the table.

"He's sweet." She said, her voice high. "He's forward." She finished her margarita, setting it rather loudly on the table. I wasn't sure how it was possible, but she turned even more pink; I could feel the nervous energy radiating off of her. My hand found her knee under the table and gave a little squeeze. I watched the rise and fall of her chest, nodding when it was slower than the last.

"Is he making you uncomfortable?" I leaned close, whispering. It was one thing for me to be jealous because another successful man was talking to a woman I wanted to marry—it was another thing entirely if his advances were making her uncomfortable, and I wouldn't hesitate to put Naji in his place.

"No!" She said, then lowered her voice. "No, he is sweet, I just..." She trailed off, nerves rising again. I squeezed her knee. "Thank you." I cocked my head to the side.

She sighed, and I couldn't help but watch the movement, admiring the silhouette on her dress and how timeless it was, how tight on her waist, how classic and beautiful she looked. I swallowed.

"The *money*, Amanté." She gritted her teeth. My mouth dropped open, and just as it did, everyone was finally situated, and Khalil and Amina stood with Safiya at the front of the table.

"Thank you, everyone, for taking the time out of your week to celebrate our daughter. As some of you know, Safiya was dearly wanted and long awaited, and to celebrate her fourth birthday is as great a blessing as we've ever felt. Safiya is the most beautiful, beloved girl, and we truly appreciate how many of you see the sweet, kind, smart girl she has grown into." Amina looked at Safiya, who gave a little nod, and began to speak.

"Thank you everyone for coming to my party." She sounded like she'd rehearsed this little speech. "I love my dad and I want to be a football player just like him when I grow up." A chorus of 'aww's swept across the table. "And thank you for all the gifts." She climbed back down into her seat, and Khalil clapped his hands.

"Enjoy the food!" Everyone sat, and I waited eagerly to receive the food. I'd only had Chadian food one other time, also at one of Khalil's events, and it was delicious. I appreciated that Amina cared to introduce the culture to her daughter, and part of me envied her connection to her roots. I squeezed Calla's knee again and reached for my martini while dishes began to be served.

"I don't know how to thank you." She said softly, and I finally turned back to look at her, taking in the openness of her eyes, the crease between her brows, the pinch of her lips.

"You don't need to thank me. I did what was right." This wasn't how I wanted this conversation to go, if I was being honest. I'd wanted to get her alone and tell her everything, tell her how I feel, tell her I wanted to take her on a real date and give her all the romance she deserved, but I'd let my social awkwardness keep me from stealing her away and now we were at a table full of people and I had no idea what to do.

"Amanté." Her voice was low, and my name—I squeezed her knee without thinking.

Leaning close, I told her, "I would love to get you alone after dinner. I am sorry I did not steal you away earlier," one of the servers set down a plate, "thank you," and walked away, "but for now, accept the money as a token of appreciation for you." I sat back up straight and adjusted my napkin.

The food was incredible, the conversation flowed beautifully, and Safiya was thoroughly enjoying her grown-up birthday meal—the evening could not have been going better. Every few minutes, Calla's elbow brushed mine, or she placed her hand on my arm as she laughed, or her leg nudged mine under the table. I couldn't honestly tell if she meant to be doing it—if she realized I was noticing and savoring every time her skin touched mine—but I was, and I could almost pretend that we were there together.

There was so much food I could hardly finish my far-too-generous serving of bangaou and rice, but it was so delicious I ate until I could see my stomach bursting. Safiya was fading fast, the rich dishes settling in her stomach until the sweet child was fighting sleep at the head of the table. The conversation was slow as everyone focused on eating, and I let slip a laugh when I looked beside me and saw that Calla had cleaned her plate.

"It's delicious!" She protested, leaning back with a hand of her own on her belly. We shared another look and burst into giggles. Amina was saying something to Safiya, and when the little girl nodded, I knew it was time for bed. All the excitement of the evening had worn her out. Khalil, Amina, and Safiya stood—well, Khalil and Amina stood, while Safiya was lifted into her father's arms, and bid everyone a sleepy wave goodnight. We were invited to the massive terrace, where the rest of the evening would continue, so while the staff they'd hired cleaned our mess, we found ourselves outside, overlooking the unbelievable view they had from their penthouse.

Calla was quiet, too, and when she walked to the edge of the terrace it was like watching a scene from a movie. Her hair whipped across her back in the wind, her tidy curls twisting together, and the flowing skirt of her dress went with it, revealing the length of her calf as it flitted up. She'd left her jacket inside, and I fought the urge to go wrap my arms around her.

Why, though? I straightened my posture and walked towards her until I was leaning against the railing at her side. She didn't look at me, but leaned into my arm, just enough pressure to know she was there. I turned to her then, looking down, studying her face as she studied the skyline, and, throwing caution to the wind, slid a hand across the small of her back.

She looked up at me then, her expression so endearing that I just—I just lifted my other hand to her cheek, turned to face her, and pressed a gentle, oh-so gentle, kiss to her forehead. She turned towards me, my hand shifting across her waist, and I felt her ribs expand at the contact. When I pulled back, she was looking at me already, up through dark lashes and darkened eyes.

"That's it?" She breathed, and I pulled her against me, kissing her deeply, trying to infuse every drop of longing I'd felt for so long. Her body pressed against mine as she rose on her toes, wrapping her arms around my neck, and when she pulled back, her smile could have powered the world. She dropped back to her heels, letting her hands slowly drag down my neck until they rested on my chest, one finger still hooked on my chain. That smile was mischievous—it was coy, it was Calla, and I wanted to make her smile like that for the rest of my life.

31

Calla

I t had taken every ounce of my energy to focus on anything other than Amanté during that entire dinner. Every single bite of decadent food was tinted with his scent, every time I brushed against him and he didn't move away, every time his eyes met mine as he laughed—I was aware of all of it, and aware of how embarrassing that was. I couldn't help it, though. I was finally in a room with him, a normal room, and I wanted to know what he wanted to say to me. A part of me knew what he wanted to say—how he felt—but the other part was loud with doubt, wondering if he wanted to speak to me because sending all that money had been a mistake or someone had actually stolen his identity or he'd sent it as some kind of hush money so I would go away forever.

It was like I'd been split in two, one half of me the Calla who loves social events and children and meeting new people, the other half the Calla who is so terrified to be abandoned. It sounded dramatic, but it felt dramatic, and when we walked outside and I felt that whip of cold air and it looked like the whole world was ahead of me, I felt like I could finally breathe.

So, when Amanté sauntered up next to me, not immediately invading my space but joining me at my side, joining my moment without interrupting it, I shivered, my entire body reacting to his huge presence beside me, thinking about all the tiny moments we'd shared through the night, and wanting to know—wanting to *know*.

And then, it felt different. It was different, somehow. He kissed me and it no longer felt like we were running out of time. He kissed me, and it felt like the beginning.

Amanté's hand didn't leave my hip for the entire rest of the night and, even though I'd stopped drinking after my one margarita before dinner, I felt a completely heady, pleasant buzz. I didn't have to confess anything; I didn't have to explain myself or beg for his attention. He just was there for me, and I was there for him, and it felt right. It felt perfect, and I felt like I was floating and his hand, where it pressed against my hip, was my tether to the earth. Amanté sent me fifty thousand dollars to be generous, not to expunge his guilt. God, I'd always prayed for a generous man, and for whatever reason I did not deserve in this life, Amanté had been delivered.

When we bid Amina and Khalil a final goodnight, with the promise that I would keep in touch, he walked me downstairs and waited by my car and asked me probably twenty times if I was okay to drive, even though I was as sober as a bird, although I couldn't stop squeezing his hand and staring into his eyes, so it was understandable. I felt like I was dreaming. It hadn't been that long, I knew, but the passion between us had always been so intense that, after being casual and teasing for so long, filling our conversations with banter and unsaid underlying potential, being real and open was refreshing. Maybe it was cringey, but it was a gut feeling that this was correct. It was like his hand was made to intertwine with mine, to mold to my hips, and I was made to fit in his palm.

Part of me never wanted to leave his side, but the rational part pulled him down for a kiss before driving off, music blasting, windows down. It was freezing and I didn't care. I had been terrified of this night and it went better than I could've imagined—I deserved cold air reminding me that I was alive.

The next day, I still felt like I was dreaming, and I couldn't wipe the stupid smile off my face. The sun had yet to rise, and I was getting ready to open the coffee shop, and I had more energy than when I took a double shot of caffeine halfway through my shift.

I was at the shop by six-thirty, and the sun was set to rise right when I unlocked the doors. I liked Saturday mornings, as odd as that sounded. It was always so slow that I could keep everything pristine for hours before it started picking up—and I usually got off right around then. Before the rush, it was just me and the occasional guest, usually someone wanting to read in the shop or bring a latte to tackle whatever Saturday errands they intended to run.

I'd even dressed up a little, today, choosing my most flattering jeans (my ass looked very, very good) and my favorite cozy pullover. I felt like the perfect stereotypical barista that people went to social media to write stories about; the type of barista that inspired aspiring writers to start a coffee shop fanfiction. I pulled myself a shot and sipped it until it was time to unlock the doors. The sun had almost crested the horizon as I settled back behind the bar, the floor to ceiling windows a perfect view. If opening the shop did anything good for me, it was that I was forced to take in the glorious rising of the sun every day, and that was a little magic I probably wouldn't witness otherwise.

The bell on the door dinged and I chirped, "Good morning!"

"Good morning." I blinked, eyes focusing in the glare of the sun, and grinned. Amanté fucking Houston was here. At the crack of dawn. "I thought we could watch the sunrise together before I head to practice." He sidled up to the bar, and every little butterfly I'd had in my stomach last night had grown enough that I could hardly stand still when I was separated.

"Hi." I said, at a loss for words. He did not need to be awake this early. I knew that. He knew that I knew that. I reached across the bar to grab his hand before I could stop myself, and he intertwined our fingers while we both turned to watch the sun finish its journey upwards. When it was done, he turned back to me, and I warmed under his devout gaze.

"You're glowing." He complimented, and I must've been glowing with the golden rays of the sun. He was glowing, too, silhouetted against the sun like a god from ancient myth. The bell rang.

"Good morning!" I said, and Amanté stepped away, gesturing for the man to go ahead and order.

One americano later and he was back in front of me.

"Can I have one of those drinks you got me in the hospital?" He asked. I didn't think I would ever forget just how fragile he'd looked in that hospital bed that first day, when he still had the tube sticking out of him and the oxygen line. I nodded and punched it into the cashier so I could track the inventory, fully intending not to charge him, but he dropped a twenty and had already walked to the other end of the bar by the time I noticed.

Starting on the drink, I apologized. "I should have come back to visit you. It was selfish not to."

"You lost your job because of me. Please, do not apologize for the time you took to process it." He replied.

"I knew it wasn't your fault, though. I was just freaking out and afraid and I used it as an excuse." I put the finishing touches on the drink and slid it across to him. He smiled when he picked it up and saw the little heart I drew next to his name.

"Well, I forgive you." He quipped, and took a sip. "Dinner, Tuesday night?"

My heart did a little backflip. I nodded.

"Great, I'll pick you up at seven." He blew a kiss—so cheesy—and walked out.

Shay was taking over for me at 10:30 (someone must've called off, because it was unusual for her to work a Saturday) and I stayed an extra half-hour to help take orders during the rush. And, maybe, to tell her everything that had happened. She was the best listener in the world, because she gasped everywhere I wanted to gasp and scoffed everywhere I wanted her to scoff. She thought Naji flirting with me was hilarious, and wanted me to pass along his number. She told me she would have sobbed if she'd seen Safiya dressed up like her dad, and whined about how jealous she was that I got to try authentic Chadian food. Then, she'd faked a swoon so convincing that three separate customers jumped up to make sure she was okay when I told her Amanté had been here the moment we opened today so we could watch the sunrise together.

Realistically, I knew everything was still brand new and we had a messy start and there was nothing to indicate that going on a date with Amanté would turn into something massive and romantic and lasting. I knew that. Realistically. But I couldn't pretend it didn't *feel* that way. Sure, the circumstances were ridiculous, but fate intervened to give us an opportunity to give this a real try right now. Not at the end of the season, not while we were sneaking around as co-workers, but as somewhat normal people who know they care about each other.

32

Calla

All the panic and anxiety of the last few weeks dissipated, and my period conveniently arrived a day later. There was nothing like the always-surprising elevated moods of the luteal phase to turn even a hint of nerves into a full—blown freak out, but a piece of me was relieved to realize that was a good chunk of the cause. Not all of it, of course, but I felt like I could safely blame at least sixty percent of my panic on the hormones. My periods usually weren't too bad, but some cycles brought worse cramps or bigger mood swings. Nothing too out of the ordinary, and I felt pretty much like myself as Tuesday arrived and it was time to dress my bloated uterus for a fancy night out.

I hadn't gotten dressed up for a date in—God, had I ever really gotten dressed up for a date? All the dates I'd ever been on were coffee or more of a hang out than a date. I hated wearing pants on my period, but he'd just seen me in my favorite dress, so I stood in front of the closet with my hands on my hips for at least fifteen minutes before pulling a sweater dress I hadn't worn in years out of the back.

I'd probably bought the dress back in high school, if I remembered correctly, but it was nice enough to wear out while still being comfortable. I filled it out quite a bit more than I remembered the last time I'd put it on, but it still fit—just a bit more snug. It looked cute, I thought, in a sort of romantic autumn lover type of way. A pair of tights and knee-high leather boots later and I was ready. Hopefully. I fastened the belt of the dress a rung tighter, trying to snatch my waist, and took a step back. I felt like the star of a nineties rom-com.

Amanté knocked on the door at exactly seven, and greeted me at the door with a single rose. He was wearing a nice pair of jeans and a well-made sweater, so I'd guessed the dress code well enough, and it looked like he'd just got his hair redone. His braids were always the same, and they flattered his jawline and sharp cheekbones and showed off his expressive eyes perfectly.

"You look beautiful." He held out a hand, and I took it, making sure to lock the door behind me before he walked me down the stairs and outside. I blinked a few times, realizing that he had not driven here in his little red pickup. Instead, a glossy black sports car was parked out front. I was sure that if I knew anything about cars, I would be wildly impressed, but as things stood, I knew nothing about them and was still fascinated by the very expensive looking vehicle. He opened the passenger door for me, and when I got in it felt like I was sitting on the floor. It even smelled brand new.

Before we took off, he interlaced our fingers together over the gear shift, which did something very unexpected to my body, and although we made brief small talk I really had no idea what we were talking about. The car, the weather, my dress—but when he turned on the music and we started to drive, all I could do was feel his hand on mine as he adjusted, watching cars as we darted through the streets.

We pulled up to what looked like an old mansion and he tossed the keys to the notably excited valet guy. He offered his arm and I took it as we walked up to the door, which he opened into an elaborately decorated lobby.

"You've been quiet." He said, and though his voice was light I could feel the tension in his arm—he was just as nervous as me.

"I get shy around attractive gentlemen." I replied, and he laughed, pulling my arm further into his side. We approached the host stand and the girls immediately stood up straight.

"Good evening, Mr. Houston. Your table is ready." One of the girls—dressed like an old-school flight attendant, I noticed—walked us to our table, and I took in the restaurant. It was an old mansion, as far as I could tell, with ornate molding and elaborate portraits covering the walls. Our seat was a small booth tucked into the corner of what appeared to be the bar area, although it was the fanciest bar I'd ever seen. A grand piano sat not too far away, and I hoped someone would be playing tonight. I slid into the red velvet seat and as soon as we were both situated a server brought two flutes of champagne, setting them before us.

I wasn't sure what I had expected, not entirely, but part of me had assumed he would take me out somewhere a little more... normal. Maybe we'd go to a little Italian chain and drive around in his truck. This was the nicest date I'd ever been on, and we hadn't even ordered anything yet.

"This place is gorgeous." I said, reaching for my flute. He took his and held it up.

"To us." We met eyes and clinked our glasses. It was the best champagne I'd ever had.

"This is..." I wasn't sure how to say what I was thinking without sounding offensive. "I'm nervous." I was honest instead, smiling up at him.

"Me too." He replied, taking another sip. "It's weird, a little. Just going on a real date."

"I thought you'd take me somewhere more normal." I giggled, and he slid a hand onto my thigh.

"Welcome to your new normal, Calla." He teased, lowering his voice, and giggles bubbled out of me again. It was easy to forget he was a millionaire when we were with other people, or at my shitty food service job, or at the club. Now, on a random Tuesday night, I was being driven around in a sports car and drinking champagne. His jewelry alone could probably pay my rent for the year.

I took another sip. Why was this so awkward? I knew Amanté, we knew how to talk to each other, but we both were sitting here with tension thick enough to slice. A server came by and introduced himself—which I instantly forgot—and asked if we wanted anything to start. Amanté told him we'd not looked yet, and when he walked away, I reached for the menu. Amanté put a hand on it.

"Are you allergic to anything?" He asked. "Or is there anything you don't really like?"

"No." I said, narrowing my eyes, edges of my mouth pulling up as I anticipated his next move.

"Can I order for us? I don't want you to worry about a thing." He seemed shy, almost, asking. "If that's too controlling, I don't have to."

"No, that sounds nice." I answered, and I was being honest. I'd never had someone want to order for me, and I did think it was sweet. I had a feeling that looking at the prices on the menu would have given me a heart attack, anyway. Maybe that's what he was anticipating—that I'd try to order something cheap instead of ordering something I really wanted.

"We'll start with an order of the crab cakes and a glass of your recommended pairing." He ordered, then opened the menu, and the way his lips pursed as he was checking his order took all my attention. Next, he dragged a finger along the wine list and pointed to a bottle. The server nodded and wrote it down, then took the menus with a little bow and left us again.

Amanté looked at me, catching me in the act, and my cheeks warmed. "Sorry." I said, looking away, taking another little sip of champagne.

"Were you watching me the whole time?"

"Maybe."

"You're adorable."

"Shut up."

"You are."

"Tell me something silly that nobody knows about you." I blurted. He was holding one of my hands in both of his, tracing each finger, outlining each French-tipped nail. When I looked back at his face, he wasn't even watching, just absently playing with my hand while he thought.

"I made a graphic novel when I was fourteen about a famous football player who's secretly a salsa dancer." He finally said, and my mouth dropped open as I imagined Amanté not only as a child, but as a child who illustrated a graphic novel. The image was adorable.

"Was it any good?" I asked, grinning.

"Awful. I cannot draw." He admitted, and we both burst into laughter, quieting ourselves when we remembered where we were, holding onto our stomachs as the laughter took over.

"Can you dance?" I asked, once I could speak again, and Amanté just shook his head, and we devolved into giggles again, tears pricking our eyes as we laughed.

I sniffed and sat back up as the server returned with our crab cakes and wine, thanking him, taking a few breaths. Amanté gestured to me, so I placed my napkin across my lap and cut a bite. I wasn't sure I'd ever had a crab cake, and I had no idea what it was supposed to taste like—or what the sauce it was sitting on was—but I took a bite and washed it down with the wine. I nodded, swallowing. When he asked how it was, I admitted that it was the best crab cake I'd ever had—because it was my first. We giggled again, and it went like that for a while, asking little questions and admitting silly little facts while we laughed and ate and settled into this new version of us.

I was certain the server had the wrong table when I spotted him rolling a cart towards us, but when I looked at Amanté, he had a mischievous smile on his face that I desperately wanted to kiss off him. The server carved a massive tomahawk steak—probably the biggest steak I'd ever seen—and placed the perfectly sliced, perfectly cooked meat onto each of our respective plates, leaving the bone and its plate at the center of the table. Then, he dished us mashed potatoes and asparagus onto our plates, setting those on the table as well, and just as I was sure he had to be finished, he reached to the bottom of the cart and took out a crystal decanter and a bottle of wine which Amanté quickly approved.

He decanted the bottle, gave it a little swirl, and then poured a taste. I sipped it, and fought the urge to groan at the richness, the decadence. I enjoyed red wine but this—this was completely different. I nodded at the server, who smiled and poured a glass for Amanté before pouring the rest of mine.

"Enjoy your meal." He said, bowing slightly again, and rolled his cart away. I looked at Amanté, and it must've been quite the look, because he laughed aloud.

"Are you enjoying yourself?" He asked, and I broke into a grin, shaking my head. He turned to face me as I cut my steak. I held the bite up on my fork, inclining my head to him, and took a bite. It was the most flavorful, indulgent piece of food I'd ever consumed. As I chewed, Amanté nodded towards the wine, and I took a sip, and the combination of flavors couldn't be described as anything but completely ridiculous.

"Amanté, you've set the bar pretty high." I told him. He lifted his hand to trace my jaw with his thumb, and I nearly fell into his touch when it moved away just as quick.

"You deserve nothing less."

The rest of dinner was just as mind-blowingly amazing as we enjoyed the delicious food and amazing wine and settled into our usual banter. All of the earlier awkwardness dissipated as we spent more time together, and by the time dessert was served, we were both giggling and glaring and nudging—and were sitting far closer together than we had been.

The chocolate cake was phenomenal and I wanted badly to kiss Amanté. The wine paired beautifully with both the steak and the dessert, and *I wanted badly to kiss Amanté*. I was definitely a little tipsy—I supposed I hadn't drunk very much in a while—but only enough to be a little warm and a little extra giggly. Someone cleared our dishes. I expected the check to come, but Amanté waved the server over.

"Could you help her decide on an after-dinner drink?" He asked, and my eyebrows shot up. The server seemed amused, which was mildly embarrassing.

"Absolutely. Do you like coffee? Sweet or bitter?" The server asked, consulting a small menu he pulled from his back pocket. I had no idea—I liked coffee, sweet things, and bitter things. He noticed my indecision and a smile pulled at his lips. "Trust me?" He asked.

"That would be great." I agreed. Maybe once I tried whatever he brought I would have more of a preference.

"And for you, sir?" The server turned to Amanté, who ordered an espresso. He nodded and left again.

"Nothing for you?" I asked, facing him more, both of my hands holding both of his under the table.

"I'm driving you home, remember?" He teased, and I blushed. I did remember. I appreciated that—not everyone cared enough. Two and a half glasses of wine at 220lbs probably weren't enough to make him unable to drive regardless, but I liked that he was still planning on hanging out for a bit longer. To make sure I was safe. Suddenly, a cramp radiated out of my uterus, pulling me forward and setting a slight grimace on my lips.

Amanté immediately pulled away, holding both of my hands up, eyes scanning over my body. "What's wrong?" He asked, resting our hands back on my lap, eyes still flickering back and forth. One deep breath later and the cramp passed. I took one of my hands away and fanned my face.

"Just a cramp." I picked up my purse. "I'll be right back." I quickly changed my tampon in the bathroom—decorated with hundreds of mirrors, it seemed like—and made sure my hair and makeup still looked good. When I came back, Amanté was waiting, eyebrows slightly pursed, his hands folded on the table.

"Are you alright?" He asked when I returned to his side, and I just nodded, letting myself lean into his touch, his arm snaking around my back and rubbing small circles. I really was fine—it was just a cramp—but the tenderness with which he was holding me was too lovely to refuse.

"I want to kiss you." I said, then pursed my lips, immediately regretting saying something. His eyes lowered, flickering to my mouth, and I sucked in a breath. He leaned down, kissing me, a demure, soft kiss, one I wanted to lean into, and I did, squeezing his thigh, and he pulled away. He swallowed hard, and I knew we were both on the same page.

The server came with my drink, which he called a 'vieux carré', and waited until I took a sip and confirmed it was good before he left and returned with the espresso. I couldn't exactly place what all was in it—I thought I noted whiskey, maybe cognac? But it was a nice sipper, and when the intoxicating sound of the piano began to fill the room, I knew I would remember this night forever.

Amanté was looking at me already, smiling to himself, and I felt like curling into a little ball. I felt ridiculous, getting so excited about live music and a fancy velvet booth and an incredible man and a fun new drink. He didn't say anything, just slid an arm behind my back so he could tug me closer to his side, and I leaned into him as I enjoyed the music and the evening and the feel of his firm chest supporting me.

33

Amanté

C alla had a little smile plastered on her face the entire drive home, and I wanted to make her smile like that for the rest of my life. The date had been an exquisite success, and she'd been so excited and present for all of it, and I loved watching her taste the food and think about the pairings and sway with the music, and now, as I drove her home and she gazed out the window, in her own world, while her arm stretched to its full length to sit at the crease of my hip.

I'd never felt so driven to impress a woman—I'd certainly never felt so pleased when I successfully spoiled her. She was beautiful; everything about her was like something out of an old magazine, from her effortless aura to her enamoring curves to the way she dressed them. She made me feel normal when I usually felt like I was on a pedestal. Maybe, part of my success this season and throughout rehabilitation was more than just getting away from the Captains.

I'd made friends throughout my life, but they'd never been my priority. Amelia had been my closest confidant, and I couldn't really call her a friend. I'd been so focused on proving myself, I hadn't cared about making real connections with people. I'd been selfish.

Before tonight, when was the last time I'd gone on a date with someone who I actually liked? How long had it been since I had friendships that extended outside the confines of work, who I saw more frequently than the occasional night out? How long had it been since I lived in a regular house instead of a big, cold, empty mansion? I thought I was successful because I was making a lot of money and receiving awards and breaking records despite being on a team that couldn't get out from under. Even with all of that, I was deeply unhappy. I had money and nothing to do with it, nobody to spend it on, nothing I even cared about enough to donate to. I was completely selfish—the most selfish person in the world.

Maybe I would have grown up on my own, but the truth was, meeting Calla had made me realize a lot of things about myself. Not that first night, when we'd gone to my hotel in a frenzy of passion, but when I awoke that morning and missed her warmth. When I met her again, and realized she would be part of my life. When acting like a douche in the kitchen had inspired me to text Isaiah and start to live like a real person instead of an athlete you watch on TV.

She'd just opened her apartment door when she looked at me with concern in her eyes for the first time in the night. "Is this real, Amanté?" She asked, her voice soft. I exhaled through my nose, hating that she felt like she had to ask at all.

"It's the realest thing I've ever felt, Calla." Her eyes searched mine, scanning for evidence of a lie, but there was none. I knew—I'd known. Our relationship may have been founded on banter and flirting and fun, but tonight had proven that we could be slow and sweet and romantic, too. I wanted all of that; I wanted things to be real and fun and serious and every other little thing. I wanted something more than football for the first time in my life.

Apparently content with my words, she leaned on the doorframe and smiled. "Thank you for tonight."

"Thank you." I replied, just the ghost of the words, as I leaned down and kissed her. Then—blood buzzing and feeling like I'd just drank a shot of espresso, which I supposed I had—I walked back outside to my car and drove home.

34

Calla

A manté was scheduled to return to play for the first game of the postseason, and I couldn't have been any more proud. As fun as it was to experience him outside football for the last few weeks, I missed the undeniable energy he had when he was playing. It was like part of him lit up; he was so talented you couldn't tear your eyes away.

The Saints had finally confirmed our playoff berth, so as Amanté was cleared for more and more involvement in practice, his time spent at the facility increased, too, until our main hangout time during the week was grabbing coffee—whether I was on shift or not—before he spent the full day and half the night at practice. According to the players I was still in contact with, which was only a few of them, mostly via social media, Connor was having a bad time trying to do his job and everything I'd been doing. From the outside looking in, it was pretty clear that I'd dodged a bullet. What kind of multimillion dollar business didn't have a dedicated social media team? They were clearly behind the times, and as much as I'd loved doing it, I was being massively taken advantage of. The Saints had gotten by for too long with just a marketing manager and a few underpaid social media interns—if they wanted to stay competitive, they needed to flesh out all of their teams. Or not, I supposed. Multimillion dollar profession- al football teams probably made ridiculous profit even without any marketing, but even so, I didn't want to work somewhere that I was so undervalued.

Not to mention that I didn't even really want to do social media. I wanted to be a sideline reporter, and social media for the St. Clair Saints wasn't the only way I could break into the industry. I'd done the interview with Amanté, which would be helpful on a portfolio, but I needed to figure out how to build an actual portfolio that was good enough to outweigh the fact that I was fired from my only sports-related job. Fuck Connor, honestly. He deserved the mess he was in.

As much as I could manage, I wasn't worrying about it. No team I would want to work for was hiring so far into the season, and I needed to strengthen my application anyway. For now, I was content enjoying football as a fan.

It felt like I'd blinked and we were already here. It felt like I'd met Amanté two weeks ago, and he'd gotten hurt last week, and then suddenly he was returning to play. Time was going too fast for my taste. I wanted to savor all these moments. Most of all, I wanted to make them mean something. Amanté had been an exemplary boyfriend. He'd asked me officially just a few days after our first date, giving me a bouquet of a hundred red roses and one of those cute vintage cakes. Since then, we'd gone to dinner a few more times, talked on the phone nearly every night, enjoyed coffee together nearly every morning, and even gone on a few physical therapist-approved runs together. He'd bought me a sick retro Saints jacket to wear to his first game back, a pair of sneakers I'd wanted for years, and a prepaid gas card with an amount he refused to disclose—all 'just because'.

I wanted to do something nice for him, but what the fuck did he want? What did he need? He didn't really want things—I supposed nothing being out of reach did that to you—and anything he wouldn't get for himself was something I couldn't afford to get him. The holidays had come and gone, and we'd agreed to go small: I got him a bath towel designed for gigantic men like him, which he'd thought was hilarious and thoughtful—"I can actually dry myself!"—and he bought me a little stuffed cow that I could heat in the microwave to help with my cramps. Not wanting to compromise his recovery, we'd spent New Year's Eve on Isaiah's couch, playing cards and drinking champagne.

He deserved something incredible; he hadn't even gotten to celebrate his record-breaking success, since he'd spent most of the following week in the hospital and had to take it easy. Amanté Houston was not easy to buy for, that was for sure.

He didn't talk about it, but I knew he was nervous to return to the field. Not because he thought he'd be bad or something, but because things were so incredibly different. He'd been reminded of his mortality. He seemed different to me, even, before and after the injury. Before, he was untouchable, charismatic yet slightly aloof, open yet slightly guarded. Now, his openness drew you in like a moth to a flame. His charisma was fueled by more than media training; he was full of this energy, purpose.

I liked to see it. I got to watch some of his training sessions he did on his own, and even those individual ones were filled with a spark I'd not seen from him. He'd always been a magnetic player: unbelievably athletic, bodily control like I'd never seen, skills so elevated it was like watching a video game. Now, he was still all those things, yet *more*. Where some athletes might have understandably suffered a mental block following an injury like that, Amanté was enlightened. In short, he was going to be a big, big problem for anyone on the field.

None of that solved the question of how to reciprocate his generosity. I was deeply proud of him and I wanted to convey that. Still, my mind was empty.

I'd never seen the city as alive as when we were hosting the first round of the tournament—and Amanté was returning to the field. I was in a bus on my way to the stadium to hang out at Isaiah's tailgate until I was allowed on the field, when I'd wish Amanté good luck, then go back to the stands to watch. Khalil had offered for me to hang out in his box, but I wanted to be closer—I didn't like the idea of being so far away if something happened. Maybe that was me being paranoid; okay, it definitely was me being paranoid. But it was also a completely different atmosphere in the stands compared to being in a box. In the stands, I was shotgunning beer with strangers, bundled up against the January cold, screeching like a crazy person. I couldn't do that with Amina—well, I could, but I'd feel bad subjecting the woman to it, considering how miserably pregnant she was.

Isaiah threw a great party, and that extended to his tailgate. There was a DJ—the same girl as his fundraising party—and a fancy grill with a dedicated chef. Beer pong was set up, and although the parking lot wasn't too busy just yet, it was already a vibe. It wasn't as miserably cold today as they'd forecasted, which I was grateful for. Still, I wore leggings under my baggy cargos, a hoodie under my Houston jersey, and the jacket he'd bought me over it all, with a cute Saints beanie to match.

I brought a pack of the cheapest beer I could find as my contribution to the tailgate, and rocked up to the pong table holding my beer in the air and dancing to the amapiano beats the DJ was putting down. Isaiah matched my vibes as soon as he spotted me, pointing at me and climbing onto the table to shake his ass. He jumped down when I was close enough and pulled me into a hug, both of us cracking up.

"Let's do a shot!" He said, directing me towards his little bar.

"No fucking way!" I protested over the music, but when he held out a nip of very fancy tequila complete with a wedge of lime and a salt shaker, I rolled my eyes and grinned. "Just one!" I acquiesced, and he agreed, clinking a mini bottle of his own as we shot it.

Just like that, the party was started, and the parking lot quickly began to fill, and maybe it wasn't so bad being on the outside looking in. This was a lot more fun than my pregame routine had been when I actually worked for the Saints.

Isaiah and I swept the beer pong tournament, and before I knew it, it was time for me to get on the field and wish Amanté good luck. I'd just had the one shot and one beer, so I was feeling great heading into the stadium, getting shuffled into the proper tunnels to send me to the sideline so I could see him. There were still a few hours until the game, so the parking lot was far more lit than the stadium, but they still had some good music playing. The sun was high in the sky, and I squinted, searching for Amanté in the crowd of light-clad men.

We saw each other at the same time, and I didn't think before running to him, and he picked me up, kissing me deeply. His hands were firmly on my ass, holding me up as I wrapped my legs around him, and we walked further down the sideline.

"You taste like tequila." He smiled, giving my ass another little squeeze.

"Isaiah and I won the pong tournament." I informed him, taking in his slightly sweaty face, the utter joy on it. "I can't fucking wait to watch you."

"Really?" He asked, and I thought I could see some warmth creep onto his cheeks. He set me down, finally, and I pushed him. Taking a few steps back, I slowly took him in, the very tight cutoff, the tight, tight pants, his arms—fucking loved his arms—and the steam that was emanating from him. He laughed, watching me watch him.

"I love watching you, Amanté Houston." I said, and I was sure it was just the little buzz talking, but I wanted to tell him I loved more than just watching him. I held off, though. It didn't feel like the right time. "I feel like I'm watching an ancient god show us all how it's done."

He laughed aloud. "How much tequila did you have?"

"Not enough to use as an excuse." I grinned, and told him all about the tailgate. "So, not drunk. Just excited to see you." In response, he wrapped a hand around my waist and yanked me against him again, kissing me.

"Where did we say your seats are?" He asked. His new agent had bought them, so I didn't know either, and I took a second to find my tickets in my phone, pulling up the map while we spun around trying to orient ourselves. Finally, he pointed to one of the corners—right by the endzone. Easily the nicest seats I'd ever sat in, and Isaiah and I were sure to be the most obnoxious football-goers St. Clair had ever seen.

"I'm proud of you." I told him, and he pulled me tight into his chest. It felt like just a few seconds went by, but somehow it was time to let the boys focus, so I bid him farewell and emerged in the now-packed stadium to search for Isaiah.

wya I texted, and he immediately replied.

Hot dogs acquired. Bucket of beer? I chuckled. *Between our seats n bathroom.* I looked up, spotting the area for our seats, doing a 180 before I saw the bathroom sign in the distance—and there Isaiah was, holding a tray of hot dogs in line for beer.

"How is he?" He asked when I came up beside him.

"He's good. Excited, I think. High energy." I answered, taking a fry from his tray.

"Think we're going to win?" I elbowed him, eliciting a loud oof. We stepped up to order.

"Hi!" I greeted, looking at the menu, "We'll have a bucket." I handed over my card, throwing Isaiah a wink, which made him laugh hard enough I almost elbowed him again. "Make it two."

Climbing over people's laps with two buckets of beer and a tray full of hot dogs was hilariously awkward, but luckily, we were all in such high spirits that nobody cared. I handed out the first bucket of beer—then the second, as I kept making friends—and was climbing back over everyone to wait in line for another two.

It was my fucking boyfriend's first game back *and* the first game of the postseason—I was going to be (mildly) generous and fun. I'd made everyone agree that we'd shotgun the beers at kickoff, all together, so as the Saints set up to kick it away, all twenty of us in the vicinity who were over 21 were holding our beers, preparing to crack and chug. The ball sailed through the air and Isaiah was the first one to finish. I was close to last, if not dead last, and we were all laughing and cheering, and this was definitely way better than being at work.

35

Amanté

The defense shut them down so fast we might as well have started with the ball, and when I jogged out onto the field with the rest of the offense, the stadium erupted into a cheer that consumed my entire consciousness. I looked around, just for a second, but it was long enough to see it—to see that they were cheering for me, the entire stadium, and I let the wave of energy fill me. I wouldn't win MVP having been out almost half the season—but I could still bring us a ring. And that started today.

Our first drive was great—first down after first down after first down, until we were first & goal. I was being double-teamed and had yet to be targeted, but it still felt amazing to be back on the field, and I blocked like a motherfucker, threw up my hands like the ball was coming when it was on the other side of the field, and ran my two guys all over the end. No luck, though, and I smirked when—despite it being fourth & goal—we kept our offense out on the field. Khalil called the play, clapping as we left the huddle, and I lined up as wide out as I could. Just before the ball was snapped, I darted inside, to line up right by the o-line, my two defenders coming with me. The ball was snapped, Khalil stepped back, and I blocked like I was a third grader playing offensive line, leaving the entire sideline wide open for Khalil to take it himself, practically jogging in. The crowd erupted, and I ran to him, joining in his stupid dance his daughter had begged and begged us to do.

I was winded—I'd been doing a lot of work to stay in gametime shape, but playing in a game was different than pretending to, and I was breathing heavy after playing every snap of that drive. Bunch of guys smacked my helmet and I just nodded at them all, throwing a thumbs up. Fuck, I missed this shit, I missed the adrenaline, I missed feeling tired like this. My rest was cut short, though, when we all jumped up as Cornell snagged his first interception of the season, if I was remembering correctly, and made it halfway back down the field before he was tackled out of bounds. I jogged out; I'd probably play almost every snap today. That was the plan—I wouldn't be getting as many targets as usual, but we needed me in true game form for the rest of the postseason, and there was no better way to prepare than by doing it. So, here I was, lining up, running routes.

Khalil launched one to me as I darted across the middle. It was a great ball, but I was supposed to be the last resort, and as such he had to thread it through two defenders to end in my hands—but when I turned up field, I had nothing but open space in front of me. I probably got thirty yards after the pass before someone flew across the field to tackle me. I jumped up quick, the stadium once again erupting into what might've been a chant of my name, and held up my hands like a gladiator in the colosseum.

It wasn't the postseason for no reason, and their defense was good. We had a solid drive, quality passes out of Khalil and impressive runs, but they managed to hold us to a kick. Still, it put more points on the board, and I liked the way the scoreboard looked: 10-0. I liked the sound of that.

As good as their defense was, ours was still dominating, holding them to another three and out, and they punted the ball back to us. Our defensive coordinator was great; I liked him, when I got to see him, and based on the morale of our defense he was a good guy to have in the locker room. I didn't want to jinx anything, but our defense looked as good as it had all season. As a receiver, I loved when my defense pulled their weight—and I loved it even more when they dominated so hard that I felt like I was being carried.

"Careful out here, bro." The safety covering me said, and I ignored him. "One good hit and it's back to IR." I clenched my jaw, fighting a smile. I liked trash talk. It always fired me up, especially when I knew I could smoke lil bro, which I definitely could. I just waited for the snap, and as soon as it did, I hit that boy hard enough that he was barely off the ground at the end of the play, when I was jogging back to the line of scrimmage after catching an easy pass for first down. Legally hit him, of course. He didn't say anything after that, but he was doing a better job of covering me—maybe a little reminder of who I was helped him lock in.

Khalil was on fire today. I wasn't sure of the actual stats, but it seemed like every pass he threw was a completion, every throw landing exactly where he wanted it to be. The drive ended with an easy toss for the touchdown, and I jogged off the field with a big grin. 17-0 was a very comfortable lead heading into the half—and we still had six minutes, plenty of time to score again. Of course, I wanted to score one for myself, but what we were doing now was working. We were diversifying targets, using all the guys who'd gotten more confident while I was out, and I couldn't blame Khalil for tossing the ball elsewhere when I was being double teamed.

Still, I sat on the bench and watched the film, preparing myself to level up. I wasn't playing poorly, but I knew I could take it up a notch. In the second half, Calla would be at our endzone, and if I didn't bring one in then, I'd be beating myself up for sure. Our defense was great, again, holding them to a kick, although I was disappointed that we weren't going to actually blow them out. They had a stellar kick, and our returner only made it to the fifteen before he was taken down.

I didn't mind a long drive—I was starting to acclimate to the tiredness, feeling that runner's high I was accustomed to, feeling like I was unstoppable—all of us were. I told Khalil as much, who shared with the OC, and sure enough, for the entire drive, I was open every time. Snap, Khalil, me. Snap, Khalil, me. I felt like I was flying on the field, not running routes but creating them, losing defenders like they'd never been there to begin with, catching pass after pass as we made our way to the other side of the field. They took a timeout.

Quick squirt of water and boost of energy later, we were back—and they'd adjusted their defensive scheme. The kid who'd said something to me earlier was in front of me.

"Scared, huh?" I said, and had a great laugh as he was on me so hard they threw a flag.

"Defensive holding, number 9. Five-yard penalty, automatic first down." The ref's voice boomed throughout the stadium, eliciting a roar from the crowd. We rushed a few yards, letting me breathe a little, and as I blocked for the next play, Young went flying through the gap we'd made, hurtling over the last line of defense and making it into the end zone with ease.

"Let's go!" I reached him, smacking his helmet, and we ran back to the sideline while special teams set up the extra point. It was good—we had a reliable kicker, so of course it was—and the score sat at a comfortable 24 us, 3 them. First half was pretty much over, and we got the ball to start the second. I was feeling great, to be honest. I was feeling as good as I'd ever felt on the field, having fun and feeling truly present in a way I rarely felt outside the game.

We kicked it back towards them, and I grimaced as their returner dodged every tackle, turning up the speed until he was past everybody, running it in for a special teams touchdown. I put my hands over my head, groaning. 24 us, 10 them. I wasn't worried, but a return touchdown was always brutal for the energy in the stadium. It was decently quiet, except for some boos, and I patted all the guys who ran off. Their frustration was understandably palpable, but I took a deep breath. It's the postseason—we're supposed to all be good. They were allowed to do good stuff—we were better, and we knew it. We had just enough time to get back on the field and reclaim the energy. Just enough time for Khalil to launch the ball to the endzone while we all sprinted down to catch it.

The Hail Mary was exactly what you want out of that kind of play: perfect spiral, arcing through the air in slow motion, ready to land right in the center of the end zone. We were all sprinting down the field to where the defense awaited our arrival, everyone's eyes on the ball, all of us tracking its path in the sky. It began its descent beautifully, and I knew it was coming to me. I launched myself into the air, hoping to snag it before anyone could bat it down, and as my fingers brushed the leather, air rushed out of my lungs, an ache blooming in my ribs, and all I could think was *fuck* as I hit the field.

Flag was thrown, but whoever had tackled me was lucky I didn't catch his number, because he would've caught my fucking hands in the second half. That was a cheap hit, and watching it on the replay, I muttered a few more profanities under my breath. He easily could've swatted the ball away from me—and he chose blatant pass interference instead. Well, lucky for us, we got an untimed down, which I almost regretted, because they refused to let me play it.

If I had been re-injured, I wouldn't be fucking breathing. There was no reason for me not to play, especially when I knew—I knew—I would catch the fucking ball. Coach Frye kept saying it was the smart thing to do, and I kept walking away, because if I heard him say it one more time I was going to have a meltdown. We didn't score, and walking to the locker room, he took my shoulder and stopped me.

"I need you more at the end of the game than at the end of the half." He said, and I knew he wasn't trying to hurt my pride, but my adrenaline was racing and I really, really didn't feel like being rational.

"I get it, coach. Let me cool off before I crash out." I snapped, and he moved to my side, matching my pace as we went to the locker room.

Coaches talked us up, brought the energy up, told us what to fix and what to look out for. They reiterated that if we lose, it's over, and that we're the better team. They talked about energy, keeping our head in the game, and not letting them get under our skin. They hyped up our young guys who were bringing the pressure—and our veterans holding it down. They reminded us that, whatever happened right before the half, we had a nice-looking lead, and they were playing on their heels the whole game. We broke down a few more minute issues, and when we were about ready to head back out there, I stood up.

"You know what, let me say somethin'," I looked around at my team, the team that held it down the last eight, nine weeks, the team that made it possible for me to even return this year. "First off, it feels fucking good to be back on the field with my boys." A few 'yeah's echoed. "Second, I'm glad they're sittin' in their locker room talkin' bout how they got the upper hand. I'm glad somebody's yellin' bout puttin' us in our place. I'm fucking glad they think they have a chance. You know why?"

"Why?" A few guys asked, nodding, bouncing with the adrenaline that was fueling me, too.

"Because it's going to feel fucking great," I raised my voice, looking at each of them, "watching them realize that they gave us everything, and they're still going to Cabo."

They came out of the locker room just as hyped as they expected, and managed to hold us to another 3 and out. I was antsy, but I wasn't worried. We'd prepared for a close game all week. We knew how to play from behind, and we knew how to hold onto a lead when things picked up. It was all good, and I trusted our defense—trust that was well placed, because they held them to a kick. 24 us, 13 them. Still a two-score game, three if they had to kick again, but I wanted to make it a little more comfortable. I nodded along on the sideline as we received some more coaching, adapting to their adjusted defense and taking advantage of a few newer guys who might be more likely to foul.

When it was time to get back out on the field, I was lined up across from a different guy than before, and he was fired up. He was muttering shit under his breath, and when his middle linebacker yelled at him, he yelled right back. My eyebrows shot up, and I couldn't help myself.

"You good, bro?" He either ignored me or didn't hear me, but barked something at his teammate again, so I said, "Maybe focus on me instead, my guy."

We snapped the ball, and Khalil threw it to the other side—incomplete. My cover—number 28—lined up in front of me again. He said something under his breath.

"Speak up." I said, trying to bait him.

"I said, I've locked down tougher guys who actually played a whole season." He looked me in the eye. "You just here for the photo op." That one actually stung a little, and when the ball snapped, I may have done my job a little too well; maybe, I threw him onto the ground after the play was dead. Who knew. The yellow flag flew.

"You good, bro?" He asked, once he got up, getting in my face. A ref pulled us apart and I jogged back to the huddle.

"Unnecessary roughness, offense, number 1. Fifteen-yard penalty, repeat second down." Fuck. Khalil smacked my helmet.

"Head in the game." He said, then launched into the plan. Second and twenty-five wasn't exactly where we wanted to be. My route was straight up the sideline. If I couldn't shake my defender, I was a good distraction. If I could...

I lined up, and when the ball was snapped, I lunged toward the middle—then dodged out, leaving my boy on the ground, streaking up the sideline. I threw my hand up, waving it, begging Khalil to see me, and he did. There was no one around for miles when I caught the ball and jogged the last few yards into the end zone, crowd going wild for my obscenely long touchdown—so long I had to wait for everyone to run to the end zone to celebrate with me.

Instead of waiting, I threw off my helmet and ran to the corner, scanning the wild crowd to find her, and once I did, everything else faded away. Only Calla, who, to my great amusement, was chugging a beer with four other people around her, and who locked eyes with me only once she crushed the can, spraying the remaining beer all over. Everything slowed down as I sprinted, jumping up onto the stands, grabbing her by the neck, and kissing her.

I was being drenched with beer, I was pretty sure, and just like that I hopped off the stand into the crowd of my teammates, and we skipped and cheered our way back to the sideline.

I felt better than I'd felt in years. This game, this team, this was why I played football. I was great for the Captains—I broke a longstanding league record for receiving touchdowns, primarily by being the only guy who could catch the ball—but I hadn't been playing football. Not like this, with a team I trust, a team that roots for me on and off the field.

"Bro! Bro!" I yelled, pushing through to Khalil, who was talking to somebody, probably interviewing for some network I didn't care about. He saw me and threw an arm around my neck, pulling me into the video. "This my first playoff win!" I yelled at him, over the noise.

"What?" He asked, genuinely incredulous, and we both burst into laughter. Someone else with a microphone tapped my shoulder and I turned around to stare into a massive camera—an interview of my own.

36

Calla

I'd never been to a home playoff game before, let alone one we won, and the atmosphere was more than electric. It was chaos, pure joyful chaos, and it took me a while to find a quiet corner to wait for Amanté to come out. My skin was buzzing from the adrenaline and the fucking kiss and I wanted to see him, wanted to jump up and down and scream and celebrate. It was far more fun to watch and cheer and be part of the community than it had been to hold down the social media on my own.

The more I thought about it, the crazier I realized my job had been. The Saints' front office was so behind the times that they'd only wanted to pay one person—with minimal experience—to run their billion-dollar social media. This thought hit me across the face multiple times in a day, constantly over the last few weeks, but seeing the game, the thousands of people who paid to be there, and realizing I'd been willing to get walked all over, hit me harder and harder every time. Still, waiting here for my famous boyfriend to be done with work, exposed an uncomfortable bit of jealousy. I wanted to be in that room being celebrated. I wanted to be part of the team, as they continued to exceed expectations, situating themselves as real contenders for the championship. I didn't like feeling jealousy, but I definitely didn't like feeling it about a man who'd been nothing but good to me.

I was proud of him, though, and I reminded myself that jealousy itself was natural—dwelling on it, letting it fester, wasn't. The truth was, I had felt that pang of jealousy, but it was far outweighed by my pride in my man. And I was, truly, proud. I had no idea how I'd bagged such an incredible man. I'd always been magnetic—attributed to a combination of my confidence and my genetics, I thought—but the result always seemed to be less than stellar guys, usually with a below average emotional intelligence and a not-awful face that I still had to justify in the group chat. Amanté was none of that; he was wildly successful, unafraid to be honest and open with me, and the man of literally everyone's dreams. It almost seemed unfair for everyone else that this picturesque man was on my arm, was mine to send silly texts and watch sunrises and curl up into.

Almost as if it was reading my mind, my phone pinged. Two messages popped up: one from Amanté, and one from Amina. I had to read them each twice to make sure I wasn't mixing them up.

Amanté: *it ok if we take javon home?* Of course it was—and I shot him a quick text saying as much. But I stared at Amina's text for a long, long time. Long enough that Amanté's response came through: *everything ok?* I blinked, realizing it was now nearly empty and I was moments away from being escorted out by security—I'd been staring for, what, ten minutes? I replied.

Sorry bb. Sent. Then realized that didn't answer the question. *All good be there in 2.* And I was, walking the short distance to the player parking where I saw Javon and Amanté chatting at his truck. Javon waved and some of the tightness in my chest released. When I approached them, it was Javon who hugged me first, drawing an eyeroll out of his mentor.

"You comin' out with us, Calla?" Javon asked, opening the passenger door and giving me a little raise of his eyebrows. Looking into the cab, I remembered that there really was not a whole lot of room for two people, let alone two football players and me. With a little giggle, I pushed the middle console up and perched precariously on the little cushion that could hardly be called a middle seat.

"I hope we don't get pulled over." I was so close to the stick Amanté would barely be able to drive. "And, I don't know." Amanté held the door open for me, giving me a questioning look as Javon climbed in beside me and he shut the door.

"No shot you're not celebrating your boy's return to play." Javon said, doing his best to give me some room while Amanté opened his door. "Even if unc's gonna be in the ice bath all day tomorrow." Amanté laughed at the rookie's call-out, but the kid was probably right. Amanté hadn't played in a game, let alone that many snaps, in so long he'd probably be sore til next Sunday. Amanté climbed in, wedging me tightly between the two men—and Javon sent a look over my head that I was sure was incredulous. "Man, why'd you offer to drive me?" I couldn't stop the laughter, then, as I really took in how stupid we looked all crammed into this old ass truck.

I wasn't sure where to put my arms, and my knees were propped up, and I felt so, so ridiculous, and soon tears were squeezing out as I attempted to stifle the laughter that had taken me. When I blinked them away, Amanté was looking at me, this light, bright smile across his face, and I took in the glow—the glow of a game well fought, and won, where he was able to truly unleash for the first time in forever. I dropped a hand to his thigh and squeezed.

"Yeah, let's go out." He shot me a look that was less than innocent and I fought a smirk as I dared a glance at his pants. Javon threw an arm around my shoulders and pulled me into him.

"Man, I ain't know you wanted a third." Javon said, and color rushed to my cheeks immediately.

"Chill, chill, chill." Amanté said, pulling out onto the street, but the mischievous glint in his eye informed me that he was now thinking some very naughty thoughts, and every brush of his hand on my thigh as he shifted gears had me thinking the same—almost enough to forget Amina's text. Almost.

I liked Javon, but he was a cheeky motherfucker, and I wasn't sure I could get any redder by the time we climbed into the car, Ron holding the door for us, already looking tired of our shit. He was funny, too, and Amanté matched his energy, the two of them getting hyped up for their celebratory night out, doing shots and yelling along to music while I fixed up my hair.

Now that we were at the bar—and I hadn't had anything to drink since the game—I was starting to feel some of the anxiety brewing from that text. I fought the urge to look at it again. It could wait. No use borrowing tomorrow's worries, or however that phrase goes.

"What's wrong?" Amanté's voice was soft in my ear. It didn't take a genius to notice I was feeling off—I usually was the one hyping up people to do shots and dancing—but it still sent a flutter of butterflies through my stomach. He noticed me. He saw me.

I didn't want to be the cause of a less than stellar celebration. We'd only been her about twenty minutes, but if I continued to let it fester, Amanté wouldn't let himself have any fun, and that wasn't okay to me.

"I've been invited to interview with a team." I breathed, the sentence far less scary now that it was out of me. Amina's friends had pulled through—she'd texted before to make sure she could pass on my information. The position was in sideline reporting—I'd be assistant to their current one, almost an apprentice—which was even more of a dream than what I'd done for the Saints. I loved the Saints and I loved creating content, but I'd always imagined myself working my way up into an actual sports reporter. The nerves—excitement? Energy? Whatever it was, it clawed at my stomach.

The job was with the Lauderville Stallions—a three-hour drive away. I knew it was stupid to even question it, especially when I hadn't even accepted the interview or been offered the job, but, truthfully, I was terrified. I didn't want to uproot everything that had been so good lately—but I couldn't abandon my dream, either. The aforementioned 'everything' took my face in his hands and kissed me, his excitement buzzing across his lips.

"It's fate." He said, shaking his head, that perfect smile stretching across his face. He raised a hand for the bartender.

"What do you mean?" I asked. The bartender made his way towards us.

"When we met," he paused, "pop a bottle of bubbly for me, man," and the bartender dug around a fridge, "Calla, when we met..." He trailed off, his warm eyes searching mine.

When we met, I'd been celebrating an interview. He'd been celebrating a big step in his career. I felt my own smile match his. I didn't need to worry about the logistics of everything right now. I didn't need to wonder how things would pan out.

I did need to celebrate my wins—our wins. And with the smoldering look he was giving me, the glint of something softer there, I felt the tightness in my chest fully release. The bartender pulled a bottle of champagne out from what must've been the very back of the fridge and handed it to Amanté, who climbed his big ass up on a stool and yelled-

"To Calla!" I blushed harder than I had with Javon earlier. "And to fucking *me*!" He popped the bottle and gave me a wink that told me he knew exactly how that sounded. So, I climbed on my own stool and, safety be damned, kissed him.

37

Amanté

Calla was going to fucking kill me. How she managed to be so effortlessly enticing was thoroughly confusing to me, and the feel of her hip, where her hip creased into her thigh, fuck, just the silken skin she absently dragged across me was intoxicating. Shit, even the way she blushed when Javon was teasing her in the car—the way I could see her imagining dirty, dirty things—was hot. I'd never been afraid of having a beautiful woman. I could be jealous, but not truly jealous; not unless I had some reason to distrust them. I had no reason to distrust Calla, and instead of feeling that pang of anger when men looked at her, I felt pride.

She was the hottest girl in any room, and everyone knew it, and when she got that look in her eye—the one she had now, almost hungry, almost cavernous, like you wanted to fall into her eyes and could fall forever—she was completely irresistible. I couldn't blame anyone for wanting her, not when I burned so badly for her I could hardly breathe.

I wasn't dancing, knowing that Javon's jokes about being sore tomorrow were unfortunately true, but I kept a close enough eye on Calla that I doubted anyone thought I was here for anything else. Watching her dance had me adjusting my pants more than once. It was fucking torture, but the best kind. She'd changed out of her outfit for the game—equally adorable, considering that I loved seeing her in cozy clothing and I also loved seeing her wear my last name—into something considerably more sinful. The lines of her hamstrings accentuated just how mini her mini skirt was, and I took a long gulp of my drink—just water, now that the bubbly was gone—to stifle the urge to fuck her right here. She was close enough to touch, to grab, but I held myself back. We were here to celebrate. I wanted to savor this—the whole night.

She turned back around and caught my gaze as it traveled back up her body, and with that devilish smirk on her lips and the equally dark look in her eye, she took my hand and pulled me up. I fucking loved the way she looked up at me, when I stood over her. Maybe it was—fuck—maybe it was bad of me, but the fucking look she gave me, peering up at me through her dark lashes, made me feel so fucking powerful. I felt like a great knight, and she was the damsel I'd saved.

Calla turned around, dancing just close enough that her perfect fucking ass barely brushed the growing bulge in my pants, and I couldn't keep my hands to myself anymore—I pulled her tight, a hand splayed across her abdomen, while she danced against me. I felt like a heroic fucking knight, and she was the damsel who wanted to thank me for saving her.

Other scenarios swiftly exited my mind as I hardened against her. A new DJ was starting their set, and the bar was quickly becoming more club-like as newcomers flooded the space. As if my ego couldn't get any bigger, at least half were wearing my jersey. We weren't in a VIP section at some club, we weren't out at a fancy dinner—we, the handful of teammates who'd come out, were in the thick of it, getting down with St. Clair locals, and it was electric.

Calla took my hand and pulled me away from the crowd, and before I knew it we were snaking past groups until we reached a grungy little door, which she opened and pushed me inside. My question died on my lips when I turned around and found her tying her hair back, pure seduction in her eyes. I cleared my throat.

"What are you doing?" I asked, knowing, or hoping I knew, but wanting to hear the husky voice I knew would come out of her.

"Thanking you." She smirked, stepping closer, undoing my belt. My mouth dried. "Showing you exactly," her fingers moved to my button, the zipper, "how proud I am." I exhaled as she knelt in front of me. Flashbacks of her in my hotel room, her skin, her perfect breasts, made me drop my head back and brace myself. Cool air rushed over me as she freed my dick from its confines. "Something wrong?" She asked, and she knew exactly what she was doing with that coy tone.

"Absolutely nothing could be wrong right now."

38

Calla

Things had been wonderful. Truly, my life hadn't felt this good in a long, long time, and while Amanté was largely to blame, I also thought I could take some of the credit for myself. I was less high strung; not less ambitious, but less... basing my self worth on what type of work I was doing. It was good for me, working at the coffee shop while I got my head on straight. Okay, maybe that was a little bit of a lie; it was good for me, working at the coffee shop while I prepared for my second interview with the Lauderville Stallions—the first one had been over the phone and absolutely fantastic—and soaked in how simple life currently was. I was developing real friendships with actual good people, like Isaiah, and I was getting to know Amanté more deeply than I'd ever known someone.

It wasn't a bad thing, but—well, Amanté and I hadn't had sex since that morning we decided to be just friends. It wasn't that the attraction wasn't there, because it was. I mean, I'd sucked his dick in the bathroom after his first playoff win. He was still mouthwateringly delicious, and when he occasionally joined me at the gym it was an effort to keep focused, and he still squeezed my thighs and smacked my ass and kissed me like I was the air he needed to breathe. Sometimes, I would say something or do something and find him staring at me like he wanted to devour me. No sex, though.

Shay said that he was probably still trying to take it slow, like we'd agreed to before his injury, before everything, and it wasn't that I didn't believe her. She was usually right about things in my life, and I trusted her, but part of me was scared. What if what we had was purely physical, and now that we were bringing real romance into it, the sex appeal was gone? What if, when I'd told him I wanted to try being just friends, it had cursed us? That was silly—I hadn't cursed us. I didn't think. I'd just been on my knees for him! Although, what man would say no to that?

Still, he was less forward than he'd been when we hardly knew each other. As much as I loved being courted, romanced, however you wanted to call it, I was feeling a little bit put off. Was I less attractive, now that I wasn't dressing up in heels for work? Or was he bored now that I was his, no longer an ideal to chase? Photos of us kissing after his touchdown had been all over the internet once he returned to the field—did I embarrass him, somehow?

Frequency of sex with my hot boyfriend was the last thing I needed to be worrying about, but it did a great job of helping me procrastinate. Any and all nerves developed while scheduling and preparing for this interview were quickly rerouted into concerns about fucking. While I could acknowledge that this wasn't exactly the healthiest way to handle stress, the result was that I had little to no nerves preparing for my second interview, compiling clips for my portfolio, and planning the best time to drive down to Lauderville. I was hardly even thinking about how they'd told me over the phone that the in-person interview was just a formality. That I was one interview away from moving three hours south. Hardly.

My doorbell rang, and I shot to my feet, realizing that I'd been zoned out, staring at the wall for—I checked my phone—half an hour. God. That meant it was Amanté at the door, coming over for a lunch date. I buzzed him up, opening the door with a smile on my face. I was wearing a pair of his sweats I'd stolen the first time I slept at his place, one of his massive hoodies on top, and my rarely-seen glasses. When he rounded the corner, takeout in hand, I bit my lip to keep from laughing at his nearly identical outfit.

He didn't say anything, just walked to the door and wrapped me into a tight hug, pressing a gentle kiss to my head, and walked in. It was the first time Amanté was at my apartment. Ever. Seeing him inside the tiny space had me scanning the room to make sure I'd cleaned it adequately.

"Calla, I love it." Amanté announced, after a moment, then plopped onto the couch and started unpacking the food—a shitload of sushi. My stomach grumbled, so I poured us some water and joined him on the couch, claiming one of his arms for my own while he laid out everything.

"Thanks for bringing food." I planted a kiss on his bicep, then sat up and took in the spread. I could feel him watching me out of the corner of my eye, so I turned to face him, propping one leg up on the couch, and really took him in.

Things had been moving so fast in life, his career, my new job and this new opportunity, and I wasn't sure if we were really serious enough to consider changing anything with this interview. I'd been drawn to Amanté since I met him, and my entire life had changed due to him, and I wanted him, wanted this. But I couldn't pretend that it all felt a bit distant. Maybe that was just the sex, but even the lack of sex was making me feel like it was all a dream. Everything had felt more real when all the odds were stacked against us.

"Can I ask a question that's kind of embarrassing?" I blurted, placing a hand on his thigh. He cocked his head to the side, that beautiful little smirk coming out, and I squeezed his thigh.

"Always." He took my hand from his thigh and intertwined our fingers.

"Why haven't we had sex?" I watched his face, searching for any reaction, any shock or anger or discomfort, and was somewhat confused to see only a sort of shyness that dusted over his features.

He laughed, a breathy laugh that brought an unexpected smile to my face, and replied, "I didn't want you to think this was just sexual. I meant what I said, before. This could be something real. This *is* something real."

I exhaled, feeling the blush stain my cheeks. "I was worried you weren't attracted to me like that anymore." Amanté laughed for real, this time, and kissed my knuckles.

"No, Calla, fuck." He grinned. "It's been miserable, controlling myself around you." I narrowed my eyes, ready to tease him. "Not that I don't love spending time with you, I do."

"I know."

"But yes, Calla, I am still attracted to you like that. Very attracted to you like that." The look he was giving me confirmed it, and I felt the wave of shyness wash over me, instead. "Actually, before we eat, I wanted to talk about something." He said, and the shyness was replaced with anxiety. Before I could think about it, I blurted it out:

"I think the Stallions are going to offer me the job." I slapped a hand over my mouth, wide eyes searching his for a reaction. He seemed taken off guard, and my throat tightened.

"Calla, holy shit." He had me in his lap before I could react, standing up to jump with me in his arms. "That's amazing!" I pulled my head back to look at him.

"It would mean I'd have to move." I said, my voice quiet.

"Your first time in a new city—have you been to Lauderville? It's a great city, totally underrated. I think it's a lot like St. Clair, honestly.

You'd love it." He set me down and kissed me, warm yet hard and God, this reaction was nothing like I'd expected and it made me feel that intense wholeness in my chest I'd refused to label.

"You aren't worried about us? About the distance?" I asked, and he took my face in his hands.

"Not even a little, Calla." He kissed the tip of my nose, the gesture so endearing I nearly broke right there and told him I was in love. "Of course, I want to be with you—I would rather be with you all the time, every day—but the season is only 18 weeks. We have the other eight months of the year to be together." The tingling in my hands began to subside.

"What if it's a year-round position?" I asked, half teasing, half genuinely curious how he'd respond.

"Then I guess I'm buying you a fancy house in Lauderville." He grinned at my expression, brushing the hair out of my face. "I love you, Calla Monroe. A few hours can't get in the way of that." Just like that, tears pricked my eyes, and he was kissing me—kissing me with abandon, holding me tight, and I was happy—I was so exceedingly happy, words couldn't do it justice.

"I love you, Amanté." His answering grin nearly made me cry again.

"Let's eat, my love."

39

Amanté

I loved being on a winning team. After so many years of wishing I was in the postseason, enduring relentless teasing about heading to Mexico rather than the big game, it was exhilarating to be one of the guys fighting to be in the final game. Even though I wasn't getting a whole lot of action on the field—I was back to being double covered, triple once—I was doing my job as best I could, blocking and feinting and generally just enjoying being back on the field.

I was sitting in the ice bath, chatting with Khalil; we had a bye week, this week, and I was trying to be chill about it—but it was hard to be chill when I was officially about to be playing for a ring.

"And, my wife might give birth during the damn game." Khalil finished his thought, then dunked his head under the frigid water. When he popped back up, he was laughing. "Man, I'm glad we got you."

"Yeah?" Some of the tension left my shoulders.

"Yeah, bro, we wouldn't be where we are without you." The timer went off and we both stood, stepping out of our respective tubs, and Khalil shook my hand. "Always knew you were a G, but for real, you bring a vibe to the team that we needed." He wrapped his towel around his shoulders while I soaked in the compliment. It, freely given, meant a lot to me. I could've cried if I wasn't frozen.

My phone buzzed and I picked it up. Calla was in Lauderville, finally having that second interview, and I'd set her up in my favorite hotel down there. Based on the time, she should've been on her way to the facility.

Baaaaabe was the first text, pulling out a smile. *I just fucking landed. Gotta call stallions so they don't think I'm standing them up lmao. So mad.* My smile dropped.

Everything ok? Need me to call a car? I can have somebody pick up your bags. I typed and sent as quick as I could, slinging my towel over my shoulder.

No baby thank you. I'll lyk when I'm on my way. Love you! Her message would've had me giggling and kicking my feet if I was alone—but as it was, Khalil was giving me a knowing look.

"Calla?" He asked; I nodded. "Amina told me her interview's today."

"It is." I confirmed, drying off.

"She also told me that they basically already offered her the job." Khalil said, grinning, and I mirrored him.

"I'm proud of her, man." I gushed, "I can't imagine dealing with what she's dealt with this year, and she's still going after it."

"You okay with long distance if she gets it?" He asked, and I had a feeling Amina was the driving force of these questions. I sighed, thinking about it. Long distance wouldn't be fun, but not being with her would be worse. And, I'd meant what I said the other day—worst case scenario, we were long distance for four months out of the year. I could handle four months—easy. Khalil and I walked to our lockers, finally done with recovery for the day, and my phone buzzed again. I whipped it out, scanning quickly to make sure Calla was good.

Games tonight? Isaiah asked, and I liked the message before tucking it away, tuning back into my conversation with Khalil.

"I love her. I'd make it work even if she moved to fuckin' Ridgeway to work for the Eagles."

Isaiah loved playing games—video games, board games, card games, games with girls, occasionally—and he loved to host a good time. As a result, when we played games at Isaiah's, you could always count on good music, great snacks, and fun beverages, which is exactly what he delivered tonight.

I would move out of Isaiah's eventually, but right now? I was in no rush. I loved having a roommate again. It was almost like being back at the dorms, crashing RA meetings just to eat the food and forge lifelong friendships. I badly wished Calla was here, but it was still a fun time. Speaking of Calla, my phone rang, and I stepped away from the table.

"Hi, my love." I answered, and she sounded immediately out of breath.

"Thank God for Amina, honestly." She said, and I heard the sound of a car door. "I messaged her asking what to do and they were willing to reschedule to tomorrow morning."

"That's great!" I replied.

"Honestly, I'm thrilled. I didn't sleep well at all last night, and I smell gross, and something about the airport always makes my skin age fifty years." She groaned; I laughed, glad to hear she was doing okay. I heard a yawn.

"Sleepy?" I teased, and her crystalline giggle filled my ear.

"Yes, I am, so I'm going to order a slice of cake from room service and go to sleep." Glancing at the clock, it was only 7pm. "I hear you're having a fun night without me." I could hear her smile, imagine it like she was in front of me.

"You know Isaiah. All he needs is a thumbs up and he'll curate the best party you've ever been to."

"Tea." She laughed. "Shay's already texted me about three separate incidents."

"Incidents?" I asked, lowering my voice.

"She says that Isaiah is lowkey flirting with Lucy." Lucy... Lucy, Benjamin's little sister?

"No shot." I protested, and her affirmative *mhmm* made me laugh.

"Go be my eyes and ears, babe. I love you."

"Text me when you're in the room."

"I will."

"I love you."

"I love you." The line was quiet for a moment, and she hung up. I returned to the game room with a smile, taking in its contents. Isaiah had gotten close with Shay, somehow, since meeting her at the Saints & Sinners party, and they were sharing the couch while Lucy sat on the floor beside them, Ben opposite her, me taking the final chair on the other side.

Isaiah did seem a little more stiff than usual, which was unusual considering how much of a flirt he usually was, but, Ben's little sister? Wasn't that off limits?

"How's Calla?" Isaiah asked.

"She's good, heading to her hotel now. Interview in the morning." I plopped back in my chair, drinking my water, feeling a little jealous of all of their glasses of wine. Something about playing board games while drinking wine felt like it was supposed to happen, but I'd live—I'd much rather be 100% for the game than have a glass.

"Your turn!" Shay chirped, pointing at the table, and I picked up my cards. We were playing a game I'd not heard of before, couldn't remember the name, but I was supposed to be guessing how many tricks I'd take based on the trump. Looking at my hand, I could very confidently guess.

"Zero." Everyone laughed, but the game continued, and I was completely ass all night until Shay—of course—officially won, and we decided to see if there were any board games we wanted to play.

Ben, Isaiah, and I lounged around the table while Lucy and Shay discussed which game they wanted to play next. I fought the urge to tease Isaiah, not totally sure how Ben would react to that, or Isaiah, so I just drank some water.

"Thinks looking serious with Calla?" Ben asked, breaking the silence, and I nodded slowly.

"I bought a ring, dude." I replied, half-regretting it as soon as I did, especially when Isaiah and Ben both sat up straight, looking at me with concern.

"What?" Ben asked, and I laughed.

"I bought it before I even asked her out." I elaborated, laughing at how insane it sounded out loud. "You're telling me you didn't notice $10k on my card? What kind of financial planner are you?" Everyone laughed then, and Ben threw a punch at my shoulder.

"You're serious, aren't you?" Isaiah said, less a question than an incredulous statement. I shrugged.

"You fucking are!" Ben said, but now he sounded excited. I liked that about my guys—they wouldn't jump in too quick if they thought I was being crazy, but if it was clear that I was for real, they were true ride or dies.

"I've loved her since I saw her at the club, I think." I admitted, knowing that I was beginning to sound truly ridiculous. "I know it's fast."

"Very fast." Isaiah agreed.

"How long has it been?" Ben asked.

"Two months, almost three. Almost five since we met." God, it sounded short. But, I was confident. I'd never felt this confident about anything.

"The kids in Utah have it in writing in about six, so I guess you're fine." Isaiah joked, and we all laughed just in time for Shay and Lucy to return with a board game—an ancient looking one.

"I hope you all know trivia!" Lucy grinned, and I covered my face and groaned.

40

Calla

A manté Houston was a fucking saint. No pun intended. When I walked into my hotel room, exhausted from a day of traveling, delays, and freaking out about missing my interview, all I could do was burst into tears. Why, one might ask?

There was a bottle of champagne and a bouquet of roses on the side table. He was so thoughtful, even hours away, and just when I thought the tears had subsided, there was a knock on my door, and when I looked through the peephole it was a man holding a tray with an entire chocolate cake.

So, now, I was sitting in bed, watching a rom com, eating cake, enjoying occasional updates from Amanté regarding game night and whether or not he thought Isaiah was into Lucy. It could not have been a more perfect night—unless Amanté was curled up in bed with me. The rom com I was watching was one of those accidental engagement ring ones, where the guy thinks he bought earrings or whatever but instead opens up a ring.

I was alone in my room and I was blushing brighter than a tomato, because I was imagining Amanté proposing. It was way, way too early to start even daydreaming about that unless I was trying to break my own heart, but I couldn't help it. I imagined it anyway, if I'd react how the leading lady did or if I'd do one of those cute sob-and-squat things some girls did. Amanté was such a romantic—would he organize some kind of elaborate private dinner, or fly me to Paris or the Maldives? If you were supposed to spend three months' salary on a ring... I burst into giggles.

Imagine a seven-million-dollar engagement ring—how big would something that expensive be? How gaudy would it look on my finger? I held out my hands. I'd never even owned something worth seven hundred dollars, let alone million. Any engagement ring would be extravagant.

You might be right. Isaiah is acting weird af. Amanté texted, and I nodded to myself, mouth full of cake. I didn't know Lucy very well, but Shay had been confident that Isaiah was into her. If even Amanté could tell, it was almost definitely true. I replied with a selfie: a messy bun fit for fanfiction, glasses, and the slice of cake, all cozied up under the covers.

He replied almost immediately. *I am a lucky man.*

I'd never been more prepared for an interview than I was today. I was due in the office at 9am, and I was awake at 6am, watching the sky beginning to lighten and getting ready to go for a quick run, hoping for endorphins to fuel the good vibes of the day. It was a bit warmer in Lauderville than St. Clair, but still cold, so after putting in my contacts and covering my face in a thick layer of moisturizer, I went out to brave the cold. It wasn't too bad out, but still cold enough that I wished I'd brought something to cover my ears. I didn't want to be gone too long, so I did a 30-minute loop while the city woke up.

When I got back to my room, I cracked the energy drink I'd stashed in the mini fridge and did a few sun salutations. I didn't do yoga very often—I wasn't flexible and didn't really enjoy it—I couldn't deny the mental and physical benefits of an early morning practice. That, and I was really trying to get into the habit of stretching after my runs.

After a quick but luxurious shower (I double shampooed and shaved my armpits), I massaged a teensy bit of coconut oil into my hair and left it plopped in a t-shirt on my head. Still wearing my robe, I snuck outside to get some ice from the machine, then filled the sink, added some water, and dunked my face in it. I'd spent the last week and a half studying up on the Stallions. Everything I thought might be useful, I learned. Everything I wished I'd known at the Saints, I learned. Every question I had about why things ran the way they did at the Saints, I wrote down to make sure I asked. Most importantly, I practiced how exactly I would explain why I got fired. They hadn't asked on the phone, but I was sure the hard-hitting questions were coming today, and I would hate for that to ruin yet another opportunity just because I didn't explain it right.

Being dropped off at the facility brought an odd feeling of déjà vu. I half expected to see Connor waiting for me at the desk.

"Hi, you must be Calla?" The woman at the front desk had a very upbeat customer service voice that did not match the look in her eyes in the slightest. Been there.

"Yes, good morning." I replied, unsure what exactly to say. She saved me the awkwardness of attempting small talk and directed me to a small but very well stocked lounge where I made myself a coffee and helped myself to a few mini muffins. Taking a few deep breaths, I envisioned what working here might look like. Lauderville was a bit less expensive of a city, per my research, so my money would go a little farther. I wouldn't know anyone, so life would be fairly simple. I didn't know how much money I would be making or how labor-intensive my job would be, but maybe I'd finally have a simple life, with a simple routine. That didn't sound too bad.

"Ms. Monroe?" I turned around. In the doorway, a tall man—probably mid-forties, if I had to guess—was wearing a fancy grey suit and checking his watch.

"Yes, that's me." I smiled, picking up my coffee and closing the space between us with an outstretched hand. "It's nice to meet you." He took my hand, shaking it firmly, and I decided that I was not the biggest fan of how he was looking at me. Taking a deep breath, I allowed my shoulders to relax and willed a casual smile onto my lips.

"Chip Mahon." He released my hand and gestured towards the door. Chip Mahon was not a name I'd ever heard before, nor was it who I expected to see. I exited anyway, waiting until he fell into step beside me.

"Forgive me, but I was expecting to meet with Meredith today." Meredith was the iconic reporter I'd be shadowing—the woman I'd spoken with on the phone. Chip gestured towards an office and I entered, taking a seat across from the desk as he settled into his own chair.

"Yes, and Meredith told me you were a charming candidate for the position." This man was less likable by the second. "You understand how *quickly* hiring moves in our world." He gave me a little smirk that made my skin crawl. Yes, I did know how quickly hiring moved, and the way he said it gave me the feeling that he knew exactly why I understood it.

"Yes." I said, sipping the coffee to avoid making a face.

"Our sweet Meredith has been poached by a network to cover the big game, so I'll be serving in her place while we search for a replacement." His awkward commentary faded as a bloom of hope burst open within me. If they were hiring—I could do that job. I'd do it for next to nothing, too. I smiled to keep myself from saying as much. We looked at each other for a long moment. "Well, I'm willing to offer you the job."

I blinked. "Sorry?"

"Meredith vouched for you, you're in with some big names, and you carry yourself well. I'm sure you can handle whatever I need, and I hate doing these interviews." He leaned back, dragging his eyes down my seated frame. This was... What was happening? Was this some sort of nightmare, and I'd wake up for the interview any minute?

"I'm a bit confused. Don't you need to ask me about my experience, my skills?" I asked, and he actually laughed—guffawed.

"No one needs experience to pick up dry cleaning and order coffee, darling." He said it so genuinely it actually turned my stomach. This entire thing, the job, the interview, all of it was a complete waste of time. This man was talking about me like some pretty little maid when I thought I was getting close to doing something I was actually passionate about. I couldn't fight the displeasure from showing through the wrinkle in my nose. "I've offended you?"

Understatement. "When I spoke with Meredith, I was under the impression that this job would provide training so that I could become a sideline reporter myself."

"Oh." He made an exaggerated face. "I've never been one for training newcomers, unfortunately. You do have the face for it, though." I fought the tears pricking my eyes. "It will still look good on a resume, sweetheart. Take some time to think about it. A few good months learning from Chip and I'll getcha a job anywhere."

I managed not to cry until I made it to the hotel. Until I was standing at the mirror, staring.

Fuck Chip Mahon. Fuck him even more because he was probably right. If I spent a season as his assistant, even if I learned absolutely nothing except how he takes his coffee, I would be able to get a job anywhere. I glanced at my phone. Was five hours too early to get to the airport? I didn't care. I packed everything up as quickly as I could, changing into a pair of sweatpants and a hoodie big enough I could hide in it, and sat at my gate with a book I wasn't reading. Maybe I'd buy an energy drink and a pack of cookies. Maybe I'd buy a glass of wine.

Amanté's name popped up on my screen. "Hi, baby." I forced my voice to be light.

"The hotel told me you checked out already, what happened?" He asked, and I blinked furiously as tears began to flow. I shot a glare at the man sitting across from me, and he quickly looked down at his phone.

"They offered me the job." I choked out. He didn't respond. "He made me feel gross." My voice cracked. It had been a long, long time since a man had made me feel this way—made me feel lesser, like an object for his enjoyment. I felt small.

41

Amanté

C alla was not taking that job. I did not give a single fuck that it would supposedly be good for her career. I did not care that she was working as a barista and wanted something better. I did not care about prestige or money or even the requirements of the job.

Chip Mahon had made Calla feel like her brilliance, her gifts and talents, were nothing. I wanted to punch him. Instead, I picked up a bouquet of flowers and a teddy bear and stood outside waiting for Calla to walk out of the terminal.

The surprised smile that spread across her face was enough for me, but then she ran towards me, throwing herself into my arms, and I could've been the happiest man alive.

"I'm sorry, Calla." I murmured into her hair, and she squeezed tighter.

"Fuck men." She whined, then shot me a look with raised brow, and we both burst into giggles. She was in a better mood than she had been on the phone, and I was relieved to hear her humming along to music as we drove back to her place. She was cuddling the teddy bear, which was adorable, and had her head resting on the window. I wished I knew what to say—what would make her feel better. I didn't want to scare her by telling her there was no way in hell I was letting her work with a man like that... so I just played her music and let her have a moment to herself.

Her apartment was frigid, and I quickly turned on the heat while she dropped everything and plopped face-first into the couch. "You shouldn't turn this off while you're gone." I teased, taking her flowers and searching for a vase. She moaned something unintelligible. I rooted around for a pair of scissors, finding a junk drawer full of matches, lighters, and two pocket knives instead.

Once the flowers were situated on the counter, I went into her tiny bathroom and turned on the shower.

"Do I stink?" She asked, sitting up.

"No, but it'll make you feel better." I replied, turning the water as hot as it would go.

"I am irritated that you're right." She sighed, and soon her arms were around me, a tight little hug from behind, her head resting on my back. I turned around to return the hug, pulling her against my chest. "I'm upset."

"You should be."

"It's the opposite of what they told me it would be."

"I know."

"Why?" She asked, and the vulnerability—the youthfulness—in her voice caused me to pull her even tighter.

"I wish I had an answer for you." Was my reply, and I meant it. "Sometimes people suck."

"He was so nice about it, too. Like, nothing overtly inappropriate, just, the way he looked at me. He called me sweetheart. He didn't even ask about my qualifications." I took a deep breath to push the anger at bay. "I think he knew I was fired, too." I pulled her away, then, holding her at arm's length.

"I'm sorry this happened." I said, and she sighed.

"The anger is fading a little. Now I'm just sad." She sounded defeated, almost. I tried to imagine being condescended to in that way while I was trying to find a team of my own. It would never have happened.

"Your beauty is nothing to be ashamed of, and it doesn't take away from your drive and talent." Leaning down, I kissed her, softly. "Your beauty is a gift."

Steam filled the bathroom, and she started to shrug off her clothes. I swallowed.

"I'd invite you to join me, but the shower's a little small." She winked—actually winked—and pushed my chest. I made a show of stumbling backwards. Unbelievable. Calla Monroe was unbelievable in the best way.

"You know I love you?" Calla finally emerged from the bathroom, hair up in a towel, another wrapped around her body, a ridiculous looking mask covering her face. I just smiled at her, taking in every detail. "Hello?"

"Hello?" I echoed.

"I said, you know I love you?" She cocked a hip and crossed her arms. She had said that, hadn't she.

"I do know." I stood from the couch, stretching big before closing the space between us and pulling her into a hug. While doing everything I could to forget that she was in a towel. Only a towel.

"And?" She asked, and I pulled my head back as far as I could to look down at her head against my chest.

"And I love you." I smirked. She rose up on her tiptoes to peck a kiss on my lips, careful to avoid moving her face mask.

"I know it's on the calendar, but tell me again—when do you leave?" A jitter of excitement wound its way through me. We were leaving on Tuesday for Albuquerque, where we'd have the honors ceremony—a couple of us were nominated, including Javon for defensive rookie of the year—and then the championship. Equally as exciting but somehow more nerve-wracking was the fact that on Monday, I was picking up the ring.

He'd done a stellar job, if the last time I saw it was any indication. It was a gorgeous stone, and the setting looked like it was made for Calla. Fuck, I was terrified to propose. Was it even a good idea? Was it smart to propose to a woman before even meeting her family? I didn't care, really, and yet I did care—because I wanted her to know that this was real, this was genuine. I was going to get on one knee and ask her to marry me and if she couldn't accept without the blessing of her family...

"Can I meet your parents?" I asked, and she tipped her head to the side, narrowing her eyes. Oh—that's right. She'd asked me a question. "Sorry, I leave Tuesday. Can I meet your parents, though?" A little smile crept onto her face.

"Are we at meet-the-parents level, Amanté?" She teased, and I loved the way my name sounded on her lips. "Of course, you can meet them. They're very chill."

"Why not tomorrow? We can do brunch." I suggested, and her eyebrows shot up. "What? I love you; you love me. I want to meet your parents."

Her smile grew larger. "I'll see if they're available." A few moments later, after her furiously typing thumbs slowed, she confirmed. "Brunch tomorrow." I'd have to wait until she went to the bathroom or something to ask for their blessing. What if they thought it was archaic, or something? Or—worse—what if they were hesitant to give their blessing to a man she'd only known for, what, three months? Four? The football season made the timeline confusing—it felt like a million years and none at the same time.

"Did you decide when you're flying to Albuquerque?" I didn't care when, so long as it was in time for the game, and we wouldn't have a whole lot of time to spend together—but I thought she might find it fun to be my date to the awards ceremony. She dug around in her closet for a comfortable pair of pajamas, and all the blood rushed quickly away from my head as she dropped her towel to put them on. Fuck, she was perfect, and fuck, it had been much, much too long since I'd had her.

When I looked up from her round ass she was smiling at me, the mischievous smile that made my blood heat.

"I was thinking I'd fly out Wednesday, if that's okay. There's lots of museums and it seems like there's cool hiking." Something I'd learned about Calla was that she loved to tease—she'd do all these little seductive things so subtly that I was just constantly wanting—needing her. Or, maybe, she was just that enticing on her own that every little thing she did was addicting.

"I'll get it booked, my love." I said, opening my arms for her to sit across my lap. She blushed at my words. I loved how I could still make her blush. I hoped I could make her blush the rest of our lives.

"My dad is going to love you." She said, absently, placing a kiss behind my ear.

"Big Saints fan?" I asked, sighing as she nuzzled her head between my shoulder and jaw.

"No, he wanted me to go to Princeton so bad." She chuckled, but tears pricked my eyes, and my throat tightened, and I felt myself putting up a wall. Princeton—not that I had money, not that I played football—that I was intelligent enough to graduate from Princeton. "Amanté?"

"I love you, Calla Monroe." I managed, and something in my chest warmed, and I could have sworn that the world got a bit lighter.

42

Calla

I couldn't figure out why I had nerves before brunch. I got along fine with my parents—much better now than I had in high school—and texted fairly regularly. They knew about Amanté, of course, and knew who he was, of course. I'd had nothing but great things to say about him. They'd seen and read nothing but great things about him. Why the nerves?

Amanté was impossible to dislike, and even if they were hesitant, he could win anyone over. He was a millionaire professional football player and Ivy League graduate—he was any parent's dream partner for their daughter. He'd like them, too, I thought. My mother was the most loving person in the world, and my dad could talk to anyone about anything, and it would be interesting. Not to mention—the brunch spot was known for their espresso martinis and their eggs benedict. Literally nothing could go wrong. My phone buzzed.

On our way! In the family group chat. Almost immediately my door buzzed, and I let Amanté in. I was ready to go, wearing jeans and a soft blue sweater, and when I opened the door, I couldn't fight the blush that overcame me. Amanté—fuck, Amanté looked good, and he was wearing a pair of sneakers the exact color of my top, and—

"Interesting choice of hoodie." I smiled, pulling him down by the collar to kiss him, my smile fighting through the embrace. He grinned, gesturing for me to step outside.

"You don't like it?" He asked, taking my keys and locking the door. I rolled my eyes, grinning up at him as he pulled out the sweatshirt to look at the design for himself. "Princeton University, established 1746. Simple facts." I smacked his arm.

"You look very good." I begrudgingly complimented, secretly thrilled that he was going out of his way to make a good impression.

Buckling up in his truck, I couldn't help but watch his hands and laughed aloud again when I spotted a new ring on his right hand—a signet ring with a suspicious looking shield. He followed my gaze and wiggled his fingers at me.

"What, I'm using all the tools I got!" He said, turning down the blasting music and pulling out onto the road. We listened quietly for a while, watching him and the road, until I could literally see a thought form inside his head.

"What?" I asked, and he narrowed his eyes, giving me a very well-formed side eye.

"I was thinking..." He trailed off, seeming actually nervous. "They aren't, like, racist, right?" I fought the urge to burst into laughter, because it was a valid question and an understandable fear, but I swallowed my giggle and squeezed his thigh instead.

"They are not racist, Amanté. And if they are, we'll never speak to them again." My response was simple but clear—if my parents, as much as I loved them, were closet racists, they wouldn't be in my life anymore. Imagine racist grandparents with a biracial child—I wouldn't do it. I wasn't worried, though. I just wanted him to know that I had his back.

"Really?"

"Really."

"Swear, this is the best espresso martini I've ever had. Ever!" My dad gushed, making my mom try it, then me—even though I had one of my own on the way. "Can't believe we caught you before the big game, Amanté." He said, then, inclining his head to Amanté, who was chugging a fresh glass of orange juice.

"Yeah, it was spontaneous for sure, but I'm glad we got to." Amanté replied, looking a little more stiff than usual but otherwise fine. "I hope Calla told you she'll be going, too." An eyebrow raised on my dad, and I fought the urge to elbow my lover.

"I hadn't mentioned it, yet." I smiled, giving him a look I knew he'd understand. He just smiled, his stupid eyes crinkling and stupid cheeks warming. Ugh.

"Hopefully, she'll be my date to the awards ceremony." He continued, and I watched my mom's face light up—she loved shopping with me, especially for special occasions, and hadn't gotten to do so since senior prom.

"Oh, Calla, how fun!" She replied, and I relaxed a bit. I loved my parents, and their approval was important to me. Maybe, if Amanté went to the bathroom, I could ask them what they really thought and explain, face-to-face, how genuinely good a person he is. When I glanced back towards him, he was watching me, that sweet look on his face that always made my ovaries tremble, and I squeezed his hand under the table.

"I know we don't have a lot of time, but maybe we can dress shop?" I offered, and the pleased nod from my mother was everything. "I'm going to run to the bathroom." All I offered was an apologetic smile, but I wasn't too worried. Half his job was talking to strangers, he could handle my parents.

The bathroom was just as cute as the rest of the restaurant, with cute tile and fun signs and a massive mirror I couldn't help but snap a few photos in. Looking back at them, I was smiling in each one—when was the last time I willingly smiled for a photo, especially without thinking about it? Honestly, I couldn't remember, but the smile in the photo—as well as the one on my face, which I caught unexpectedly in the mirror—was genuine. It was real, and the happiness was real, too. Even with all the bullshit I'd dealt with recently, I felt lighter with Amanté by my side.

Walking back to the table, they all looked completely engrossed in conversation, a warm, almost sappy smile on both my parents' faces, and I felt tears prick my eyes. Something about seeing them all together slid that final piece of the puzzle into place. Amanté was mine, and he'd always be mine, and wherever he or I went, we would be together.

I settled back into my seat just in time for food. "Thank you." I smiled, sliding my eggs benedict my way, stifling a laugh at the three plates set before Amanté, and the spread looked phenomenal. Amanté was great about his eating—he'd been doing this long enough that he knew exactly how much he needed to eat, when, and of what. He knew what different foods would do to his body, and he knew how different combinations made him feel. It was wildly impressive, especially because he managed to balance all the details with really delicious foods. Most people seemed to think eating healthy meant eating a lot of really plain, boring foods that make you wish you could just take a nutrition pill and be done with it. Amanté ate like a king. It was a wonderful benefit of being in love with him—I got to eat all his delicious food, too.

We talked about a million different things while we ate, from Amanté's time at school to my own time at school to hobbies and interests and foods we grew up on. It was good, really good, far better than I'd even anticipated, and when Amanté stood up to go to the bathroom himself, I turned quickly on my parents.

"So?" I asked, unable to stop the smile. "He's great, right?"

"He seems like a very genuine young man." My dad agreed, and my mom took my hand.

"You like him?"

"A lot."

"Well, it sure seems like more than a little crush." She teased, sharing a look with my dad. "I like the way he talks about you."

"And I must admit, he seems to treat you well." My dad agreed, a good-natured eye roll really sealing it. "Doesn't hurt he went to Princeton." We all laughed.

Swallowing hard, I looked at my plate. "I think this is serious." My eyes darted back up to check their reactions. My mom was smiling that same sappy smile from before.

"You think he's, like, the one?" My dad asked, and I let the brewing smile grow wider as I nodded.

"I think, yeah." He smiled then, putting an arm around my mom.

"We think he's a good man, Calla."

Amanté walked me to my door, like the perfect gentleman he is, kissed me, then stood. Waited. Waiting for me to open the door, bid him farewell, and shut it behind me. I gulped.

"Stay." Barely above a whisper, I looked up through my lashes to see if he'd even heard me. The moment our eyes met, he had me in his grasp, one hand in my hair, bracing us as he backed me against the door. I melted into him, a giggle bubbling into me as my keys jingled in my hand. He stepped away, eyes dark, that smirk I absolutely loved on his face, and gestured widely towards the door.

"After you." I smirked up at him, but shook my head, turning to unlock the door.

His hands found my hips as I did so, whisking my breath away. "Ridiculous."

As soon as the door was open, he spun me to him again, kissing me like—well, like it had been a long time. Or would be. He kicked the door shut behind him, his arm around my waist guiding me further into the apartment, until he paused.

"What's wrong?" I asked, feeling heat warm my cheeks. He was looking at me, directly into my eyes, with an intent and earnestness pulled me in faster than any embrace.

"Is this okay?" He asked, and I felt my love for him swell. He'd remembered—I'd never brought someone back to my apartment, had never in my life had sex in my own bed. It was mine, my safe place, my home, and I didn't want it tainted by memories. I'd told him that the morning after the first time he stayed the night. We just slept, no fucking, and I'd told him because it was the first time I'd had anyone in *my* bed and it felt good. It felt great. He made me comfortable and safe and home.

"More than okay, Amanté." He groaned as his name left my lips, and within seconds, I was in his arms, his hands grasping my ass as he carried us to the bed, dropping me on my back and immediately pulling at his shirt. I fucking loved watching him—even this, something as mundane as taking off a shirt, was decadent, each muscle activating to toss the shirt aside, each inch of his bare, massive, powerful body better than a wet dream. I leaned up on my elbows, reaching one hand to his hip, to trail the waistband, finally meeting his eyes as I unbuttoned and unzipped his pants. I pushed them down his legs, placing a kiss on his hip, then his thick quads, before letting them drop to the floor. Then, I sat back again, drinking in this godly man who was completely and entirely mine.

"You are far too clothed." He announced, so I pulled my sweater and top over my head, handing it to him, unveiling my unencumbered breasts. He set it aside, watching me, those dark eyes raking over my body, and I felt a hint of shyness that I pushed back down. "I love that."

"What?" I asked, unbuttoning my jeans, shimmying them over my hips and letting him pull them off.

"That I still make you shy." My blush came out in full force, then. "I fucking love that look you give me." He didn't waste any time, hooking my legs over his shoulders and dragging my lacy thong off by himself. I pulled my legs back into a butterfly, leaning back and watching him watch me with pure fire in my blood. I could feel how wet I was; I wondered if he could see it.

"Now I'm underdressed." I teased, and he pushed his underwear down, kicking it aside, and I took him in, in his entirety, every ounce of him absolutely delectable I almost moaned just imagining him pushing inside me. "How do you want me, Amanté?"

"Fuck." He muttered, under his breath, thinking, examining, finally reaching out to palm my breast and lazily flick at my wetness—smiling, at the confirmation of my arousal.

I gasped as he leaned down and picked me up, my legs instinctively wrapping around him. The warmth emanating from him was ecstasy, and I kissed and nipped down his neck as he maneuvered us. He sat on the corner of the bed, and I ground my hips against him, my head lolling back as we both groaned, and I slid along his length before slowly, gasping, slowly, sinking onto him. Amanté's hold on me tightened, his hands surely leaving a peppering of bruises along the round of my ass, and when I'd fully taken him, it was over.

I gripped him against me, every brush of skin against his heightening my pleasure as we fucked, heart to heart, face to face, his lips warm and hungry as he thrust up into me, my own core tightening with each luxurious beat, and a cry escaped my lips as he stood, driving into me a few more times in the air before taking us down to the bed. I put a hand on his hip, pausing him, and turned onto my knees, pushing my chest down, arching my back, the cool air giving me a shiver, and just before I was about to turn around and ask him what the issue was, he smacked my ass, grabbing it tight, and wrapped his generous hands around my hips.

"Fuck, Calla, your body is fucking perfect." And then he thrust into me, so blindingly perfect it was astonishing, how he had been truly made for me. I could feel he was close, so was I, my moans growing louder, my muscles clenching, his rhythm growing relentless, and then we were lying side by side, breathing heavily, and Amanté pulled me against his chest, placing a kiss on the top of my shoulder.

"That was incredible." I breathed, knowing it was silly to say but saying it anyway.

"I fucking love your pussy, Calla. I love you, too." We giggled. "But fuck, your pussy is unbelievable." It didn't even occur to me to doubt him.

43

Amanté

In three days, I was playing in the biggest game of my career. In three days, I would be redeemed.

Tonight, though, I was hopefully going to win some kind of award. I didn't have to go to the ceremony, considering that I was playing on Sunday, but I wanted to go. I wanted to bring Calla, for one, but I also thought Javon might actually win rookie of the year, and I wanted to be there for him. I was nominated because of my redemption season—because I'd left a team and then took them to the championship, and because I'd had my injury and was still fucking it up on the field afterward. I wasn't sure I'd win—there were a few guys who'd been out all last season who had great years, and the award was really tailored to that type of come-back, but either way. If I won, I wanted to be there; if Javon won, I wanted to be there. Calla dressed fancy and on my arm wouldn't hurt.

Really wouldn't hurt, I realized, standing outside the car, waiting for her to walk out of the hotel. I saw her before she saw me, and she was breathtaking. Every person she walked past just stared at her, a few saying something I couldn't hear that made her stunning cheeks deepen, and suddenly, the ring box was feeling very, very heavy in my pocket.

When she looked up and saw me, the spark that lit up her eyes warmed through my entire body. She looked truly stunning, and I almost couldn't believe that she had done her hair and makeup herself. Her hair—I loved her hair, anyway, how it somehow always looked tousled—fell in loose, soft curls down her back, and her makeup was so subtle and yet exaggerated every stunning feature she possessed. Her always-rosy cheeks were flawlessly flushed, her lips a devastatingly pouty dark pink to match, and her eyes—fuck, her eyes.

She was right in front of me now, looking up at me, surely awaiting my response to her look, but I didn't have any words. I was taken away in her eyes, the enamoring pull I couldn't get away from, and I could almost see our entire future reflected in her dilating pupils. Almost, because I knew she had no idea what this weekend held. I cleared my throat. I hadn't even really examined her dress, yet, and when I looked her up and down, my mouth dried further. On anyone else it might've been boring, but on Calla, it was the type of subtle sexiness that she always managed to exude. It was rich, deep blue, formed so perfectly to her body it was like a second skin. There was next to no skin, showing—the sleeves reached her wrists, and the top cut across her neck in a straight line, and the skirt extended to the floor, revealing only French-painted toes. I took her hand and spun her around.

The back was just as sinfully tight as the front, not tight so much as it looked like someone poured paint on her perfect body and called it a day.

"You are going to make a lot of people very angry, tonight." I grinned, my voice low, and she leaned her head up for a barely-there kiss—I had no desire to smudge that beautiful lip. I opened the door for her, and once I slid in, we were off.

Calla told me about her week, on the way. She'd been hiking all day, every day—maybe that contributed to the warmth on her cheekbones—and was absolutely gushing about how beautiful the desert is and how much cooler it is than she thought it would be and how fun choosing cute hiking outfits was. I wasn't saying much, mostly because I didn't trust myself not to break the little control I had and launch myself at her. Calla knew she was beautiful, and that confidence had drawn me to her, but I didn't think she had a real, full grasp on how actually gorgeous she was. I'd never seen anyone like her.

It wasn't a long drive, though, and we arrived within minutes of the rest of the team—those who'd come, anyway, which was only Javon, Tyler, and Khalil. Amina was back at her hotel, far too pregnant to want to attend.

"Calla!" Javon saw us first, completely ignoring me and running up to pull Calla into a hug. He held her at arm's length, giving her a once-over I didn't entirely appreciate, and raised his eyebrows at me. "Unc, you gotta show up cleaner than that if you're bringing a girl like that in here!" He pulled me into a hug next, the kid was ridiculous, and when we looked at each other again, we burst into laughter. We were dressed almost identically; in fact, as I looked closer, we were wearing the exact same suit—classic, but enough flair to not be boring—only his was a rich red and mine was simple black.

"You look good, man." I complimented, and he cheesed. I liked Javon—he was mature enough to be a friend, but young enough that I felt like I could help him out. It felt good to mentor someone, especially someone who wanted it all so bad.

"Alright, boys, which one of you is taking me on the carpet?" Calla asked. Javon winked, and she rolled her eyes. "Stop it." I held out my arm, and she took it, and then—somehow—my future wife and I were posing on the red carpet.

I wasn't sure I'd ever loved Calla more than I did right now. Every time someone came over to talk to us, I'd say enough polite niceties that no one would be offended and then they'd talk to Calla for however long, always leaving perkier than when they came. They hardly realized they weren't talking to me anymore, she was so sweet and engaging, and I was free to squeeze her hip or her thigh and look around the room for anyone else I recognized. No one from my old team was here—not shocking—but I did spot the kid who'd put me in the hospital. Unfortunately, we accidentally made eye contact, and soon he was walking over. I stood up to greet him, dapping him up like an old friend. I felt Calla's hand on the small of my back and relaxed a little.

"Tyriek Johnson." He held out a hand to Calla.

"Calla Monroe." She replied, shaking his. "Although I know who you are." She quirked an eyebrow. Tyriek chuckled, turning back to me.

"Listen, man, I know I was talking a lot of shit that game, but I ain't mean to do you like that." He actually looked a little nervous, and I softened a bit. Thinking back to the list of finalists, I thought Tyriek Johnson might've been one of the names.

"You're nominated?" I asked.

"Yessir. Against your boy." That's right—against Javon. He was just a kid.

"Can't say I'm rooting for you." I replied, starting to smile. "But I am looking forward to smoking your ass on the field again next year." I grinned, and he laughed. I held out a hand, and pulled him in for a hug, sure a picture would be all over the news tomorrow. When he walked away, I sat back down, Calla taking my hand.

"That was nice of you." She said, and I laughed at the skepticism in her voice.

"He's just a kid. The fire is good. He'll figure it out." I said, and I couldn't figure out the look she gave me—but I wanted her to look at me like that forever.

Finally, it was time for awards. Khalil and I didn't win ours, which was fine, but it was time for Javon's category. I smiled, glancing at Calla and seeing that she was grasping both my and Javon's hand like a vice. The announcer was talking a lot, dropping in a few jokes, and when I met Javon's eyes all his bravado was gone and he just looked nervous; a glance back down at his hand and I realized he was squeezing her hand just as hard. He deserved it—he fucking deserved it—and this announcer needed to say who won or shut up.

"Defensive rookie of the year," they opened their little envelope, pulling out the paper, "Javon Al-Qasim, St. Clair Saints." I was on my feet in an instant, our whole table was, except Javon, who took a second to blink furiously before standing and pulling us all into a squished hug, Khalil on one side, Calla and I on the other, before making his way to the stage.

Calla dabbed away tears before they could slide down her cheeks, and I put an arm around her neck, pulling her close. Javon had a solid little speech prepared, and he looked every bit the professional as he stood at the microphone.

"Finally, I want to thank Amanté Houston, whose mentorship and friendship has taught me more than I realized I could learn about not only football, but life." Fuck. Then, I was crying, too.

44

Calla

I woke up obscenely early on Sunday morning like it was Christmas. Of course I loved Amanté and was incredibly proud of him—but I also loved football, loved the Saints, and couldn't believe I was going to the biggest game of the year. I stayed in bed, scrolling through social media until I decided it was a reasonable time to start getting ready. I was picking up Isaiah and Benjamin from the airport so they didn't have to get a rental car, and then we were going to some kind of pre-game party, and then we'd be watching the game from a box.

I'd brought a frankly comical number of options. Did I want to lean into the girlfriend thing, dressing like a state-school sweetheart? Like a sorority girl on game day? Or did I want to be subtle, casual, super chill—Amanté who? The championship was generally a bit more formal than other games, so I'd almost definitely be wearing heels. That was fine—I'd conditioned myself to be able to wear them for hours back when I was a bottle girl—and we'd be able to sit in the box, anyway. Subtle was the move, I decided—although, looking at the 'subtle' option, I wasn't sure that descriptor was quite accurate. I had a deep red bodysuit, just a shade or two darker than the Saints red, with long sleeves and a mock turtleneck, and overtop I would wear a Saints blue, paillette mini skirt. For shoes, I had knee high leather heels that matched the color of my top perfectly. Subtle would not be the word to describe my look—but honestly, I didn't want it to be. I wanted to look great, not only for my confidence but so that everyone saw how hot Amanté's girl was.

It took longer than I expected to put my hair into a high ponytail, but once I'd curled the ends and the little strands that fell out the front, I felt like a bouncy cheerleader-turned-runway model. Checking the time, I didn't have too much longer before I needed to leave, so I carefully put on my outfit, cursing myself for not putting the turtleneck on *before* doing my hair, but successfully had everything situated with about ten minutes for makeup. I kept it simple like I had for the awards ceremony, going for that flushed, just-been-kissed, 90s romcom look.

Assessing myself in the mirror, I smiled. I looked fucking hot. Win #1 of the day.

It shouldn't have been surprising that the traffic was atrocious heading to the airport today, but it was frustrating anyway, and by the time I picked up Isaiah & Benjamin I was in desperate need of something to loosen the tension. Isaiah, pulling open the front seat, presented me with an energy drink, and I decided he was my new favorite person.

"You're a life saver. I fucking hate traffic." It was my favorite flavor, too, and I cracked it with joy. Isaiah took the aux, turning on a banging playlist, and we headed back towards the hotel. They'd gotten a room in the same one as me, which was convenient, and when we swung open the door to their suite, it was decorated for newlyweds. Two bottles of champagne sat next to a vase with a singular rose. I raised an eyebrow at Isaiah, who shrugged.

"I told them we were on our honeymoon." Benjamin grinned, kicking off his shoes and going straight to the champagne. "What, I wanted free champagne!" Isaiah and I shared a look before Benjamin popped the bubbly, pouring us each a glass—his own in one of the water cups by the sink—and we toasted to Amanté's success today.

"You look hot, by the way." Isaiah complimented, shouting from the bedroom where he was changing into his clothes for the day.

"Thank you." I gushed, examining myself in the mirror.

Isaiah walked out, arms wide, and gave me a spin. "Yeah?" He was wearing very nicely tailored pants and—my mouth dropped open.

"Phenomenal. Yes, absolutely." I turned him around again, surveying the jersey. Amanté's Princeton jersey, to be specific. It looked game-worn, even. "That's amazing. I love it. Does he know?"

"Nope." He poured himself another glass of champagne. Benjamin was in the bathroom changing, and a loud thunk caused us both to look his way. "You good?"

The door slowly opened to reveal Benjamin, wearing a very nice suit that he somehow made look casual and unassuming. I leaned to the side and spotted the hair dryer, soap dish, and all the other little toiletries on the ground. "I almost spilled my champagne," he stepped out, "and in the process of saving it, may have knocked over a few other things."

He picked it all up, pushing it back onto the counter, and stepped outside. We all looked at ourselves in the mirror—what a vain bunch. I turned to Isaiah.

"Tuck it." I pursed my lips, watching him adjust the jersey, then stepped back. We all looked at ourselves in the mirror again.

"Good choice." Benjamin nodded his agreement, and with a glance at his very fancy watch, he clapped his hands. "I'll call a car."

We were very close to the bar that was hosting the party, and it was complete chaos when we stepped outside—so much so that the three of us held hands like elementary school kids on a field trip. It did feel fancy to be on the list and escorted further inside to a VIP area, though, and I felt a little pang in my chest that Amanté wasn't here with me. I intended to stick to water, knowing I wanted to have a cocktail or two at the game without worrying about getting drunk at all, and to my absolute pleasure they actually had a robust mocktail menu. The cucumber-lime agua fresca caught my eye, and soon, we were all three standing in a crowd, enjoying the DJ.

I loved to people watch, so I was scanning the crowd, assessing outfits, and did a double take when I saw Connor across the room. Fucking Connor. I turned around before he could notice me.

"What's up?" Isaiah asked, following where I'd been looking. "Oh, doesn't he work for the Saints?"

"Yep." I replied, realizing that, yes, he did work for the Saints—why wasn't he at the stadium? To my dismay, he saw me, and began pushing his way towards me. "Fuck."

"Want me to tell him to fuck off?" Benjamin offered, although I wasn't sure he knew exactly what I was upset about.

"That's okay." I sighed, and Connor reached us, pulling me into a hug.

"Calla, it's so good to see you!" He greeted, then held out a hand to Isaiah and Benjamin in turn. "Connor Matthews."

"My brother is a wrongful termination lawyer." Benjamin smiled, shaking his hand, and Connor's smile dropped. I smacked Ben's arm; I didn't even think he had a brother.

"Right." Connor swallowed, tucking his hands into his pockets. "I got fired, actually. They're contracting some ad agency to cover the rest of the season." I nodded, only feeling slightly bad for him. "I'm sorry about everything."

"Sure." I sipped my drink, feeling the tension. I liked Connor, when we worked together, but not enough to act like he was my bestie now that we were both unemployed. "You know, the Lauderville Stallions are hiring. I could put you in touch." God knew I didn't want to take the job.

"Thanks, Calla, I appreciate that." He said, and I was once again grateful for the music to fill what was a very, very awkward silence.

Benjamin clapped him on the shoulder. "Well, nice meeting you, man." Connor took the cue and moved back towards whoever he was here with, and I turned on Ben with a look of pure astonishment.

"You're hilarious." I shook my head, and he smiled, raising his glass to me. Isaiah laughed, too, and just like that, all awkwardness dissipated.

45

Amanté

I could remember the first time I realized I was serious about football. I was in middle school, fifth grade, staring at my ceiling after losing a game I knew we could've won. I'd given it my everything—carried the team nearly to victory, yet when the time ran out, we were still short. I was 10 years old, and I'd never felt this emotion—it was anger, but something more than that. I was angry and upset, but it felt different. It felt like determination and resolve. So, I stared at my ceiling, feeling that purpose blooming in my chest, envisioning every ounce of effort and fortitude I could give. I envisioned how far that effort and fortitude would take me. I imagined myself pushing harder and harder at practice, until no one could come close to my speed. I imagined lifting weights before school like all the older kids on varsity, until I outlifted even them. Then, I imagined my momma's face when I told her I had a full ride to school. I imagined her face when I told her I was drafted to the NFL. I imagined her face when I paid off all her debts and retired her to a big, fancy mansion where she never had to worry about a thing.

That's what I imagined, now—my momma's face, telling me she was proud of me. That I made it here, after all my hard work. I squeezed my eyes shut, trying to suppress the tear, unable to stop one as it trickled down my cheek to the field.

I stood from where I'd been kneeling, brushing the tear aside, and took a deep breath. Everything I'd ever worked for, everything my mom had ever sacrificed, everything came down to today. Was it tough to be here without her support, without her getting to see the fruit of her labor? Of course it was. But I also knew my momma—and I knew she would be the loudest person in the crowd, hyping me up. She'd tell me to keep my head up and show those boys what I'm made of.

I laughed, then, practically hearing her say it. Purpose—that was why I was here today. Fuck if I wouldn't enjoy it.

We lost the coin toss, unfortunately, but I had faith that we could start with a bang and make them regret giving us the ball. Everyone was in the right mindset, prepared and energized and completely locked in. As I jogged out onto the field, everything went quiet, and the world slowed down around me. This was living.

Determined to shove a score down their throat, we were starting out with a no-huddle offense, letting Khalil call quick plays and snapping the ball as fast as possible. Lining up, glancing at Khalil, that look in his eye—it was fucking over. I let myself smile.

"White 80! White 80!" Khalil yelled, and I took a deep breath, steadying into my stance. "Set—hut!"

I was off, running a deep route, only intended to be an option if they were stupid enough to let me run that far uncovered. As I ran, adrenaline rising, I took in my surroundings—no one within ten yards of me. I laughed, throwing my hand up for Khalil, and it was a beautiful spiral straight to me, and holy fucking shit. I caught the ball, two defenders a little closer now, and they were quick—quick feet, too, and I braced myself to power through the first hit, and the second one completely whiffed.

I was in the end zone, the crowd was deafening, and I ran to the camera, blowing them a little kiss. Khalil caught up, his hands raised for the touchdown, and we did a handshake we've been practicing. I watched the replay on the big screen as we ran off the field, laughing at how truly wide open I'd been.

Coach was yelling something as we got close, and he smacked my back. "That's how we start, that's how we start!" I sat on the bench, taking my helmet off, head buzzing, and finally—really—took it in. This game was ours, we just had to take it. God willing, it was already mine.

The first quarter went pretty quick, and by the start of the second, we were up 10-0, and I was standing with coach, just watching our defense. The Gators had a great offense, and they'd scored the most points of any team this season. Their quarterback was young and sharp, and they had a young, fast team overall. That was their weakness, though—we could keep our momentum, keep our cool, the entire game. They could score all the points they wanted, because we'd score more. One of their rookie wide receivers had come out of Princeton, I was pretty sure, and I searched for him on the field.

He caught a short pass as I watched, speeding up and weaving through four of our guys before finally getting tackled to the ground. "Damn." I nodded; he was shifty. Two more snaps and they were in the endzone, crowd roaring again, and I secured my helmet back on my head. Their kick was good, and special teams went with a fair catch—but as I was heading back out onto the field, I did a double take at the big screen. Calla Monroe, looking as beautiful as fucking ever, was grinning and waving, holding a sign that said "#1 on the field, #1 in my heart". I couldn't stop my cheeks from rising, even despite the cheesiness. I was locked in already, but with the reminder that Calla was watching me, screaming my name, believing in me? I was about to be unstoppable. I almost felt bad for whoever was guarding me.

Khalil saw my expression and nodded, the buzzing energy rising through the huddle, until I was pretty sure I could run faster than light. We started out with a surprisingly effective run, getting the first down, then threw it away after a blitz. Calling a similar run play as before, we set up, and I prepared to block. Looking out, it was a stacked box—we'd get stuffed if we ran. Eyeing Khalil, I cursed under my breath; I wasn't sure he'd noticed.

"Can! Can!" Khalil yelled, and I mentally switched plays in my head, looking out at the field and seeing Tyler likely would have the field, "Y-Deep," I nodded, "White 80! White 80! Set—hut!"

I took off, waving my hand in the air like I was wide open, begging the defenders to be too afraid to get toasted like last time, and two guys stumbled after me. Their coverage was top tier, I could admit that, but by the time the whistle blew Tyler had already gotten our first down and some on the other side of the field. Success.

"Good shit, Tyler." I complimented, listening to the next plan, executing, and executing, until we were two yards from the end zone on third down. They'd anticipated our every move, stuffing the run and almost intercepting a pass. We didn't usually run a QB sneak with Khalil, but it was starting to look dire, and it was either that, or some kind of rugby-style trick play, or settling for a kick to go into halftime. I had no desire to settle for a kick.

I caught the nerves in Khalil's eyes. "I got you." I said, and as we lined up, I sized up the guy I would be blocking. He was bigger than me, but not too much bigger.

The ball was snapped and I put my hands up, becoming as wall-like as I could manage, and my coverage nearly bounced himself to the ground when he met my hands. Khalil was right behind me, almost to the fucking line, and I drove my feet into the ground, pretending I was just pushing a sled at the gym, and someone else was behind me pushing, and then it was cheers all around as Khalil spiked the ball.

"Fuck yeah!"

Halftime speech was short and sweet, and when we came out onto the field, it was Gators' ball. We'd talked about adjustments, the usual stuff, sure—but more importantly, we made a decision: they would not score again, and we would. Many times, preferably.

"Here we go!" I yelled, eyeing Javon. If there was ever a time for one of his impressive interceptions, it was now.

They snapped the ball, completing a short pass, second and two. Come on, Gators, target Javon. They snapped the ball again, running it, and I held my breath watching as—they were short. Everyone was in an uproar, arguing whether they made it or not, and I watched the replay on the big screen. "Clearly short", I yelled, while the referees deliberated. "They're going to fucking give it to them." I complained, pacing between the bench and the sideline.

"Ball was short of the line of gain, fourth down." They announced, and I jumped up, celebrating their correct call. Their offense stayed on the field, though. If we could hold them on the tush push, we'd be starting with insane positioning, but it would have to be nearly a miracle. They lined up, and I found myself watching the Princeton kid, and—fuck if I didn't recognize that formation. I sprinted to our defensive coordinator, hoping our middle linebacker identified it, and before I could say anything at all they snapped the ball. Princeton kid must've brought this play to the Gators, because it was one of my favorites in college, and it meant they were going deep when we'd set up to stop a run. Fuck.

The quarterback stepped back into the pocket, avoiding the sack and running out to his right while Princeton boy ran down the field. Motherfucker. He threw, a big toss with lots of hang time, and I crouched into a squat watching it spin through the air directly to Princeton kid. The ball was caught, and I smacked the ground, watching as Javon ran at him—and ripped the fucking ball out of his hands, sprinting in the opposite direction. I jumped up, mouth wide open, and started running after him along the sideline, yelling as he sprinted, before he finally was tackled out of bounds at the five-yard line. He held onto the ball, running towards us, jumping up and screaming a bunch of stuff I couldn't' hear.

We all stared at the replay, as Princeton clearly caught the ball, and before he could make a football move, had it wrenched out of his hands.

"That's the best shit I've ever seen!" Someone yelled, smacking Javon's helmet, and I had to agree. Now, it was our turn to run away with it.

By the end of the third quarter, we were up by two touchdowns and a kick. I told the guys on the sideline that I wanted to personally score two more.

By halfway through the fourth, we were up by four touchdowns and a kick, and the game was ours. The game was ours, and it felt like being a kid at recess every snap. As I glanced at the clock, the time slowly ticking away, I started to laugh. Khalil just needed to kneel, and the game was over. My first touchdown in the first seconds of the game would be on my highlight reel forever. My second touchdown was in double coverage, and Khalil had threaded it through to me like it was nothing. My *third* touchdown—the defenders would dream about that touchdown for the rest of their lives, because by that point, I was just having fun, and I'd caught the 12-yard pass before simply outrunning everyone in the 63 yards between me and the end zone.

The clock ran out, and confetti rained down on us, and I dropped to my knees. Everything was a blur—was that the adrenaline or the tears in my eyes? And I could barely breathe, could barely think, I just won the biggest game I could ever win. I won. We won.

Tyler ran up to me, grabbing me by the shoulders and hoisting me to my feet, dangling my goat chain in front of my face. I grinned, taking it from him and pulling him into a hug, his presence pulling me back into the present, into the blasting music and announcers and TV people starting to flood the field. I didn't care about any of that—I just started to scan the field, searching for Calla.

46

Calla

"Amanté!" I screamed, seeing him looking around, and when his head swiveled towards me, and our eyes met, nothing else existed. I ran towards him, through falling confetti in blue and red, past hugging teammates and massive camera crews, until I was in his arms, being spun around like we were the only two people in the world. "Amanté." I said, again, grabbing his face and kissing him.

He kept holding me, one arm around my waist as he shook hands with people as we made our way to midfield, where they'd give out the trophy—and the MVP. Amanté had been absolutely magnificent, and I could see it from the first moment he stepped on the field. Today was different, it was essential, and instead of caving under the pressure, he'd thrived in it. He was resilient and talented and fucking amazing, and I was so unbelievably proud to be by his side. We reached Khalil, who was on the phone, eyes wide and nodding vigorously.

"You good?" Amanté asked, and he hung up, facing us.

"Baby's coming." He breathed, then burst into laughter. "I'm having another baby!" He screamed, jumping up and down, and when he calmed down, he clasped Amanté's shoulder. "Today is the best day of my fucking life, but I have to go." Amanté nodded, and Khalil ran off, saying goodbye to everyone he ran into, grabbing a reporter's microphone and telling the world his wife was in labor.

"What a good life." I said, drinking it all in, the joyous laughter and cheering all around us, the tears of disbelief and pure delight, and all the loved ones gathered with the men they're so proud of. Amanté looked down at me, his warm eyes comforting and thrilling me all at once, and kissed me, deep, passionate, his hand gripping my hair. I wrapped my arms around his neck, reaching up on my toes as much as I could in these boots, feeling like we were in our own world.

There was some kind of speech, and then the captains went up to accept the trophy, along with the head coach, who pulled Amanté up with them. I was practically bursting with pride, seeing him up there, holding up the most iconic trophy in the world.

"Now time for the MVP," The announcer said, the stage full of players ogling the trophy, "Amanté Houston." Holy shit. I screamed louder than I'd literally ever screamed before, jumping up and down as he turned back around, face blank, eyes widening as he looked at the announcer. The man inclined his head and held out the microphone. Amanté just stood there.

"THAT'S MY MVP!" I screeched, as loud as I could handle, and he blinked, pushing out a breath as he made his way back to the front of the stage.

He took the trophy, and tears filled his eyes as the crowd began to chant his name. God, he deserved this. He deserved every good thing life could offer. He was looking out at the crowd, at the trophy in his hands, and I could see it beginning to sink in.

"Amanté, we all loved that opening snap touchdown—but then you did it two more times. Tell us about the chemistry you share with Khalil, and what it's been like to play with this team this year."

He leaned towards the mic. "It all comes down to believing in each other. Khalil is a good man, a great man, and he trusts me, and I trust him, and I trust these guys with anything." He swallowed, his voice breaking. "I couldn't have had the year I've had without the support and encouragement of this amazing team. These guys are like my brothers, man, and this whole team worked their asses off to get us to this moment."

"It all started in St. Clair, and now you got them a ring. Think of all the people who brought you here, everything you've done to get here, how does it feel?"

Amanté handed the trophy back to his teammates, who shoved the thing in the air. "I couldn't be more thankful. Everyone who pushed me, who believed in me, I'm so grateful. To my mom, who isn't here with us anymore, who made this all possible." Tears pricked my eyes, and he met mine through the crowd. "Hold on." My eyebrows raised as he climbed off the stage, running towards me and grabbing my hand, dragging me up there with him.

"Amanté!" I scolded under my breath, but he picked me up and set me onto the stage, climbing back up after me.

"There is one person I want to thank very specifically, and it is this incredible woman, Calla Monroe." He said, sliding an arm to rest on the ridge of my hip, leaning forward to make sure he was talking in the mic. I attempted to school my face into something calm and elegant, instead of the shock and shyness that was flowing through me. "Some of you may recognize Calla from an interview mid-season, or as the woman who saved my life when I went down, but to me, she is my best friend and the love of my life." He moved his hand away, and I looked over my shoulder to see him on one knee, holding up a ring. I smacked my hands over my mouth.

"Calla Monroe, I have had many dreams in my life, and I already fulfilled one today. Will you do me the honor of being my wife, and fulfill another?" I couldn't speak, could only throw my arms around him, sobbing as he held me on his knee with one hand and slid the ring onto my finger with the other. I kissed him—then pulled him into the tightest hug I'd ever given. He stood, up, holding me tight, and when he released me, he threw his fists into the air. The cheering finally registered, and I realized with a giggle that everyone was cheering for us—for Amanté's happiness and mine.

"I cannot believe you." I breathed, staring at him like he was an angel. "I love you so fucking much."

He kissed the top of my head. "I had a longer speech planned out, but," he brushed his lips against my neck, "I'll give it to you later. I'll propose to you every day until the day we marry, then I'll marry you every day until the day we die."

The afterparty was spectacular, but all I could do was show off my ring. It was a rock, that was for sure, but it was unlike any ring I'd ever seen before, the band like interwoven strands of gold, designed to be wrapped around my finger alone. We were making small talk, and rehashing the game, and congratulating Amanté, then congratulating me, then doing shots, then dancing, then doing it all over again. The whole time, Amanté never once left my side—if his hand wasn't intertwined in mine, it was on my hip, or the small of my back, or caressing my jaw.

I loved him, I loved him, I loved him. Amanté had taken his perfect, once-in-a-lifetime moment, and eagerly brought me in to be with him. He'd thought of me, even at his greatest height. Amanté was being celebrated for the unbelievable talent he was—and he thought that I could make it even better. I felt honored. I felt truly chosen. My heart was light. I saw a million different futures for us, and all of them were beautiful. I had known for a long time that he was the one, early enough that it had terrified me, and still the pieces had fallen into place to bring us together.

"I love you." I said, interrupting my train of thought, and he smiled, that sweet, mischievous smile.

"I love *you*." He replied. A new DJ was starting their set, and he held out his hand. I took it, and he walked us out to the dance floor like we were at some regency ball. He even bowed, and I giggled, giving him a curtsey. The music started, something I didn't know layered overtop a classic salsa rhythm, and he took my hand, and we danced.

"I'm not taking the job." I said, in his ear, as he spun me close and away again.

"Don't do that for me." He replied, following the music, effortlessly leading me.

"I'm doing it for me." I said, pausing as we pulled apart again for a moment. "That guy was a douche." I explained, and Amanté laughed, pulling me close and resting his hands on the small of my back.

"I completely agree." Amanté kissed me, and then we just swayed together, occasionally spinning or stepping or whatever else the music called for, but mostly enjoying the feel of him against me, the sturdiness he brought, the safety I felt in his arms.

Just a few weeks ago, I'd fantasized about Amanté on one knee. I'd giggled and closed my eyes and imagined the ring he'd get me, the size of the diamond, and what he'd say. I'd been embarrassed, almost, even having those thoughts in the comfort of my own, private head, in the comfort of my own, private room. It hadn't even occurred to me that he might be thinking those things, too—that he might be imagining a ring, a perfect diamond, and a speech. He hadn't said much, understandably, but even what he did say was straight out of a romance novel. *Will you do me the honor of being my wife, and fulfill another?* God, it was hopelessly romantic, and yet here we were. Romantic and cheesy and completely devoted. I loved him, and I'd loved him for a long time—it wasn't the first time we'd met, that was pure lust, but it hadn't been long after. When I realized that this incredibly impressive man also had a deep heart and a warm soul, when I realized he could live anywhere he wanted and still chose to be with his friend, when he went out of his way to give me an opportunity to skyrocket my career—when he paid my entire salary because his miscommunication had caused me harm. He was selfless, and kind, and it felt like loving my best friend.

I was proud of us, honestly. Sure, we hadn't been strictly friends before—and I didn't regret any of the sex, at all, even a little—but we'd allowed that natural connection to form and grow however it wanted, until it blossomed into a deeply rooted relationship. It wasn't that doing this—getting engaged after only dating a short time—wasn't scary, but even though it felt scary, it also felt right and natural. Like, with Amanté by my side, the scary things were easy. I pulled him closer to me, if that was even possible.

I gradually became aware of a near-constant buzzing in my purse. Taking Amanté's hand, I maneuvered us to an empty table at the edge of the room and checked my phone. So many missed messages. All from...

"Shay." I laughed, shaking my head.

"Shay?" Amanté asked, chugging a glass of water he'd procured out of nowhere, nudging another towards me.

I took a sip. "I have a million new messages and all of them are her freaking out." I scrolled through, the smile growing on my lips as I took in all the photos she'd sent, the excitement and surprise, the bachelor party she'd already planned. After the game was over, she'd pulled up the post-game celebrations on her phone so she could actually hear the speeches over roar of the St. Clair watch party. As such, she'd sent about fifteen high quality screenshots of the moment—of my oblivious face as Amanté slowly lowered to one knee, of all the moments after. Tears pricked my eyes.

"Is everything okay?" Amanté asked, taking my hand, nervous eyes frantically searching. I just turned my phone around. Swiping through, his smile soon matched my own. "Fuck, we're hot." He said, and I laughed aloud. He loosened his hold on my hand, holding me delicately, and examined the ring.

"It's beautiful." I said, staring unabashedly. I couldn't even pretend I wasn't thrilled about the gorgeous new piece of jewelry.

He brought it to his lips, kissing it lightly, then turning my hand over and placing another soft kiss on my palm. "I designed it just for you." I peered up at him, suddenly warm, at my hand in his, and swallowed.

"My love?" I asked.

"Yes?"

"Would you like to take me home?" I asked, giving him the little grin I knew made him crazy—and that's all it took.

47

Amanté

B y the time we were dropped off at the hotel, Calla had fallen
asleep across my lap. She awoke as the door opened—foiling my
opportunity to carry her to bed like a hero with his princess—and we
made our way to the room in a cozy, warm silence that radiated con-
tentment. Looking down at her, her sleepy eyes and slightly rumpled
hair, I was filled with more love than I knew what to do with. No
matter what came next, this was right. She was right.

I was pleased she'd decided not to go to Lauderville—even more
pleased that I didn't have anything to do with it. I would never stop
her from doing something she wanted to do, but I could still be
uncomfortable with the way they treated her. If that was her interview, imagine the actual job. She didn't deserve to be belittled and
condescended to just to get a good recommendation for the rest of the
industry. She was already talented and hardworking; I had no doubt
that she would succeed wherever she sought to.

Honestly, she didn't need to work, either. If she decided she wanted
to stay home, I wouldn't mind it at all. In fact, the thought of coming
home to her every day brought a smile to my face, so much so that she
raised her goofy little eyebrow at me, even half-awake in the bathroom.

"Just imagining life with you." I teased, and she narrowed her eyes
but couldn't hide the rising smile and reddened cheeks.

We brushed our teeth, climbed into bed, and I pulled her tight to my chest. Her breaths steadied almost immediately, and, despite how creepy I felt, I watched her face as it softened. This was my future. Not glitzy parties and crazy sex—well, not *not* those things, but, whatever—Calla in my arms, so safe and comforted that she falls asleep almost immediately.

I wasn't quite tired yet, so I laid my head back, closed my eyes, and went back over the day. Breakfast with the team, Khalil—fuck!

I reached across to the nightstand as slowly as I could, careful not to disturb her, and turned my brightness down all the way before writing out a text.

Baby here? I typed, sending it off. A few seconds later, he was typing.

Meet Ali. Attached was a photo of the four of them, all crowded together around Amina, their not-so-tiny bundle of joy mid-cry.

Congratulations man. Tell Amina I appreciate her waiting until after the game was over. I locked the phone, setting it back on the nightstand. Today had been—today had been the greatest day of my entire life. I wasn't sure what could compare. My phone buzzed again.

Amina told me congratulations are in order for you, too. I guess I missed it on the road. She wants to see the rock. lol. I exhaled through my nose, the little snort as much of a laugh as I could risk, and put the phone away for good. I wanted to bask in the gratitude for a moment. Everything had happened so fast, especially once the game was over. It had been a good game, a thrilling game, and the fact that we were able to run away with it and just enjoy playing football like a bunch of kids was a blessing. When the clock hit zero, I knew the only thing that could make this day even better was to finally give Calla that ring, so I'd tucked it into my uniform and hatched a plan.

A plan that went to shit, because I was hauled onstage. And I won MVP. Fuck, I hadn't really soaked that in, had I? I could hardly think, let alone speak. I'd admired championship MVPs since childhood, most of them quarterbacks but a rare few receivers or linebackers. I'd pretended to give acceptance speeches in the shower, in my head on long walks, out loud on long drives. I'd dreamed of being recognized by my peers as exemplary—seen by those around me as someone to aspire to. It was an incredible honor, and sitting in bed, my arms around the woman I loved, I wasn't sure I really felt it yet. Maybe tomorrow, maybe months or years from now, it would all really hit me. I am truly the luckiest man alive, lucky and blessed beyond belief, to be able to play the sport I love for a living, and do it with a beautiful woman at my side. Slowly, surely, Calla's deep, steady breaths lulled me to sleep, too.

When I woke up, Calla was already awake, creeping around the hotel room trying to keep quiet.

"Good morning." I greeted, and she immediately skipped the two steps to the side of the bed, kissing me and plopping atop me.

"Good morning!" She sang, kissing me again before pushing off me and going to the window, opening the curtains and showering us with bright desert sun. It hadn't fully risen yet, but was almost there, prompting me to check the clock—almost 7am. Thank God we'd gone home instead of following the crowd to an after party after last call. I was willing to bet some of my teammates were still partying in some mansion somewhere. Although, they didn't have the added impetus of getting to a morning press conference. I did. Because I was the MVP. I climbed out of bed, following Calla to the window and spinning her around in my arms.

"My love." I said, and she nodded, smiling as I set her back down. "I'm the most valuable player of the championship. The whole championship. We won the game."

She poked me in the center of my chest. "Because of you." I shook my head. Unbelievable. My lifelong dream come true. I took Calla's hands, examining the ring and how it looked on her hand.

"I fucking love you." I reiterated, wanting to bask in the moment forever. Calla pulled away, walking back to the window and pointing.

"You see the museum?" I walked over and nodded—I hadn't expected much from Albuquerque, to be honest, but I had been pleased to discover that the architecture is really nice. "There's a really cute coffee shop on the other side of it." She turned around with this precious warmth in her cheeks, like she was waiting for the punchline of some incredible joke. I looked at her, really looked into her eyes, and laughed.

"Hey, Calla." I said, fighting to keep my voice steady.

"Mhmm." She replied, fighting her own smile off her face.

"I heard about a really fun cafe not too far from our hotel." I took a deep breath to continue, but Calla interrupted, her bright eyes literally sparkling in the sun.

"Oh, wow, really?" She gushed, allowing a laugh to escape.

I nodded, very solemnly. "Since it's only 7 in the morning, would you like to get some coffee with me?"

She swayed side to side, hands clasped behind her back. "Why yes, Amanté, I surely would."

We quickly got dressed—it was chilly in the mornings, here, so pants and hoodies were the move—and walked to the coffee shop. Calla was glowing—I mean, she looked truly happy, like someone had lit a candle within. A surge of pride flowed through me as I considered that it might just have been me. Walking inside, I was immediately distracted by the building. It had a rustic look, with massive murals covering the walls and colorful booths for seating.

"Good morning, welcome in." The barista greeted, and after a pause, "oh, good morning!" I looked towards her, expecting to see a fan, but she was looking at Calla, who looked sheepishly up at me.

"I may have come here every day." She smiled. "Can I order for you?" She asked, and I nodded.

"Same as usual?" The barista asked, and Calla nodded.

"Plus one with honey, iced please. Thanks, Soph." It didn't take long, and soon we were finding a seat outside as the sun slowly began to warm the chilly air. The outdoor tables all had mosaics on top, the entire atmosphere completely unique and lively.

"Mine has honey?" I asked, taking it as she slid it across to me. Calla nodded, popping a straw into mine and then her own. Even that little gesture—putting my straw in my coffee—made me want to run around like a schoolgirl with a crush.

"Yours is local honey and cinnamon and it's delicious." Calla told me, then shook her drink and took a sip, wiggling with pleasure. "Try." She slid hers over; I wasn't sure what I was expecting, but it definitely wasn't dark chocolate and...

"Spicy? What's in this?" I asked, taking a sip of mine, which was delicious. Much better than hers.

"It's espresso shaken with dark chocolate and homemade red chile sauce. Sophia told me to try it topped with half and half and I'm indebted to her forever." She took another sip, enjoying the odd drink, and I smiled at how genuinely happy she was drinking her special little coffee outside in the cool air. "What! It's a special New Mexico thing!" She protested.

"This is nice." I acknowledged, and we sat, watching the air, the sun continuing its path—and for a second, I saw us old and wrinkled and still enjoying the mornings together with a cup of coffee.

"I was thinking," Calla began, leaning forward to prop her elbows on the table, "this morning before you woke up, I was thinking..." She trailed off, blushing into her coffee. "Since we're engaged," Her cheeks were redder than I'd ever seen them, "maybe we should talk about getting a place together."

I reached across to take her hand. "Are you asking me to move in together?" She pulled her hand away and punched my arm, and we both laughed. "Not funny, got it."

"You're ridiculous."

"You love me."

"I do."

48

Calla

I watched Amanté's press conference on my phone in the airport. He was so fucking handsome that I couldn't care less what they were asking—although I forced myself to listen to his responses so we could talk about them later. I could just sit and stare at him for the rest of my life. I just might.

One reporter asked about the proposal and I smiled to myself—then a call interrupted the stream. I declined quickly, waiting for the reporter to finish his question, and a voicemail popped up. Sighing, I opened the notification. Missed call from an unknown number, who cares, voicemail... My heartrate tripled.

"Good morning, Calla, my name is Jordan and I'm the hiring director here at St. Clair Problems, the most followed St. Clair fan page on social media. We post about all of St. Clair's sports, among other things. I know you've had a busy weekend, but I have a few things I'd love to talk to you about, so go ahead and give me a call back at your soonest convenience. Thanks!" My hands were shaking as I quickly redialed.

A different voice answered. "St. Clair Problems, this is Anna speaking."

"Hi, Anna, I just missed a call from Jordan." I replied quickly.

"Let me transfer you over!" She chirped, and I got about half a second of hold music before the line opened again.

"St. Clair Problems, this is Jordan." Jordan greeted.

"Hi, Jordan, I just missed your call, my name is Calla Monroe." I heard what sounded like a bunch of papers rustling around on the other line, and Jordan clapped loudly.

"Calla! Amazing! How are you doing? Good, I'm sure. Can't wait for you to post that ring on the internet so we can all envy you." Jordan's voice was professional yet teasing, and some of my nerves dissipated.

"I am pretty good, you're right." I laughed. "You?"

"Great, great, listen." More rustling, a distant bang. "Sorry. Listen, I don't know if you've heard of us, but St. Clair Problems runs all the top social media pages for St. Clair and we're currently working on expanding into longer form content, and we saw your work with the Saints team and thought you'd be great talent for the project." I didn't say anything, absorbing what exactly she was trying to say. Jordan cleared her throat. "Basically, you'd start on a shorter-term contract—3 months, 6 months—to host our weekly podcast, and if everything went well, we'd obviously want to keep you longer."

I cleared my throat, this time. "Wow, that sounds exciting. What kind of podcast? I don't really have experience outside football."

"We're hoping to have a different show for each team in the area, but we'd be starting with the Saints, so you'd just be covering football. Off season, drama, interviews, whatever." Jordan's chair creaked audibly as she presumably leaned back in it. "We don't have a number finalized yet, but since we already have like a million followers across channels, my guess is we'll be able to offer you $500 an episode on the first contract. Subject to increase upon renewal, of course." My eyes widened. "I know it doesn't sound like a whole lot, but you're still a pretty new face and you wouldn't be doing much of the behind-the-scenes stuff, so hopefully it sounds bearable." Bearable? It sounded amazing.

"That sounds great, Jordan, thank you for thinking of me." I didn't know what to do with my hands. "Can I give you my email, you can send something over to me, and we can set up something in person?"

"Sounds perfect, Calla, thanks for your time and get home safe." She hung up, leaving me cross-legged on the uncomfortable airport chair, wiggling because I couldn't scream.

It wasn't network television, but honestly, that shit was kind of overrated! $500 an episode to basically show up and live my dream sounded incredible. I know St. Clair Problems—I followed their meme account and their main, and you know what, now that I thought about it, they'd followed me back a week ago. I smiled to myself, pulling up the press conference and seeing that Amanté was done with his segment. Damn.

Obsessively checking the clock every thirty seconds was becoming tiresome, but I couldn't stop it. Amanté would be here any moment, knocking on my door, my *betrothed*, and I couldn't wait to tell him everything. My little apartment was now decked out in Saints decor—garlands, balloons, a bunch of little plastic trophies scattered everywhere—and I had just put a bottle of champagne in the freezer so it was hopefully cold by the time he walked in. Which should be any second now.

The door buzzed, and I let him in, then snatched the champagne and swung the door open.

"Congratulations!" I yelled, popping the champagne, and it startled him so bad he dropped what he was holding—a bouquet of roses and a bottle of champagne, one that luckily was sturdy enough to survive the fall.

"Fuck, Calla," Amanté laughed, picking everything up and tackling me into a massive hug as he dragged everything inside. "You did all this in a couple hours?" He asked, looking around. I nodded, pouring us glasses.

"I have news." I said, almost jumping up and down. Amanté tucked his bottle in the fridge and gestured for me to continue. "I got offered a job." His eyes lit up, but I held up my hand before he could speak. "I'd host a podcast for St. Clair Problems, and they want to pay me $500 per show, and I'd get a raise after the initial contract." Instead of clinking my glass as I'd intended, he swept me into his arms, and what was a mostly benign celebration became frenzied. He was kissing me like I was oxygen, and champagne sloshed on the floor before I set it on the counter behind me, and he picked me up to set me there, too, my legs wrapped around his hips, his hands everywhere, in my hair, down my back, under my shirt. His skin against mine gave me goosebumps, even his scent made me lightheaded.

"I love you." He breathed, and I needed him closer. He smiled against my lips. "I love fucking you, but I don't want to fuck right now." I pulled back, confused. "I want to make love."

And he did, lifting me from the counter, bringing me carefully to the bed, gently setting me down and kissing my neck, my stomach as he pulled my shirt over my head, my hips as he pulled down my pants, painstakingly slow and soft and sensuous. He looked me in the eye, and I swear, our souls merged as he removed his clothes and climbed over me, peppering soft, warm kisses across all the skin he encountered. My mouth was dry; I was slick with anticipation—desire—and every time his hand skimmed mine a spark arced through me, every nerve on edge, every moment unspeakable pleasure.

I reached between us to touch him, and the groan that escaped his lips heated my blood even more. I loved his sounds, his noises. He made me feel like the sexiest woman in the world—like every time I touched him, he was on fire. Impatient, I placed a hand on his hip, arching mine, and pushed him inside me, both of us groaning as he moved, slowly, deeply.

Slow, passionate, intentional, deep, I didn't know what to do with my hands, didn't know how to think or breathe beyond raising my hips to meet his perfect thrusts, pleasure rising miserably as he kept his steady beat. He reached a hand between us and my pleasure increased, tripled and then I was probably screaming, crying out his name even as he continued, relentless, determined to bring me over the edge.

Over the edge I slipped, moaning his name, over, and over, writhing beneath him—but he had purpose. He didn't stop for a second, but flipped me to my stomach and drove into me from behind, his rhythm increasing in intensity and speed, and, "Fuck," was all I could groan as I felt his weight on me, bearing down, allowing himself to truly thrust, hard and deep, knowing the bed would take our weights, support us as he hit that perfect spot time and time and time again, the friction of the sheets undoing me again, and I was over the edge again, faster this time, unable to even say his name. He slid his hands beneath my hips and grabbed tight, the sensation overwhelming, and this—this was fucking, and Amanté fucked me better than any dream, hard and steady and fast and so intense that I could physically feel his need, feel how much he was truly enjoying this moment, and when his thrusts turned sloppier, frantic, I knew he was about to finish.

His heavy breathing tickled my back as he ran his hands across my skin. "I want to do that again."

"Do it, then." I replied, my own breath coming in pants, already aching once again for the feeling of him inside me. He smacked my ass.

"Really?" He asked, kissing up my spine. "You want that?" He slid a finger between my legs, the remnants of his pleasure and my own, and my hips twitched under his cruel touch. "Tell me, Calla."

I raised my hips further into his hand and he acquiesced, pushing a finger inside me. "Please." I breathed, hardly able to think around the sensation.

"Please, what?" He teased, standing, his presence a disappointing loss, until I gasped at his lips against my inner thigh. "Please, what, Calla?"

I swallowed as he ate me like a fucking king, one hand keeping my body pinned to the bed, the other inside me, and—I couldn't think. I couldn't hardly breathe, I was close again, but him—I needed him, all of him, now. Immediately. "Please." Was all I managed, the word more of a whine than a command, and he stood back up. I twisted back to look at him, his fucking stunning body, and was pleased to find that he was already hard again.

"You're greedy." His hungry eyes were, too.

"You've already made love." I said, turning fully around until I was sitting. "Now, I'd like you to fuck me."

49

Amanté

SIX MONTHS
LATER

"**B**abe, we're going to be late!" Calla's voice echoed through the bedroom to where I was, the closet, standing in front of the full-length mirror with some vague disappointment. "Babe?"

"I heard you!" I called back, cracking my neck and looking back at the rack of shoes. "Give me five, my love!" It was my own fault for not checking before actually getting ready, but—I wasn't sure I had any shoes suitable to wear with a tux.

"Do you need help?" She was closer, now, and I waited until she poked her head around the doorframe.

"What shoes do you wear with tuxedos?" I asked, and her smile lit the room.

"Hmm..." She pondered, eyes scanning the shelf. "Ooh! Do the loafers with the tassel." I followed her eyes, stopping on the pair she was talking about—classic black leather with a tassel. I never wore them.

"The tassel isn't trying too hard?" I asked, and she rolled her eyes so hard I was shocked she didn't literally spin.

"The tassel says I'm fancy, rich, and stylish." She countered, and I grinned as I shook my head, dropping them to the ground and slipping my feet in. "You're the one who wanted black tie, anyway."

Calla winked, and stepped into the closet, standing beside me in the mirror. I was breathless, looking at her.

"Calla," I breathed, running my hand down the silken fabric. "Maybe we should stay here." I murmured in her ear, gaining a deep satisfaction from the slightly shaky inhale I received in response. The fabric clung to her curves like she was a statue of Aphrodite, the deep purple making her eyes look startlingly blue. I brushed my hand across her stomach, then up, across her temptingly braless—and sensitive, apparently—breasts.

"Enough." Calla breathed, but when she looked at me like that...

"I want to bend you over and fuck you in the mirror."

"Don't tempt me."

"Please?" I pulled her hips flush against mine. After placing a kiss behind her ear, I stood upright, straightening my jacket and appreciating the view from behind. "I know we can't. But I really, really want to later."

"Please." She smirked, leading the way out of the closet. I followed at a short distance, admiring the way her hips swayed from side to side, effortlessly feminine and frustratingly sexy.

I followed her to the top of the staircase, where she turned around, mouth tight. I reached for her, holding her face in my palm, and softly caressed her cheek. "This is going to be fun."

She held my arm as we walked down the stairs, and as we turned the corner, "Calla!"

The room was packed with people, but Shay, Calla's best friend, closed the distance first, pulling Calla into a tight hug before spinning her around with a few exaggerated 'oo's and 'aa's.

"It's stupid as shit to throw a black tie housewarming party, man," Javon came up beside me, martini in hand, looking sharp, "but I gotta admit, this is pretty tough." I dapped him up before he held out a hand to Calla, kissing it like the idiot he is.

"It's also a hilarious choice to show up fashionably late to your own party." Shay chimed in, and Javon pointed at her appreciatively.

"Hey, Isaiah's hosting, we're the guests of honor!" Calla protested, and we made our way to the bar. Spicy margaritas were on the menu, of course, and I ordered two of them before wrapping an arm around Calla's waist and beginning to make our way through the crowd, greeting people as we passed. The house looked amazing, and I could hardly believe we lived here. It had taken six months to find the perfect one, but it certainly was perfect, and we'd decided to throw a ridiculously fancy party before it was fully furnished so we could take advantage of the space. The living room opened up to the outside, the floor-to-ceiling windows folding away to make a seamless transition, and half our party was outside enjoying the remainders of the August sun.

We set up long tables in the backyard, and after about an hour of mingling, we began to shuffle everyone into their seats and the music transitioned into some vibey bossa nova. I grabbed a microphone and my woman and waited for it to settle down.

"Thank you everyone for coming to celebrate our new home with us tonight." I began, squeezing Calla's hand. "We do have a few other special announcements." I paused and smiled, looking out at the crowd—until Calla snatched the microphone away.

"I am not pregnant." She clarified quickly, earning a lot of laughs, and she elbowed me in the ribs. "These announcements are very special, though, and we're excited to celebrate them with you tonight!" Calla looked around for a second, searching for something, until she spotted her drink. Raising it in the air, she brought the microphone back to her lips. "As of last week, The Ciara Houston Foundation is fully funded and dedicated to serving women and girls in our community." My heart swelled with pride at the cheers that rang out—and Calla's fingers interlaced with mine, squeezing tight. "The Ciara Houston Foundation will provide funding, training, equipment, scholarships, and after-school programs in flag football beginning this fall." She looked up at me, then, stepping closer to rub my back. "Amanté has always been inspired by his mother, and I am so proud of how he is continuing her legacy of love and opportunity." Tears welled up, then, and I gave her a tight-lipped smile in an effort to keep from crying in earnest.

We clinked glasses, hugged, and drank, and I had a moment to collect myself. "The other big news," I said, leaning over to the microphone before taking it myself, "is for Ms. Calla Monroe." I gestured for her to step in front of me, and she did, cheeks strawberry-red. "As many of you know, Calla hosts a Saints podcast."

"Let's go Saints!" Someone yelled, and giggles spread across the tables.

"As of last night, at midnight, *Saintly Sports with Calla Monroe* has reached 100,000 total downloads. For those of you who don't know podcast metrics, that's incredibly impressive." I watched the tension leech from her shoulders as whoops rang through the guests, her posture straightening even further at the praise and attention. I was so, so incredibly proud of her. I was proud of us, really—we'd more than persevered. We'd both gone above and beyond to get what we want in life. I had everything I'd ever dreamed of.

My life was good. I was entering my sixth pre-season healthier and more focused than I'd ever been, ready to win season MVP this time. My soon-to-be wife was the most gorgeous woman in the world, my team—great guys, even if they were goofy—was tight, the entire franchise was locked in, if I was being honest. Every week was the same: I worked hard, mostly just hanging out playing ball with my friends, consistently saw strength and speed gains in my workouts, and went home to a beautiful house where a woman was always waiting with some sort of insanely high protein meal and—usually—an unparalleled fuck. I knew I was lucky, but if any reporters asked me about my mindset and my goals heading into the season, I would talk about it 'til they cut the cameras. I could talk about how blessed I was forever, speak Calla's praises, describe all the ways she made my life better that I didn't know was possible. Fans would call me a simp—even guys in the *Saintly Sports with Calla Monroe* comments would clown me for being so in love—but everyone could see it. I was at the top of my game, and she had allowed me to rise to it.

I couldn't help but reminisce on my time with the Captains; it felt so long ago, now. When I went pro, I had imagined staying with the Captains my entire career. I was hesitant to speak too badly about them—without my time there, I couldn't have gotten to this point, and a lot of my darker feelings were fueled by bitterness that healed, slightly, as time went on. The Saints, though? They'd saved my career. They reminded me why I loved playing football, and how a supportive, secure team should take care of each other. I'd punctured a lung and missed the second half of the season, and still no one hesitated to rely on me. They trusted me, and I trusted them. Together, we got the job done. *Life is good*, I thought, over and over, while I finished my workout.

Our house included a very robust home gym, and it was one of my favorite parts of the whole floorplan—because Calla and I could work out together, like we were now. We had massive mirrors, grungy flooring, and top-tier lighting to show off the gains. Today, I was hitting a light recovery day, while Calla worked back and biceps. It was one of my favorite days, because she always wore a pair of my sweatpants with one of her tinier sports bras. It had to be a good sign—that I was only getting more attracted to her. I'd never been one to obsess over a woman, but Calla was something else. I would literally watch her breathe for the next decade and I'd be rock hard the whole time. I focused back on my reflection—on my own workout.

Calla bent over, loading a barbell for rows, interrupting my clearly impenetrable focus, and I dumped my dumbbells to reach over and smack her ass. Looking at me in the mirror—messy hair falling over her shoulder—she winked. Fuck, I didn't know how many times I could say it. Life was fucking good.

"Like what you see?" She asked, not letting my touchiness get in the way of her workout.

I tried to sound like I wasn't ready to do cardio. "Definitely."

"You aren't too bad yourself."

"Calla, will you marry me?" I asked, and she grunted mid set.

"You already asked me that." She breathed, squatting down for her break.

"Why don't we just do it then?" I replied, trying to read the look on Calla's face.

"Amanté," she cocked her head to the side, "you're not serious?" I couldn't stop the excitement on my face—not as the idea took form in my head and I rushed to get it out.

"We'll buy out the steakhouse where we had our first date. I'll fly you and your mom to Paris or Milan or wherever you want to buy your dress. Everyone we love and care about already lives here. I'm sure one of us knows a photographer who's free." I paused, taking in her expression.

She stood up straight, hands on her hips, and stared into my eyes—into my soul, the way only she could. "You're being serious."

"I am."

"When?"

"Tomorrow." I replied, kissing her. She smacked my chest. "Before the season starts. I want to be a married man when I win the MVP." I smirked, and she smacked my chest again.

"Let's do it. Let's get fucking married."

It was unconventional to plan a wedding in three weeks, but what about us wasn't unconventional? Everything in my life... I blinked tears out of my eyes. One look at Calla told me she understood just how much this meant to me. I was creating my own family, designing my own life. I was free.